A NOVEL OF THE MARVEL UNIVERSE

CAPTAIN MARVEL

LIBERATION RUN

NOVELS OF THE MARVEL UNIVERSE BY TITAN BOOKS

Ant-Man: Natural Enemy by Jason Starr
Avengers: Everybody Wants to Rule the World by Dan Abnett
Avengers: Infinity by James A. Moore
Black Panther: Who is the Black Panther? by Jesse J. Holland
Captain America: Dark Designs by Stefan Petrucha (Oct 2019)
Captain Marvel: Liberation Run by Tess Sharpe
Civil War by Stuart Moore
Deadpool: Paws by Stefan Petrucha
Spider-Man: Forever Young by Stefan Petrucha
Spider-Man: Hostile Takeover by David Liss
Spider-Man: Kraven's Last Hunt by Neil Kleid
Thanos: Death Sentence by Stuart Moore
Venom: Lethal Protector by James R. Tuck
X-Men: Days of Future Past by Alex Irvine
X-Men: The Dark Phoenix Saga by Stuart Moore

X-Men: The Mutant Empire Omnibus by Christopher Golden (Nov 2019)
X-Men and the Avengers: The Gamme Quest Omnibus by Greg Cox (Jan 2020)

ALSO FROM TITAN AND TITAN BOOKS

Marvel Contest of Champions: The Art of the Battlerealm by Paul Davies
Marvel's Spider-Man: The Art of the Game by Paul Davies
Spider-Man: Into the Spider-Verse – The Art of the Movie by Ramin Zahed
The Marvel Vault by Matthew K. Manning, Peter Sanderson, and Roy Thomas

Ant-Man and the Wasp: The Official Movie Special
Avengers: Endgame – The Official Movie Special
Avengers: Infinity War – The Official Movie Special
Black Panther: The Official Movie Companion
Black Panther: The Official Movie Special
Captain Marvel: The Official Movie Special
Marvel Studios: The First Ten Years
Spider-Man: Far From Home – The Official Movie Special
Spider-Man: Into The Spider-Verse – The Official Movie Special
Thor: Ragnarok – The Official Movie Special

A NOVEL OF THE MARVEL UNIVERSE

CAPTAIN MARVEL

LIBERATION RUN

AN ORIGINAL NOVEL BY

TESS SHARPE

TITAN BOOKS

CAPTAIN MARVEL: LIBERATION RUN
Mass market edition ISBN: 9781789091670
E-book edition ISBN: 9781789091663

Published by Titan Books
A division of Titan Publishing Group Ltd
144 Southwark Street, London SE1 0UP
www.titanbooks.com

First mass market edition: October 2019
10 9 8 7 6 5 4 3 2 1

FOR MARVEL PUBLISHING
Jeff Youngquist, VP Production Special Projects
Caitlin O'Connell, Assistant Editor, Special Projects
Sven Larsen, Director, Licensed Publishing
David Gabriel, SVP Sales & Marketing, Publishing
C.B. Cebulski, Editor in Chief
Joe Quesada, Chief Creative Officer
Dan Buckley, President, Marvel Entertainment
Alan Fine, Executive Producer

Front cover art by Phil Jimenez and Marte Gracia
Back cover art by Jamie McKelvie

Special thanks to Ronald Byrd, Kevin Garcia, Daron Jensen, Chris McCarver,
Mike O'Sullivan, Roger Ott and Stuart Vandal

This is a work of fiction. Names, characters, places, and incidents either
are the product of the author's imagination or are used fictitiously, and any
resemblance to actual persons, living or dead, business establishments,
events, or locales is entirely coincidental. The publisher does not have any
control over and does not assume any responsibility for author or third-party
websites or their content.

© 2019 MARVEL

A CIP catalogue record for this title is available from the British Library.
Printed and bound in Great Britain by CPI Group Ltd.

For Elizabeth May,
A brilliant writer, a wonderful friend, and a
misogynist's worst nightmare.
Thank you for always seeing me through.

1

EVERY NIGHT in the Maiden House, they would tell the story of the woman who fell from the stars.

Hundreds of years ago, the suns went dark and a woman spilled from space itself. Though she was strange and her powers were alien, unlike anything found on Damaria, she was welcomed by the Flame Keepers as an honored guest and ally.

But she was not content to walk among them for long. She felt it was unfair that only men bore the flame of power, and her gifts were beyond even those of the Keepers that the suns had blessed with power. And so she left them behind, choosing to travel far and wide across the planet, bestowing her gifts on the chosen women of Damaria.

But all was not well.

This is the part of the story where the teller would lean forward and the girls would shrink back.

It changed each night, the painful ways the star woman's gifted powers destroyed the daughters of Damaria. The storytellers never seemed to run out of new horrors, hammering it into the girls' heads, trying to break them. Instead, it made them form even stronger armor.

The woman who burned up from the inside, her power turning her to ash. The woman who plucked her eyes out because every time she closed them, she saw flashes of the future. The woman who drove a spike into her head to stop hearing others' thoughts. The woman who wasted away to a husk, too entranced with her new gift to even eat or drink.

They were too weak to bear it—and so are you. This is why you are kept here, away from everyone. This is why, when you come of age, you will be given to a Keeper to safeguard you from your powers. For the betterment of all.

Every night for ten years, they told the story to her and to the girls who would become her sisters in suffering.

They thought it was the right kind of threat. Keep the girls scared, keep them hurting, keep them thinking they're weak, and you'll keep the women they'll grow up to be in the palm of your hand—right?

Wrong.

The girls born to this may not know the sweet taste of freedom, but she and her sisters remembered.

She saw their story for what it was. A tale born from fear: of power, of difference, of *women*.

What they thought was a warning she took as a

rallying cry. A seed to nourish her into someone strong.

Once upon a time, the Keepers had feared a woman with power.

Rhi would find a way to make them fear one again.

2

POWER.

Some people are born with it. Others stumble into it. Even more will do anything to get it.

She'd hungered for other things—mostly the sky and the stars—but in the end, power was the hand she was dealt… the mantle that was thrust on her, but one she came to value. To love. To wrap herself in until there was no difference between Carol and Captain.

But even when you're an actual super hero, sometimes a woman finds herself in a situation she just can't punch or fly her way through.

"Come on," Jess nudged Carol. "Do it!"

"No," Carol replied, even with her stomach growling as she peered over the heads of the milling crowd at Nebula, the busy restaurant where Jess had dragged her. The designers had escalated the space theme to a level of elegance that impressed even Carol, who tooled around space on the regular. But there were no space junk or abandoned alien ships found at Nebula. Above them, holograms of galaxies swirled on the ceiling, moving so slowly that unless you stared for a long time, the swath of stars and planets seemed only to glitter against the deep-blue and purple background.

"I made the reservation under my name, but the hostess will give us a table if you pull the Captain Marvel card."

She and Jess had been waiting for at least twenty minutes, and she was starting to daydream about the hot-dog stand down the street she'd passed on the way. "I'm not gonna whip out my imaginary super hero badge to get us crab cakes faster, Jess," Carol said as her friend rolled her eyes.

"Crab cakes," Jess sighed. "I hear they're *so* good."

"As you've been telling me for a week since you booked this."

"I am an attention-starved single mother," Jess declared. "I need adult time. Time that does *not* involve swinging off tall buildings saving the world and *does* involve crab cakes."

"We can wait a few more minutes."

"Girl Scout," Jess replied, with absolutely no heat and all sparkle in her eyes.

"I've still got my badges," Carol smirked.

"Do you want a seltzer while we wait?"

Carol looked over at the bar, which had hand-blown glass planets suspended above it. "I'm good."

Despite the crowd, she did like this place's

aesthetic. There were days she woke up during her leave on Earth and missed looking out her window at Alpha Flight Station into the vastness of open space. There was a loneliness to that view she missed, but the endless possibility of discovery and the imminent danger also grabbed her. It wasn't just a mere pull now; you could break that kind of tether. But the stars, they'd sunk into her very soul, and they wouldn't leave. She'd soared through them—one of the handful of people from her world to do so—no gear, no fear, no need. She was home. She was lucky.

She was restless.

"Did you get a load of this guy?" Jess muttered, not so subtly tilting her head to the side so that Carol's glance shifted to that direction. At the bar, sitting under the glass Jupiter, was a young blonde woman, her entire body stiff and tilted away from the man in a suit who wasn't just *not* taking the hint, he was full-on blasting past blinking red sirens screaming *LEAVE ME ALONE!*

"Just one drink," Carol heard him say. "C'mon."

"No, thank you," the girl said, her voice strained.

"Third time she's said that," Jess noted, throwing a disgusted look across the room.

"I'm meeting friends," she went on, "I really don't want—"

"But your friends aren't here yet," he interrupted, signaling for the bartender. The girl shifted in her seat as his hand settled between her shoulders. Carol could see it in her face, the quick mental calculation going through her mind: *What's he going to do if I move his hand? Will he get angry? Is it worth risking that?*

Carol's mouth flattened.

"You're not gonna get mad at me for people-watching now, are you?" Jess asked, misreading the look on her face. Then, in the next second, as Carol started moving toward the bar, suddenly singleminded, Jess hissed, "Carol! Wait a second!"

But that's the thing about power: It comes with privileges. It comes with responsibilities.

And one of those privileges *and* responsibilities is teaching certain people that *no* means *no*.

Jess's hand closed over her wrist, tugging. "Hey, after the last time, you promised me you'd never get us kicked out of a restaurant again."

"You won't let me forget that, will you?" Carol asked, keeping one eye on Mr. Pushy. "And technically, we didn't get kicked out."

His hand was still between the girl's shoulders, which were clenched so tight they were up near her ears, as if she was trying to turtle inside her body.

"After it nearly burned down, we were strongly encouraged never to return to Chez Maurice," Jess pointed out.

"In my defense, there were aliens."

"When *aren't* there aliens?" Jess asked, which should have been more of a joke, but if you got down to it, it was kind of Carol's life.

"I promise, I won't get us kicked out. You'll get your crab cakes," Carol said.

"No punching?"

"No punching. Cross my Hala Star."

Jess grinned. "Good enough for me. Go get 'em."

Not that she needed permission. Carol was already making her way down the steps to the bar area. Her heart wasn't thumping, her palms weren't sweating, her stomach wasn't knotted—she'd faced far worse foes than this with a smile—but still, she knew those feelings. They were hard to forget.

She remembered being fifteen, walking down the street in Boston... and the quickening of her steps when some dirtbag whistled and shouted. That hot, humiliated flush that spread up her neck and cheeks, the hooking sensation of fear in her stomach. She remembered being nineteen, out with her friends, only to get followed home by a man. Those moments of fearful calculation and quick checks behind her when the footsteps became impossible to deny were just seconds away, but they stretched into eternity. Her only saving grace that time had been the fact that she'd lived on base and he couldn't follow her beyond the checkpoint. It had kept her tossing and turning for weeks: *What if I didn't live on base?*

Her fingers clenched as she zeroed in on Mr. Pushy. His other hand had moved to the seat of the girl's stool, effectively boxing her in. She was leaning so far back, trying to prevent his fingers from grazing her thigh, that she was in danger of toppling off.

No punching. Right. Carol had promised. Why had she done that again?

"Andrea!" Just four steps away from the bar, she boomed out the name. The sound startled Mr. Pushy enough that he dropped his hands, no longer boxing the girl in. Excellent.

"There you are!" Smiling at the girl like she was her best friend, Carol fit herself in the space between her and Mr. Pushy. Her mother always said that her broad shoulders would be good for something someday. And right now, they were blocking his view perfectly.

She met the blonde's eyes steadily. *I've got you.* There was a flash of confusion in the girl's face, then realization followed by profound relief as Carol continued, "I must have walked right past you when the rest of us came in. My bad. We're all in the back at a big table already. Let's go!"

"I should've checked, so silly of me," the girl replied, hopping off the bar stool, clutching her purse in a death grip, anxiety in every line of her body as Carol took her arm.

"Hey," the man said, even as they were turning away. "We were talking."

The girl stiffened, but Carol's stride didn't break. "Just keep walking," she said under her breath.

"*Thank you,*" the girl whispered as Carol led her away, toward Jess and the hostess who was holding the menus. Perfect timing.

"No problem," Carol said. "Why don't you come sit with us until your friends show up?"

"Are you sure?" The girl looked over her shoulder, then back at Carol, relief in her eyes. "I would really appreciate it. They texted me they were held up in traffic, but they'll be here in ten minutes or so."

"We'd love to have you," Carol said, turning to the hostess with a smile. "It's going to be an extra person, just until her group arrives." The hostess's eyes widened as she recognized her.

"Of course, Ms. Danvers. I mean, Captain. I mean…"

"Carol's fine."

"Of course. This way… Carol."

The hostess led them to their table at the back of the restaurant, where Jess had already set up a third chair.

"Are you… you're *Captain Marvel*?" asked the girl in a hushed whisper, her eyes widening.

"Guilty," Carol smiled. "This is my friend, Jess."

"Nice to meet you," Jess said. "Sorry you had to deal with that jerk."

"I'm Kensie," the girl said. "And… wow. I seriously can't thank you enough. When I came back from the bathroom, I overheard the guy trying to bribe the bartender into double-pouring my drink without telling me."

Carol's eyes narrowed, and Jess's head whipped toward the bar.

"The bartender wouldn't do it," Kensie added hastily. "He had my back."

"Small mercies," Jess muttered.

"What do you do, Kensie?" Carol asked after the waiter walked up and took their drink orders—wine for Jess and Kensie, sparkling water for Carol.

"I'm studying biology. I actually just applied for an

internship at Alpha Flight for next summer. I'm very interested in the field of alien biology—the top-secret stuff. There's so much to learn from other worlds."

"Just don't ask me to be a specimen," Carol said, and Kensie's cheeks turned red.

"Oh, I didn't mean—"

"She's joking. Don't worry, you get used to it after a while," Jess said, flipping open her menu.

Carol grinned. "I'm an acquired taste, I'm told."

Kensie's phone buzzed, and she looked down. "Oh! My friends are here." She cast a glance back to the waiting area, waving at a group of young women who waved back.

"What's your last name?" Carol asked as she stood up to go.

"Hoffman… why?"

"So I know which Kensie to put in a good word for."

Kensie practically squeaked at the thought. "Thank you *so* much! And thank you again for saving me. I just… I didn't want to make a big deal out of it. I just wanted to be left alone."

Carol could feel a twinge of familiarity at her last words. So simple, right? Yet anything but, in this world. "We understand," Carol said.

"Bye!"

"Sweet kid," Jess commented, as Kensie went to join her friends, who were peering interestedly at their table. "I would've made a big deal out of it."

"We're not all so sure of ourselves. And all sorts of people freeze up."

"It's good that you stepped in," Jess went on. "A true act of heroism."

"And nothing caught on fire this time."

"We might just get through this dinner unscathed," Jess said, suppressing a smile. "Now, do you think we should split an order of crab cakes, or get one for each of us?"

"You've talked them up so much, I want my own plate," Carol said. "And the biggest steak on the menu."

The two women relaxed, the incident at the bar starting to fade with their familiar banter.

"So tell me what's new with you," Jess said.

"Not much."

"Still lone-wolfing it?"

"I'm not," Carol protested, and then she was saved by the waiter coming to take their order. But Jess was like a dog with a bone, waiting impatiently for her to elaborate. "Technically I'm on leave."

Jess snorted. "Like leave's a thing you've *ever* taken seriously. I read online that you fixed the dam break in Northern California. Did you just happen to be in the neighborhood?"

"Kind of," Carol said. "There are some very nice volcanic formations up there. And I like jumping off Burney Falls when the park's asleep. Teddy Roosevelt called it the eighth wonder of the world, you know."

"Teddy Roosevelt also wanted to breed hippos domestically for meat."

"The man had questionable ability to determine the dangers of hippos, but good taste in waterfalls."

"You're not going to distract me with trivia!" Jess shook her finger at Carol. "You've been Earthside for two weeks and you've spent the whole time zipping around the country doing the equivalent of super hero odd-jobs."

"Everybody needs a hobby," Carol shrugged.

"Somebody needs to take a spa day. And by *somebody*, I mean you."

Their bread basket arrived, and Carol grabbed one of the warm, crusty rolls. There was glitter swirled into the deep-blue glass tabletop, and she felt like a little kid, tempted to trace its whorls with her finger, so she could ignore Jess's point.

"I don't think a spa day's gonna help," she said finally.

Jess straightened in her seat, more alert than ever. "Well, what would?"

"I don't know. I just feel… unsettled, I guess. Itchy."

"Itchy?"

"It's like… I want to get back into the game. But every time I think about logistics and planning, and, God, the *paperwork*, Jess…" She took a savage bite out of her roll and sighed. Yeasty heaven. Bless Nebula's pastry chef.

"Have some chive butter." Jess pushed a ramekin across the table.

"Sometimes I miss being out there, beholden to nothing but my shipmates."

"Like back in your space pirate days?"

"I was hardly a space pirate," Carol scoffed.

"Didn't you run with a crew that broke a bunch

of people out of a prison world? The Starjammers? I've read your bio, you know. The authorized *and* unauthorized versions."

Carol rolled her eyes. "I will never forgive my mother for giving that biographer a copy of my seventh-grade school picture. I thought I'd trashed them all."

"Apparently not. The velvet scrunchie was truly epic."

Carol groaned, but their crab cakes arrived in time to distract her from more regrettable middle-school fashion choices. She was pretty sure she had taken a picture in a dress with puffed sleeves the size of her head. She really should pay a visit to her mom while she was Earthside. Maybe burn a few picture albums.

But no matter how tempting the thought, she knew she couldn't. Her mom had lost a lot of family pictures and other precious things in a flood years back, so what she still had, she treasured. Carol would just have to suffer the indignity of knowing those puffed-sleeve pics were out there—and reassure herself that she made better fashion choices these days.

The food was delicious, and once Jess decided to stop bugging Carol about how she was spending her leave and the apparently deep motivations behind it, the conversation was just as good. Even—or maybe especially—when she was being too nosy, Jess was one of the best people to have on your side. Partly because she'd get you thinking about stuff you'd been avoiding.

Which is what Carol found herself doing after dinner. She loaded Jess into a taxi and saw her off, and then began to make her own way home on foot.

She liked walking through the city streets, the hum and frenetic energy of too many people and too many buildings crammed into too small a space feeding into her bones. Sometimes, she ran into trouble.

Sometimes she went looking for it.

Being Earthside these days made her wish for the skies. For the good kind of trouble.

She'd spent her life dreaming of the stars. Of shuttle controls in her hands, the smell of rocket fuel in her hair, and nothing but endless space and discovery ahead of her. When she was young, she thought she'd reach those goals through college, but her father had no plans on ever investing any money in his daughter's future when he had sons.

But that was the thing about Carol: Once she was told she wasn't good enough, she'd go to the ends of the earth—or the universe itself—to prove you wrong.

Her pursuit of the stars had changed her in ways she'd never imagined. The Kree Captain Mar-Vell had changed her; well, technically, it was the Psyche-Magnitron's doing, but falling into that defective alien machine that turned imagination to reality during a battle would never have happened if her and Mar-Vell's paths hadn't crossed.

She had wanted to be strong. She had wanted to survive. She had just never expected to become what—and who—she had.

She used to think about her life in strict befores and afters. Sometimes she still did.

And then, sometimes, something happened that forced you into the here and now.

A sound—like the rending of a sheet down the middle, magnified ten thousand times—broke through the air. Carol's head whipped up, her entire body tensing as she searched the sky.

There. Something was forming a few blocks away, high in the air above the skyscrapers. A sparkling hole ripped out of the horizon, lit up like thousands of fireflies in the night. The whirlwind of light and sparks wavered, wobbling in on itself before spitting out a spinning, smoking sphere—a ship. The twirling light behind it narrowed to a pinpoint and disappeared, but the ship remained, stuttering in the sky, dual rings circling around the base as it coughed up black fumes with every sluggish lurch, right toward the buildings.

Carol's coat fell to the ground, and her red scarf whipped from her neck to her waist in a smooth, practiced movement, the Hala Star pin anchoring the fabric around her hips. She ran toward the ship, veering around pedestrians, her boots pounding the pavement as screams and smartphone flashes filled the night.

One step. Two. Three.

Liftoff.

3

RHI WAS going to crash.

Sirens wailed inside the ship, and the control panel flashed like coastal lights on a foggy day. But the gray haze inside the ship wasn't fog—it was thick smoke that made her cough with each putrid breath she took in. Her eyes burned as she buried her nose in her sleeve and scrambled for the manual controls. The panel was in the midst of a colorful meltdown, lights blinking and alarms blaring.

The screen had cracked down the middle and was shooting out sparks, so she was flying without visuals, relying only on what she could make out through the windows on the bridge—nothing but flames, smoke, and the hulking shadows of tall buildings looming just ahead.

The ship rumbled, and the engine room below belched more smoke up onto the deck. Rhi watched as flames licked the sides of the hull, her ship spinning higher with each contorted circle as the rings that powered it tried to gain enough power to right itself. The floor rippled beneath her feet, throwing her off balance as she careened across the sky toward the buildings.

Impact would be fatal. For her and for anyone in the area.

Panic clawed at her. She'd known that creating a tear through time and space big enough to guide the ship through was risky, but there had been no choice. At first, she had kept control, but the longer the ship moved through that place in-between, beyond nothing and something, the harder it was to keep the channel open. Her ears began to bleed, and then her eyes, and she lost her hold on the rip that she'd slashed in space. The channel closed around her, and the pressure began to crush the ship's solar rings, which were the only things keeping it in the air. She'd barely made it out of the rip when she was caught in the planet's atmosphere and spinning down across the dark sky right over a cityscape — with the tall buildings she was plummeting toward. She had just seconds.

"Switch to manual," she ordered the computer. Her gloved fingers closed around the two smooth white cylinders that would engage the ship's controls. She could do this.

She had to do this.

"Heat signature detected. Manual control engaged," the computer said.

Her arms strained as she took over the steering, the

cylinders vibrating under her hands and her muscles bunching as the power of the ship was redirected, pulsing under her hands as she *yanked*, trying to veer away from the tops of the skyscrapers just below. The ship fought the sharp turn, its damaged shell slowing down its recall. She barrel-rolled up and left, barely missing a building topped with a tall, needle-like tower. Thank the gods her controls were still working. She squinted through the smoke obscuring the window.

Where could she land? She'd seen water when she'd been spit out of the rip, but she couldn't see any blue now. Just smoke and flames, and so many buildings...

Blood trickled down Rhi's forehead as she planted her feet, trying to stay steady as her map, her notes, all the tools that she'd so carefully collected through the years to make this journey flew from the control panel. Her gravity boots were the only thing keeping her from tumbling across the floor along with them. Her hands tightened around the control cylinders.

When Rhi had guided the ship into the rip, she knew it was a probable death sentence. She'd never torn a hole that large through time and space—and now she knew why she shouldn't try it again.

Stuff caught on fire.

And one of the many things that imprisonment in a culture reliant on pyrotechnic abilities taught a girl was that fire is a pain in the ass. The ship wouldn't even turn on unless it detected an adequate heat signature, and only the Flame Keepers ran that hot. Which is why she had the gloves. They tricked the ship into thinking she was one of them.

"*Sensors overheated,*" said the computer, the voice so calm and level it made the hysteria in her chest rise into her throat. "*System failure imminent.*"

"No, no, you can't do that." She typed in the reboot sequence and pressed the red button.

Nothing.

"Come on, come on, come on!" She typed it in again. She could hear her brother's voice in her head: *Insert the launch codes. Lift the levers. Prime the fuel. And don't look back for anything, Rhi.*

Oh God, Zeke, I've failed you.

"*Impact in ten seconds. Ten. Nine. Eight.*"

"Reverse course, *reverse course!*" She scrambled to the other side of the control panel, coughing from the smoke, pressing her gloved hand against the heat sensor. But this time, it didn't spring to life.

Her heat gloves were out of juice.

"*Seven. Six. Five.*"

"No, no, please, *no!*" She slammed her palm down on the sensor, willing it to give her one last burst of heat. That's all she needed… just enough to set the ship down.

"*Four. Three. Two.*"

Impact.

This time, her gravity boots couldn't save her. White sparks filled the air as the ship jolted with a massive impact, throwing her backward, away from the control panel. The last thing she saw before she tumbled across the bridge was a flash of red and blue streaking through the flames outside the window. Her teeth clicked hard against her tongue and blood burst in her mouth as the ship strained against something. Had she hit a force field around the city? Her ship vibrated, shaking with the effort to move forward—but instead, it was moving *back*. Like it was being pushed away. A force field couldn't do that... could it?

"System failure. All systems are offline. Crew to proceed to your evacuation pods."

She tried to drag herself across the floor of the bridge, now at a 45-degree slant, toward the window so she could peer out. The control panel shot off more sparks and the ship jerked sideways, knocking her over, as if some enormous force was grabbing it from the outside.

Something was moving her ship. And Rhi had no choice but to just hang on, ride it out, and hope it'd set her down in one piece.

She had to be ready. She crawled down the bridge, keeping low where the smoke wasn't as thick, heading toward the ladder that led to the escape hatch. Just as she reached it, the ship tilted again, as if it were a ball someone had tossed in the air. She grabbed the bottom rung of the ladder as a scream ripped through her throat and she lost her footing. For a sickening moment, the ship was free-falling— no engine, no power, no lights, no computer—and then *smash*. She—and her ship—slammed down onto the planet's surface. Sparks filled the smoke-darkened cabin, lighting up the space like a battlefield.

This is it, she thought. She and the ship had both

survived the impact, but the flames would take her in the end, just as they had always said.

But instead of an explosion, there was a sudden calm, the ship swaying rhythmically. She chanced a breath, and caught a whiff of moisture through the damaged hull: water.

Rhi grabbed the bottom rung again and climbed up to the hatch, her heart in her throat. What was waiting outside? What was that streak of red and blue?

There was only one way to find out.

She pushed the escape hatch open, the smoke funneling up around her as she scrambled out onto the damaged hull, desperate for fresh air.

Taking a deep breath, she looked around her. As she'd thought, the ship was afloat in a wide, smelly river, bobbing like a bird in the water, with an ugly gash in the starboard side. She had to grab the hatch lid to keep from sliding off into the water, her footing uncertain on the slippery metal. She coughed, blinking in the smoke that billowed out of the cabin, and spat out sooty bile as she tried and failed to stand upright.

Every part of her throbbed, the battering she'd taken in the space-time rip and this strange landing catching up to her now, the adrenaline draining out of her in one sudden, vicious rush. She trembled and leaned back against the hatch lid.

She had to get up. Something—someone?—had… what? *Caught* her ship before it hit the buildings and set it down in the water? Was that possible?

Rhi wasn't about to sit around and contemplate

it. She had to act. If this was a weapon, she had to fight back.

If it was a person?

Well, she might have to fight them too.

Something swelled in her as she struggled to her feet, water splashing over her boots. It wasn't resignation or determination.

It was desperation. The only thing that had gotten her this far. Every step, every move a frantic thrum of *Find help, find help, find help!* as a darker voice—*his* voice—told her: *No one will help, Rhi. No one would dare.*

But *she* had dared. Dared to defy every edict that had been drummed into her for a decade. Dared to love someone they told her she couldn't. Dared to steal their fastest ship, to escape to this other planet. But she was just... herself. Surely here, in this strange world, there might be someone stronger. Someone who could help, who wouldn't be afraid of any of them.

Rhi squinted, eyes still stinging from the smoke as it dissipated in the breeze. Her legs trembled as she braced herself against the hatch, the current rocking what was left of her ship to and fro.

A sudden light burst through the smoke, which parted like curtains swept open to greet the day, revealing the most astonishing woman. The first thing Rhi saw was the star on her chest. It shone like a beacon against the red-and-blue suit she wore, the sash tied around her waist. The star beckoned, welcoming... and when Rhi raised her eyes up, the woman before her—floating in midair—seemed like someone out of a myth. She was *flying*. Without wings. Without any technology. How…?

She had powers. It hit Rhi just as fast as the fear did—not just for herself, but for the flying woman. They would come for her—the Keepers of this world. They'd catch her. She'd risked herself, exposed her power, to save Rhi. Oh gods, the consequences…

That's when she heard it, the ringing in her ears finally receding enough to register the sound.

To her right, there were people—men and women—standing in the street at the water's edge, clapping and shouting. She stared at them, unable to wrap her head around what she was seeing.

They weren't rushing to yank the flying woman to the ground and punish her for using her powers. They weren't jeering.

They were *cheering*. *Celebrating* her.

Tears that had nothing to do with the smoke in the air trickled down Rhi's cheeks. It was like a light had burst through her chest, dispelling a darkness that had been shadowing her for years.

"You're just a kid," the woman said, floating forward, her hands extended but her expression wary.

Rhi stared at her. Who was she? Could she do more than just fly? Was that possible here? Where *was* here?

"Why are you here? Are you okay?"

Rhi opened her mouth. She knew she should answer the woman's questions, but the *sight* of her just… using her powers. In the daylight, where everyone could see, no implant stopping her, no Keeper to control her...

It was the most beautifully terrifying thing she'd ever seen.

The elation—and the fear—was all twisted up inside Rhi, rushing through her brain, as every rule hammered into her by the Keepers told her that any second her implant would go off and shock her in punishment. She pressed her fingers against the bandage on her wrist where she'd dug it out. The wound ached in time with her pulse, a painful reminder that she still needed. She was free. She'd gotten away.

But the others weren't so lucky.

She needed to focus, to save them. But the world started spinning, the gray fuzz spreading across her field of vision, and she staggered back against the hatch.

"Are you her?" she whispered, her voice cracking. "Did I find you?"

Rhi tried to hold on for the answer, unblinking, but the gray turned to black as her fingers lost their grip. She slid, body and mind, into darkness before her savior could speak.

4

DID I *find you?*

The last thing Carol had expected when she heaved the alien ship into the Hudson like a basketball was this bloody and battered kid—couldn't be more than twenty, if that—popping out of the escape hatch and staring at her like she'd just found God. When she sagged into a dead faint, Carol hooked her arm around the girl's waist and set her safely on the flat part of the hull still bobbing above the water.

A quick sweep inside told her that the pilot had arrived alone, but the ship's technology wasn't from any world she recognized. Back on the hull, Carol studied the unconscious girl carefully. Brown hair in a haphazard braid, a cut head, dark circles and dried blood smeared under her eyes. She looked human, but that didn't say much—shape-shifters weren't uncommon. She wouldn't have come in this kind of ship if she were Skrull, though. And she wouldn't have come alone.

Carol tugged down the glove the girl was wearing to check her pulse, and that's when she saw the scars: deep grooves of damaged tissue ringing the right wrist.

That prickle in the back of her head grew stronger as she checked the other wrist and found the same marks, along with a bloody bandage slightly higher up on her wrist. Pulling it back carefully, she exposed a jagged wound and a small chunk of flesh missing from the girl's forearm. It looked as if someone had carved something out of her.

The desperation in the girl's eyes, the scars and wounds, the fact that she'd arrived alone, on a ship that was designed to be piloted by more than one person...

It seemed to Carol that she had a refugee on her hands, not an enemy.

Are you her? Did I find you?

Who was the girl looking for?

Sirens wailed around them as Carol retied the bandage on the girl's arm. Looking across the river, she saw emergency response trucks parking along the street, and the familiar agents in suits already herding people away from the shoreline.

Alpha Flight would take care of getting the ship out of the water, which meant that she was good to focus on their visitor. Carol could put her in an ambulance, but decided instead to get her to the Triskelion, Alpha Flight's headquarters, as quickly as possible. Somehow, that hole in the sky had been her doing—maybe the ship, maybe the kid herself—and it'd been unlike anything Carol had ever seen. Like the air was torn in two, with the darkness of space rippling behind it.

So she made a call to give the Triskelion a heads-up and scooped up the girl fairy-tale-princess style. Her eyes didn't even flutter as Carol pushed off, the ship bobbing under the force of takeoff. Wind rushed in their faces as they spun upward, the smells of the city and the Hudson fading to crisp, clean air in just moments.

Flying with someone clutched in your arms is always a bit of a juggle and definitely not a skill they teach in flight school. But do it enough times, and you get the hang of it. You wouldn't think it, but an unconscious person is easier to transport, since they aren't screaming or clutching you in terror as you try to move them to safety.

Because Carol was fast. And she flew high.

She sped over the city, heading toward the complex that housed Alpha Flight—among other things. The series of gray buildings weren't the prettiest, but they were secure. It was the closest—and safest—place to take the girl. The medical staff was experienced with a wide range of species. They'd be able to treat and identify her.

Carol flew over the water and circled around the perimeter of the island. The lack of moon tonight made landing a little trickier, but she ended up choosing to set down right in the middle of the copter bay's red bullseye with a less-than-graceful *thump*. No sooner did her boots hit the ground than someone came bursting out the door leading to the buildings at full tilt.

She squinted, her grip on the girl tightening when she realized it wasn't a guard as she'd expected. But she relaxed when she saw the riot of killer—literal and figurative—red curls.

Carol had never been much for monarchy, but the queen of the Inhumans was the kind of woman who redefined the word *regal*. Tall and graceful, Medusa was all piercing gazes and icy elegance. Her hair, the source of her power, tumbled nearly to the ground, and the mass of red tendrils coiled and re-coiled with each step she took toward Carol. Behind her, medical staff hurried out, pushing a stretcher, led by a doctor in a white coat, who had dark braids twisted up in a bun. Carol set the girl on the stretcher. "She's been out for at least ten minutes," she said. "Her ship was in bad shape, so she probably hit her head. And there's a wound on her arm you'll want to take a look at."

"Thanks, Captain. We'll take good care of her in the med center."

Carol watched the medical staff hurry the girl away, taming her urge to follow.

"Where did *she* come from?" Medusa demanded.

Carol raised an eyebrow. "Do you know who she is?"

"I know the distress code that Triskelion picked up from her ship as she was crashing. Where are the rest of them?"

"She came alone. Is she Inhuman?"

Medusa let out a shaky breath that troubled Carol.

"Let's go inside." Without another word, the queen swept past her, toward the door that led to the stairwell. That was the flip side of the whole regal thing—Medusa had a tendency to act like she owned the place, even when she didn't. A little annoyed, but full of curiosity, Carol followed her. She caught up with her easily, her stride longer than the queen's—plus, she was known to float down stairs rather than walk them.

There was something orderly and clean and just a little sterile about the Triskelion. Like an office, but super-charged and much, much weirder. You walked the ordinary-looking halls knowing that on the other side of a wall, an alien creature could be being inspected, or a super villain getting questioned, and technology that would change the world was being built. It was a place full of science, of wonder, and of danger. Of heroes.

She still preferred Alpha Flight Station, though. That had somehow become home when she wasn't looking and she was more aware of that than ever, now that she was on leave.

After consulting the map in the hall, Medusa took the elevator to the fifth floor. Once they reached it, Carol walked past her, hooking her fingers on the handle of a door leading to one of the empty conference rooms. "In here," Carol said. It was cool and quiet inside, the automatic blinds across the wall of windows already drawn for the night.

She flipped on the lights as Medusa muttered, "Very well," and swept in after her.

Carol took a seat at the head of a long oak table, but Medusa remained standing, her fingers knitted together.

"Must have been some distress signal to get you here so fast," Carol commented.

The queen was silent, and Carol propped her feet up on the tabletop, bracketing her fingers at the back of her neck, waiting her out. Strong and silent wasn't always her style, but Medusa's presence here so soon after the crash—and the way her hair was practically *vibrating*—put Carol on edge. Especially since the girl had the kind of marks on her that spoke of long-term imprisonment and abuse, even torture. Had she been in some sort of Inhuman prison? And how could she be important enough to warrant the immediate attention of the queen?

Carol didn't want to think Medusa was capable of something like that. She knew there were times when the queen had clashed with the expectations of her people and government. In the past, the Inhuman way of life could be hard to reckon with—their caste system had been deeply rooted in genetics, and vestiges of it remained even now as they moved past it, and that bothered Carol. That was the righteous streak in her— she liked it when things were fair and equal. When people were free to make choices and help each other. An unequal system with no freedom of choice was one that would be broken by those on the bottom.

"There was really no one else with her?" Medusa asked, finally caving in their little game of chicken.

"Who did you expect?"

"I didn't expect anything or anyone… to trust me."

"Okay, time to fill me in," Carol said, taking her feet off the table and leaning forward, because not beating around the bush was *always* her style. "Is this kid one of your people? She's got scars on her wrists that look like she was shackled or something, and a fresh wound, deep in the muscle tissue. So, is she a prisoner? Did she escape? That ship has tech I've never seen. It's certainly not yours."

"She's not a prisoner," Medusa said.

"But she *is* Inhuman."

The queen grimaced and then nodded her head, the fiery tendrils swirling around her face, agitated. "If she had that distress code, she must be… but it's impossible."

"You and I both know that's a word that doesn't much apply to lives like ours."

"I'm inclined to agree with you today," Medusa replied. "The code was given to a group of Inhumans who left Attilan many years ago."

"Why did they leave?"

"They didn't want to live as we did," Medusa said. "They had ideas that were… not compatible with our way of life. Some on the Genetic Council were displeased with the decision to let them leave, but I was able to convince the majority that letting them seek out a new world for themselves was the most compassionate solution."

"Rather than, say, eliminating them?"

Medusa's glare might intimidate most, but not Carol.

"How many people left?"

"Several hundred families."

Carol had been expecting an answer more akin to a dozen. What she knew of Inhuman history told her there had never been many of them, but the Genetic Council had exiled *hundreds* of families? Was the girl in the medical bay the sole survivor? Carol's questions multiplied with Medusa's every reply—and the possible answers to those questions looked even more sinister.

"You never thought to share this part of your history with us?" She couldn't keep the edge from her voice.

"Do you share all of Earth's dark days and secret histories with *us*, Captain?" Medusa snapped, folding her arms across her chest. "They left on a ship over a decade ago. I had hoped that they had found an empty world to settle on, and they had no need to contact us or use the distress signal. That is what they wanted, and that is what I wanted for them. Unlike some of my people, I had no wish for bloodshed."

"I believe you," Carol said. "But I'm going to need you to stay here while I go talk to the girl."

Medusa opened her mouth to object, but Carol kept talking. "I know you want answers, too. But she crash-landed on my planet. And she zipped past all of Alpha Flight Station's security. I am the commander of Alpha Flight Station, even if I am on leave right now. So, Your Majesty, this is my territory."

"I am quite aware that you prefer to use my title only when you're being bossy, Captain."

"And you prefer to use mine when you're pissed at me."

The queen's eyes narrowed. "You are truly incorrigible sometimes." It wasn't intended as a compliment, which is why Carol took it as one.

"That's the nicest thing you've ever said to me." She had to hide her grin as Medusa practically shooed her out of the room. She didn't dislike the queen. She was a useful ally. But when crossed, Medusa could also be a powerful enemy, and Carol was always aware of that line between them—she had to be, because the queen's loyalty lay with her people. And if this girl was part of a faction of Inhumans who had abandoned Medusa's people and their way of life? Watch out. Medusa might claim to have wished the ship that left Attilan well, but to believe her Carol needed to confirm it with another source.

She'd have to play this one carefully, because she didn't know Medusa's end game. Would she want to take the girl with her?

It was time to get the other side of the story.

"Captain, wait—Captain!"

Carol was only halfway down the hall when the voice stopped her. She looked over her shoulder as a man with seriously retro glasses—tiny and horn-rimmed—loped toward her. "Upstairs sent me," he explained, a little breathless. "They asked me to tell you that the ship from the incident will be ready in the quarantine area in two hours."

"I'll be down to look at it and give my report when

it arrives," she said. "Until then, I'll be in the med center with the pilot. I plan to question her once she's awake."

"I'll let upstairs know."

With her voice lowered so Medusa couldn't hear through the door, Carol continued, "Can you make sure that Queen Medusa is kept away until my say-so?"

The man gulped nervously at the thought.

"Just request a few extra security guards outside the med center," Carol said. "Tell them I ordered it."

"Of course."

He hurried off in the opposite direction toward the security sector, and Carol continued on her way to the medical center, taking the stairs and actually walking them to wear off some of the energy stirring inside her. But with each step down, her stomach tightened with an unfamiliar dread.

She was a woman who trusted her gut. Being a pilot was about skill, for sure. Knowledge. But it was also about instinct and split-second do-or-die decisions. If you couldn't trust your gut up there in the air, you were as good as gone in a battle. And useless to your fellow soldiers.

Every part of Carol screamed that this girl needed protection. She just wasn't yet sure from whom—or what.

She pushed the door leading out of the stairwell a little too hard, and the hinges rattled in protest. Stopping short, she took a deep breath, trying to gather herself. But that didn't work, so she kept walking, down the hall and through the double doors that led to the pristine white sprawl of the med center. The girl was in the quarantine area, at the end of a long corridor, and Carol spotted a figure standing at the door. For a jolting second, she thought Medusa had somehow snuck another Inhuman down here, but then she caught a glimpse of a shade of green skin she recognized.

"Mantis?"

5

MANTIS SMILED. "Hello, Carol." The woman's black hair swung against her deep-green skin, her antennae sprouting from sharply cut bangs. Her dark clothes—a black T-shirt, a leather jacket in deep burgundy over that and darkwash jeans tucked into biker boots—were a stark contrast to the white of the med center's halls. Every few seconds, muffled beeping from the machines inside the patients' rooms would sound.

Carol hadn't seen the empath in quite a while, but she'd always felt a sort of affinity with her. Mantis had her own history with the Kree—different than Carol's, but she too had had her life changed because of them. They had wiped her mind after her training with the Priests of Pama, and Carol always felt a twinge of familiarity when Mantis spoke of it. Of that time of confusion, of not trusting one's own mind or body or memories.

She remembered a time like that in her own life, those months after she'd emerged from the Psyche-Magnitron, where she didn't understand what was happening to her. What she had become. Who she had been made. How she had been changed. It had been terrifying, and she hadn't had to deal with unraveling false memories like Mantis had. Those Priests of Pama did not mess around. Carol had just blacked out all over the place as her powered personality took over. It had taken some sorting to get steady again, to bring the halves that made up Carol and Ms. Marvel together. But she'd made it work, just like Mantis had made it work.

"It's been a while," Carol said. "I didn't realize you were on Earth, otherwise I would've called you up for dinner. Are the rest of the Guardians with you?"

"No. I've been traveling on my own." Mantis turned back to the observation window cut in the wall.

The Inhuman was still unconscious—or doing a great acting job. They'd cleaned her up a bit—washed the dried blood from her face, and fresh bandages covered the arm wound and the cut on her head.

She seemed better. Still all harsh angles and skin that looked like it hadn't seen the sun often, but her face was easier. Like somehow, she knew she was finally safe.

"I came because of her," Mantis said. "My ship picked up her distress signal and when I went to investigate, her pain screamed to me across space. I had no choice but to follow and make sure she was given help."

Carol looked at the girl, pale and gaunt against the dark sheets of the bed. The scars on her wrists were old—she'd been chained up for a long time. And if Mantis had felt such a strong connection with her, that meant some serious pain.

Carol had always had a great deal of respect for empaths—and maybe a little wariness, especially because Mantis in particular could read minds as well as feel and manipulate others' emotions. But to feel what others were feeling, to experience pain and joy and grief that were not your own, seemed to Carol to be both a blessing and a curse.

She wanted to know what had happened to this girl, and where the rest of the Inhuman refugees were. And Carol worried if she didn't wake up soon, Medusa might push her way in and try to control the situation.

Mantis might just be the ally Carol needed.

"She's Inhuman," Carol explained. "Or at least, that's what we think because of the distress signal she used. Medusa's upstairs, ready to tear me a new one for banning her from coming down here and questioning the kid. According to her, the girl comes from a group of Inhumans who left Attilan a decade ago, searching for a new world."

Mantis pressed a hand against the glass, staring at the girl. "If her injuries and her fear are anything to go on, that new world wasn't a good one."

"Other than pain, did you glean any insight from her thoughts or emotions when you were up in space?"

Mantis sighed, ignoring her question. "She's young."

"I don't follow."

"To have that much pain in you, so young..." Mantis met Carol's eyes, a leveling look that sent a chill through her. "Whatever happened to her, it's very bad."

"I think so, too," Carol said, grateful for the backup.

"You spoke to her? The doctor said you brought her here."

"She was really shaken up when she got out of her ship," Carol explained. "She asked me if I was *her*. If she had found me."

"So she's looking for someone."

"Seems so."

"Medusa, perhaps?"

"I'm not sure." Carol didn't think so. If that were the case, wouldn't she have used her name? She remembered the girl's stunned expression as she said those words... as if she were seeing something imaginary suddenly become real. She knew the whole flying thing was impressive, but for some reason, the awe on her face as Carol floated above her twisted into her like a corkscrew. There had been something different in the girl's eyes, a fear that wasn't about being scared of Carol, but rather, being scared *for* her. It soured something in her stomach.

"The wound on her wrist, the shape of it, it looks like she might have dug something out of her skin."

"Maybe a tracking device?" Mantis suggested. "She could be on the run."

"Oh, she's definitely on the run. That ship of hers wasn't some dinky one-person shuttle; it wasn't designed to be flown solo. I guarantee you she stole it."

"So, a fugitive." Mantis lightly drummed her fingers against the windowsill. "But from where?"

"I don't know," Carol said. "Did you recognize the ship when you were up there? Because I went inside and I don't know the tech. There were hand-shaped sensors all over the control panel—the setup must be bio-profile touch-activated. Same thing on the doors."

"I'm not familiar with the ship. I scanned it and couldn't find it in any database I have access to, either."

"The mystery grows."

"Well, we're about to get some answers," Mantis said, looking through the window. The girl was starting to stir. "She's waking up."

○────────○

BY THE time the doctors had finished checking the girl another twenty minutes had passed, and Carol was trying not to feel impatient. But that went out the window when Medusa showed up, her locks writhing.

"Please tell me the security guards still have all their limbs intact," Carol said.

"They're fine. I can't believe you told them to detain me."

She took a step forward, but Carol planted herself firmly at the end of the hall in a wide stance, arms crossed, with Mantis right behind her.

"We had agreed you were going to stay upstairs."

The queen's eyebrows snapped together in annoyance. "She is one of my people. I have a right to be here."

"If the story you told me is correct, her people renounced yours, and you kicked them out. So technically, she's a refugee. And she came here. So you're going to follow my rules, or I'm gonna get cranky and cause a galaxy-wide incident."

"All I want is to be in the room when you speak with her," Medusa said between gritted teeth. Her hair swayed back and forth, the tendrils twitching like they yearned to reach out and strangle Carol. "You should want that as well, since I have insights that she may not—she must have been a child when her family left Attilan."

"Fine," Carol said. "Stay in the background. Let me lead. And, Medusa? I will kick you out if you upset her."

"And I will help," Mantis piped up. "We must proceed cautiously."

"Mantis is right," Carol said. "She says the kid's been through it, and she's the one who would know, being an empath and all. We want answers, but we don't want to traumatize her any further."

"I am not a monster, Captain. I do not hate those who left Attilan," Medusa said. "There were people I knew who left on that ship. People I loved. It was not an easy time in our history."

"Then let me lead this and make it easier now." Carol let her voice go gentle, just a little, but the hint of steel remained.

Finally, Medusa's hair calmed down, and she relaxed visibly. "You have my word: I will listen more than I will speak."

Behind her, Carol felt Mantis let out a little breath of relief as the tension in the hallway finally dispersed.

"Then let's do this."

The girl watched them warily as they entered the room. Medusa, to her credit, went to sit in the chair tucked in the far corner, while Mantis took the one directly next to the girl's bed on the right. Which left Carol to approach from the foot.

"Hi." She settled herself on the mattress, which squeaked as she sat. "You remember me?"

The girl nodded.

"I'm Carol. This is Mantis. What's your name?"

"Rhi." She glanced warily at Medusa, her fingers tightening on the blankets. "I know who *you* are."

Medusa's chin tilted up. "And I know you. You're the Adella girl—Aya and Rhine's daughter. Why aren't your parents with you?"

"They were murdered," Rhi said, her voice flat.

"By whom?" Medusa was up out of her seat at the news.

"Medusa, stop," Carol ordered. "Consider this the only warning you're gonna get." She turned back to Rhi, whose eyes were round, taking in the two of them. "Rhi, the queen here tells me that you sent out a distress signal. Is that right?"

The girl nodded.

"And you're part of this group of Inhumans who left Attilan years ago?"

"Yes, my parents wanted a different life for me and my brother. Especially since the Genetic Council planned to send my brother to the mines after undergoing the Terrigenesis because they deemed him unworthy." The look she shot Medusa was pure disgust. Seemed like Rhi's parents had raised a rebel. Good for them, Carol thought. "We left about ten years ago."

"And where did you go?" Mantis asked.

"We were on track to a new world suited to our needs when something went wrong with our ship. We suffered severe damage in an asteroid belt and veered off course; vital supplies were auto-vented out into space to reduce energy consumption, and the ship couldn't sustain all of us for long. We would have starved to death out there, in the nothingness."

That was the kind of thing to drive a person to the brink. Carol wanted to ask her what happened next, but Mantis quelled her with a look that made her shut her mouth and wait.

"In desperation, our parents exposed the children who hadn't yet gone through the Terrigenesis to the mists, hoping that one of us would develop a power that could save us all. And someone did." Rhi gave a shaky shrug. "I did. Or we thought so, at first."

"That tear in the sky your ship came out of," Carol said. "Is that what you can do?"

"It's not that simple," Rhi said. "I—" Her brown eyes slid to Medusa again, and then to the door, where the security guards stood on the other side. "Can I ask you something?" she asked, her voice lowering to a whisper.

"Anything."

"You're not Inhuman."

"No, I'm not."

"You have powers, though."

"I do."

"But you're a woman. They… they still don't lock women up here?"

The way she asked it, with almost childlike wonder, was spooky. Carol frowned, glancing at Mantis, who looked equally confused.

"Do they lock up women with powers where you've been?" Mantis asked.

Rhi bit her lip, which was already reddened from the habit.

"You're safe here, Rhi," Carol said gently. "No one's going to lock you up for having powers. Look." Light sprouted along her fingers, a gentle crackle rather than the full-on blast. The heat buzzed beneath her skin, a familiar tingling she had never quite gotten used to. Captivated, Rhi's eyes followed the energy dancing between Carol's fingers.

"See? No one's coming to get me. And if they did? Well, trust me—they'd be sorry."

Mantis let out a huff of breath at Carol's audacity, trying not to smile.

"So where did you land?" It was Medusa who asked the question everyone was wondering, and she asked it softly, with the sympathy it deserved. She'd returned to her seat in the corner.

"I found us a planet," Rhi said, looking across the room warily at Medusa. "One we could live on. They call it Damaria. That's what I do... I find things. Anything that's lost or hidden, I can find it. Mostly, I create little rips, tears through time and space. A kind of channel that I can reach through to grab what I'm looking for. But I have to be specific, and when I was small, just starting out, I could barely create a rip bigger than my hand for more than twenty seconds. For sure not one large enough to send a ship through, like I did to escape. And opening a rip with just the thought of *I need to find a habitable planet* is, well, not very specific. When I reached inside the rip, I pulled out a set of coordinates, scribbled on a piece of paper by someone who lost it who knows how long ago."

"And you went to those coordinates."

"We ran out of options. We used the last of our fuel to make it out that far in space, but what we found..." Tears welled in her eyes for the first time. She pressed a shaky hand to her forehead, and then flinched when her fingers grazed the bump on her head. "We thought it was our salvation. Our scanners didn't pick up any settlements, so it seemed like an empty planet, just waiting for us."

"But it wasn't empty," Mantis said.

Rhi shook her head. "As soon as we hit the atmosphere, the Damarians attacked us. Hundreds of ships like the one I arrived in brought our ship down in minutes. Our parents tried to fight back on the ground, but that's when we discovered they had more than just invisitech to mask their presence to anyone passing by. They have a weapon that sends out some sort of energy that suppresses certain powers—and enhances others out of control. It doesn't affect any of the Damarians, but it affected us. We weren't able to fight back properly, and they…"

The tears finally fell, silently, streaming down the girl's cheeks. "They took us over within a week. And that's when we discovered what kind of place I'd brought us to."

"Why don't we take a break?" Mantis said, reaching out and grabbing the pitcher of water set on the table next to the bed. She poured a glass of water and handed it to Rhi, who gulped it down. "Do you still have the coordinates to Damaria?"

Rhi nodded, rattling the numbers off from memory, and Mantis wrote them down. She got up. "Medusa, will you come with me? We're going to go hunt down the maps of this star system. See what Alpha Flight and our ally's collective knowledge says about it."

"I—" Medusa protested.

"This is for the best," Mantis said firmly. "Please trust me."

For a moment, the two women just stared at each

other, Medusa's face pinched with frustration, Mantis's calm and determined.

"It's rude to invade people's minds," Medusa finally ground out, turning on her heel and following her out. As the door closed behind them, one of the tendrils of Medusa's hair poked Mantis in the shoulder, and the empath swatted it away, shaking her head disapprovingly.

Carol turned back to Rhi, smiling. "That's better," she said. "Sorry about her. She's just…"

"She didn't expect any of us who left to ever return," Rhi finished. She'd taken advantage of the distraction of Medusa and Mantis's bickering to wipe her face free of tears and push her hair back behind her ears. Her ears were a little big for her head, like she hadn't quite finished growing into them, and for some reason, it was this that made Carol's do-gooder heart thump like she'd just seen a sad puppy in the rain.

God, she was turning into a softie.

"Do you want to talk about what happened after you were captured on the planet?" she asked. "Or do you want to take a breather?"

"If I stop now, I might not be able to start again," Rhi confessed. "And telling it… it's not as bad as living it."

"Okay," Carol leaned forward. "Then I'm here to listen."

6

Ten Years Ago, Damaria

"FASTER!"

Every time Rhi's steps weren't quick enough for the guard, he sent flames from his hands to lick at her heels, a grin spreading across his thin lips when she cried out. The metal chains shackling her ankles heated up, singeing her skin further, burn blisters bubbling up and popping.

"Careful," whispered her brother Zeke behind her.

Dirty water squelching between her bare toes, she walked through a puddle on the concrete as the guards led the half-dozen families through the corridor.

"Where are they taking us, Momma?" she heard someone ask ahead. A small voice, a baby one.

Even Rhi was old enough to know that wherever they were going, it was nowhere good.

She looked over her shoulder, where her own parents were shackled behind her. Her mother shot her a smile, but it didn't crinkle her eyes like her smiles usually did. Her father was following her mother, a dirty, bloodstained rag tied awkwardly over his head to cover what remained of his right eye.

They had lost. And now they were here, being marched out of the prison that had been their home for the last... Rhi didn't know how long. Week? Or longer? She couldn't keep track. All she knew was that every few hours, their captors would take someone off for testing, sometimes returning them to their pit of a prison cell, sometimes not.

Something had changed this morning. The guards rounded them all up and chained each family together and began marching them out to the exercise yard, family by family. The yard was just a muddy pasture surrounded by a shimmering force field that lit anything it touched on fire. They'd found that out the first time they'd let them out in the yard, and one of the teenagers had dared brush her fingers along it.

The guards had laughed as the girl burned.

Today, the guards stopped them at the door that opened to the yard.

"Line up here," the guard ordered, pointing to a spot along the wall.

They obeyed, Rhi's shoulder flattening against the cool wall.

"First group, come forward." He pointed to Rhi's father.

Rhi looked up at her father, and he nodded, stepping toward the guard. Rhi, Zeke, and her mother followed suit, Zeke's shoulders jostling against hers as the guard removed the chain linking the four of them together at the waist. The shackles on their arms and legs remained connected, but this allowed a little more freedom of movement.

"Outside," the guard said, once he'd unchained them.

"It's going to be all right, sweet ones," her mother said on her other side as the guards hustled the four of them through the doors, leaving the rest of the families behind. For the first time in her life, Rhi doubted her mother.

The light from the dual suns circling in the sky made Rhi squint. She was unused to such brightness, especially after the days spent in the dark cell. Today, an elaborately carved chair had been set in the center of the field. It was forged from a reddish metal that Rhi didn't recognize, with carvings of flames sprouting from the top. When the sunlight hit the carvings, they almost seemed to flicker like real fire.

And sitting in it was a man with silver-shot hair and deep-set eyes that sparkled like ink in his long, strong-boned face as he looked them over.

The guards hammered stakes through the ends of the chains running through their leg shackles, driving them deep into the wet soil until they were pinned, unable to move more than a foot in any direction.

There was nowhere to run. Nowhere to hide. There was only facing their captor.

Zeke grabbed Rhi's hand now that they were side

by side. Their cuffs bumped and clinked together, the metallic *tink* making her think of raindrops.

The man was dressed in a dark, somber, high-necked suit, the jacket falling all the way down to his knees, and all Rhi could think was that this was how someone who thought you were an enemy looked at you. Cold. Assessing. Combative.

Her fingers itched, the power still newly discovered inside her swirling around, unable to burst free. She couldn't use her abilities here. The buzz in her head, the ache in her body, it heightened to a fever pitch every time she tried. And the shock bracelets they'd snapped on everyone's wrists sprang to life every time she fought through that buzz and pain for more than a minute.

Their captor stood up. His hair was parted razor-sharp, and his mouth was small and seeking, like he was hungry for something, like he wanted to gorge upon it.

"I am Keeper Ansel, undersecretary to President Lee, long may he burn. I have been tasked by the president and the esteemed Council to deliver the Damarian government's complete assessment of your people."

"We did not come here meaning harm," her father said. "If we'd known this planet was inhabited, we would've sent down a distress call—a greeting to identify ourselves. But—"

The undersecretary waved her father's explanations away. "The Council has concluded that while we believe you did not come here seeking war, your presence on our planet—especially the presence of your females—is dangerous at best, and a catastrophic biological threat to our continued well-being as a society at worst."

"What does being a woman have to do with it?" her mother asked.

Without a word, he raised his hand, snapping his fingers.

The bracelet around her mother's wrist lit up, shocking her so hard she went down in a heap of blonde hair and rusty chains.

Lesson One: Women speak only when spoken to.

But Rhi had never heard such a lesson before. All she knew was her mother's screams of pain, the fear wrapping an iron hand around her own heart, and Zeke's horrified sob. Out of the corner of her eye, she could see her mother, her eyelids fluttering from the aftershocks, blood on her lips from her bitten tongue, and that was all it took. Her fingers curled into fists.

"Aya!" Her father jerked toward her mother just as Rhi lunged forward at the man who was watching them with a light in his eyes that woke an instinct she didn't know she had until that second. His gaze settled on Rhi as the shock bracelet grated against her wrist, grinding into her skin as she strained to just get close enough…

He raised his fingers, ready to snap them again.

"No!" Her father leaned over and wrapped his arm around her waist, half yanking her off her feet even as Rhi wriggled, trying to work her way free, chains clinking and swinging.

"Your women don't know when to stay down,

do they?" Ansel murmured, his fingers just an inch apart, the threat still there.

"What do you want from us?" her father's voice broke.

"As I was saying before I was interrupted," Ansel continued, his tone growing bored, "your presence on our planet presents many complications. However, our gracious president has decided to grant you amnesty. There are, of course, conditions each family must agree to."

She could feel the energy rising in her, restless, poised to spring and unable to. And all Rhi could think was: *I did this. I brought us here.*

"What are the conditions?" Her father stood tall as he asked, his shoulders straight like a free man, refusing to cower.

"There is an isolated series of large islands on the other side of our planet, typically used for grazing lands for livestock. We will allow some of your people to remain there."

"Some of us?"

The undersecretary stepped forward, closer to her father. His eyes slid to Rhi. Her mother struggled to her feet to face the threat. Her hand grabbed and squeezed Rhi's, hard. Rhi's fingers throbbed with the pressure, which briefly quelled her rising fear as the undersecretary stopped in front of her.

"This one, she's yours? Your people say she brought you all here."

Rhi's eyes burned with tears she refused to shed as

she raised them to meet his gaze. His mouth flattened, those thin lips disappearing.

"So young," he said. "But so audacious already."

Lesson Two: Women do not meet their betters' eyes.

His fingers slid under her chin, tilting it up until her neck strained, and then back and forth, as if he were examining a prize cow.

"Don't you dare touch her!" The chains rattled so hard as her father lunged against them that the guards hurried over to restrain him further.

Next to her, her mother shook, shackled and helpless, her nails biting into her palms to keep herself from doing the same.

Rhi swallowed, her heart beating so fast she was scared the man could hear it.

"How did you do it?" he asked. "See past all our shields?"

Her lips, dry from too little water and too much crying, cracked when she answered, blood dotting the corners. "Nothing stays hidden forever, not even you. Not from me."

His fingers slid from under her chin to her neck, and the smoothness of the movement made her think *he's done this before* just as his hands closed around her throat. Her mother dove for his hands, her nails sinking into his flesh. Screams filled Rhi's ears as she gasped for air, feeling herself fade, about to spill into the welcoming black. For a moment, she wanted that welcome... wanted this to be over. Because what was to come, she knew—with a prescience no child should have—would be far worse. That was what they wanted—for her to give up, all the fight draining from her. But at her core, up in the sky and down here on the ground, she was built to fight. And to rise.

The undersecretary released her, and Rhi fell to her knees, gasping. The inside of her throat felt raw, and the finger marks on her neck throbbed.

But the Inhumans, the ones watching from the windows, were restive. Voices rose from the building, her people shouting protests from inside as her parents struggled against the guards ordering them back.

The undersecretary swept a hand across the ground. Fire brighter than ever seen on Attilan sprang up in a greedy line inches from their feet, consuming the ground as it boxed them in. The heat rose, sweat trickling down the bridge of Rhi's nose as she breathed in a wretched kind of warmth, all bitter fear and no comfort.

"Our esteemed president's terms for your people's amnesty on our planet are as follows," he said. "All men and male children will be allowed to depart for the Forgotten Islands at once. You will be provided supplies to build settlements and live your lives under our watchful eye. In time, some of you may even prove trustworthy enough to be allowed to use your powers. For the betterment of Damaria, of course."

"You expect me to leave my daughter? My wife?" Her father's voice trembled. He knew, just as Rhi did, that there was no good answer for that question.

Ansel sighed, steepling his hands together in a

thoughtful, almost concerned way. Rhi didn't believe it for a second.

"Your wife will be returned to you as soon as she is outfitted with the proper technology to control her and you are instructed in its use. We are not monsters. We are not in the business of breaking up such important bonds or interfering in the households of men and what they demand of their wives. However, your daughter, like the rest of the unmarried females, must remain with us. Maiden Houses for them are being built as we speak. They will be very similar to the schools our own daughters are sent to—though our females, of course, are not afflicted as yours are."

"Afflicted? There is nothing wrong with us!" Her father's words were strong and sure, even as the guards held him in a vise grip.

A gleeful sort of pity swept over the undersecretary's face, his eyes positively shining with it as they gazed down at Rhi. "Any woman stricken with power she cannot bear is cursed. And no woman can hold a flame for long without it consuming her. I understand this is difficult, but it is for the betterment of all, including your daughter and all your people. I assure you, all the girls will be entrusted into the care of good men who will protect them from the threat of their powers—and who will take on the management of those abilities once they come of age."

"What is he talking about?" Zeke muttered to Rhi.

"They don't like girls with powers here," Rhi whispered back, though even as she spoke the words, she knew she was just grasping the edge of it. The way that man had touched her—like she wasn't a person, but a thing to be examined, to be owned—made her skin crawl.

"Just let us go," Rhi's father said, staring at the undersecretary, pleading. "If we present such a danger and problem, we will go. Give us a ship and we'll take our leave."

"That is not possible," he said. "Despite our shields, you have discovered our planet and breached our defenses. We cannot have you spreading word of us to the rest of the galaxy. We prefer our privacy, and will not allow you to disrupt it—or tell others of our location."

"We won't do anything of the sort. We—"

"You have only two choices here," the undersecretary said. "If you agree, you will be able to depart with your son, and your wife will join you soon. If not, you will all die."

For a horrible moment, Rhi considered it. Should she give herself up? Was she brave enough? Her stomach knotting in on itself, she teetered on the decision, looking at her parents desperately for some sort of answer. *What do we do?*

What do I do?

"You will have your son," Ansel said with a smile that was supposed to be encouraging, but stretched his mouth like a smear of blood on the ground. "That's what matters. Your legacy. The girl is nothing."

"You're *sick*."

This time, it wasn't her father. It was her mother, her face glowing in the flickering flames behind them.

"We will not allow it! Don't listen to him, dear heart." She focused her gaze on Rhi even as the guard jabbed her in the stomach. "You are smart... smart and strong," she gasped. "You are somebody... you are *something*. You and your brother are *everything*, do you hear me? You're *every*—"

The gunshot came out of nowhere. Her mother stiffened, a trickle of blood slipping down her forehead as she sagged to the ground, lifeless.

Rhi didn't have the mind to scream as she stared at the pool of blood spreading behind her mother's head, but Zeke did. Her brother's wail wrenched through the air, almost drowning out the sound of the second shot.

Her father had been reaching out to her, and now he wasn't. Now he was slumped in the dirt.

Dead. That impossible word was the only thing that penetrated her shock and confusion. And as the guards turned to her and Zeke, she grabbed her brother, her nails digging into his arm. A warning, built on pure survival.

Lesson One: Women speak only when spoken to.
Lesson Two: Women do not meet their betters' eyes.
Lesson Three: You rebel, you die.

She kept her eyes lowered as he approached them, tucking the gun back into the holster in his jacket. Undersecretary Ansel, her parents' murderer. Zeke sagged against her, the shock overwhelming him.

As Ansel came to a stop in front of her, Rhi stood stock still, even though every part of her body roared with the need to lash out, to rip a hole big enough to toss him inside. She wanted to split him apart with her bare hands, and tear at his skin with her nails, shredding it under her fingers. She wanted to send this man floating forever in that between place where he'd never be found, because she'd never go looking for him.

She wanted her mother to get up. She wanted her father's hand to hold, instead of forever reaching, never touching.

But that could never be. Her heart shuddered at the knowledge, the grief she couldn't afford to feel right now. Her mother's words echoed in her head: *You are smart and strong.*

When he touched her chin this time, she did not tremble. She had to be strong.

"Are you going to argue, too?" he asked her.

She had to be smart.

She shook her head. "No, sir."

Only like this could she figure out how to make him pay.

o———————o

WHEN THE girls arrived at the Maiden House in the middle of the night, Rhi's feet were still speckled with blood. Her father's? Her mother's? They'd separated her from Zeke as soon as they were off the prison field, and it would be a year before she would be allowed to see him again, though she didn't know that then.

All she knew now was the white walls of the room they'd shoved her and the other girls in, the sobbing of a little girl—Mazz—whose parents had refused to hand her over, and the other girls' terrified faces, because they knew what that meant. Half of them had started this day with parents and ended it orphaned. The other half had started this day loved and ended up betrayed.

"What are we going to do?" whispered one of them.

No one replied. No one knew the answer or had the strength to summon up a comforting lie.

When the door swung open, the girls reacted as one, huddling in a corner, their backs to the wall, aware that here, they were prey.

But this time, it wasn't a guard or the terrifying undersecretary.

It was a woman.

Her pretty blue eyes were carefully made up, and her hair was smoothed back from her face with a blue headband, which matched the skirt skimming down to her knees, and she wore shoes of the same shade. She was neat and tidy and warm-looking, like she baked cookies and gave hugs.

"Hello," she said. "My name is Miss Egrit."

Mazz, who was only three, toddled forward, almost automatically drawn to the motherly voice and smile.

"Mazz, no!" Rhi jumped forward, instinctively snatching Mazz up before she could get close to the woman. She held Mazz tight to her, the girl squirming in her arms, curious and unable to understand the other girls' fear as they circled around her.

The woman's smile turned from friendly to sharp as

she took one step forward; the girls, as a group, huddled back in their corner, drawing their youngest close.

"You won't need to bother with silly things like names anymore," she said. "But we'll get into that in a little while. First, I want to sit while I tell you a very important story. About a girl much like you. A woman who fell from the stars."

7

CAROL SAT back, absorbing the reality that Rhi had just laid out to her. The murder of her parents and all who refused to hand over their daughters, the imprisonment of her people who did obey, the cruelty of these Damarian men—and some women, who seemed to buy into this terrible, patriarchal system.

She didn't know what to say. What could she say? That she was sorry? That it was wrong; that it was evil? It was all those things and more. A world already built on oppression, adding another level to it when a new species arrived and they saw their chance to pounce.

"So you've spent all these years at this... this Maiden House?" Carol asked carefully.

"Once they were sure there would be no rebellion from the surviving parents, they allowed them to come visit. And sometimes we were sent places when the Keepers had use for our powers, but for the most part, they kept us locked up."

"How did you get free? And how did you manage to learn how to fly their ships?"

The girl looked at her, then looked away. "Everybody loses things. Everybody hides things. Sometimes, those things are useful."

She paused, and then let out a breath that could *almost* be a laugh.

"They never understood my power. I was the one who brought us to Damaria, so I was kept with the girls whose abilities were deemed most dangerous—and the most useful to the Council. Girls who could yank all the moisture out of your body with a twitch of their finger. Girls who could burst your brain by singing one note. Girls who could blend into any scenery, as good as invisible. And then me. They soon got bored with me, though. The Keepers, they like flashy powers."

"Tearing through time and space isn't flashy?"

A smile curled across her face, a flicker of rebellion in a girl who knew its cost. "Well, they never understood that part. I made sure of that. I can see flashes of where a thing is hidden if you give me a picture or description, or I'm holding something related to what you're looking for. And that's what I told them I could do—nothing more.

"They couldn't test for anything more. And there was no one to dispute it. They'd killed my parents, and my brother wasn't going to tell them. The people on our ship knew only that I'd found the coordinates, not *how* I'd done it... Those last days in space were just chaos and panic." She closed her eyes, trying to shut out the memories.

"And even after all that, you fooled them—from the start." Respect bloomed in Carol's chest like a thorny rose. "How old were you?"

"Nine. Almost ten."

Carol whistled, impressed, and when she said, "That was really smart of you," Rhi looked surprised, as if no one had told her that in a very long time.

"They replaced the shock bracelets with implants keyed to the brain pathways that activate when we use our powers. But mine was keyed only to the pathways that light up when I use the visual facet of my power— they never mapped my brain when I was creating a rip. Some of the pathways, they're the same, but some aren't. It took me a few years to work through the pain, but I kept at it."

"And here you are," Carol said encouragingly.

But instead of relief in the girl's eyes, she saw tears. "But I left them all behind," she whispered. "We had a plan, to get all of us out. Every girl in my Maiden House. We spent *five years* working out the details. But then… everything had to change."

"Why?"

"One of the conditions in Damaria was that we weren't allowed to have children," Rhi said. "I don't know what they did to the adults on the Forgotten Islands but it's against the law for Inhumans to reproduce. It was one of the last laws President Lee passed before he was ousted from office by

Undersecretary Ansel, who is now President Ansel. President Lee said the scourge of us Inhumans must be stopped, or we'd just have so many babies we'd take over."

"Well, that's messed up," Carol said.

"We heard stories. Rumors about girls in other Maiden Houses who got pregnant," Rhi said. "I always hoped they weren't true, but then… I couldn't just hope—I had to act."

"Rhi, are you pregnant?" Carol asked, alarmed. How had the doctors missed that?

Rhi shook her head. "Not me—my friend Alestra. She's next, after me, to be given to a Keeper. Or, I guess, now that I ran, she's just next." Rhi's lips trembled as she pressed them together, trying to control her emotions. "She and Zeke, my brother, have always been friends. Alestra's family doesn't visit her, so she used to spend time with us during visiting hours. And the two of them… I know it wasn't allowed. But it's not like you can stop love, can you? I know that, just as well as the two of them."

"So Alestra's pregnant," Carol said. Well, that certainly complicated things, if she had to factor in rescuing an expectant mother.

"We agreed, all of us girls, that we had to protect Alestra and the baby above everything else. Because if we didn't—" Her words faded off, as if she was too scared to voice what might come next.

"Rhi," Carol said gently. "Are you afraid they're going to kill Alestra and the baby?"

But when Rhi raised her shimmering eyes to meet Carol's, the look on her face was almost pitying, like Carol was being terribly naive.

"No," she said. "I'm afraid of the opposite. I'm afraid this will be the dawning of a new age. We're just tools to them; resources. A way to uphold their beloved motto, 'For the betterment of all.' 'All' except women and Inhumans, that is.

"And we *have* made the planet better. The crops would never have survived the droughts without Umbra's help. Because, when it comes down to it, diversity and evolution within species are necessary for survival. But the Damarians have gotten lazy and too dependent on what we provide their planet and society. And you can't grow dependent on a resource that's going to die out in a generation, can you? Unless you've ensured a second generation. And a third..."

Oh God. Carol's stomach clenched as the scope of Rhi's fear hit her, her own heart beating too fast.

"There are still men on the Council who lean toward the thinking that we should be banned from procreation," Rhi went on. "But there are others who see into the future where we've died off, and they realize what that means. It's too early for her to show yet, but that won't last forever. If Alestra's pregnancy is revealed, President Ansel might bring it up for Council debate as a test case to overthrow the procreation ban. And if he succeeds..." Studying her trembling and scraped hands, the girl didn't even look at Carol.

"They've taken everything from us," she whispered.

"I can't let them take our children. That's what they want. That's the mistake they made before. They thought they could break us, like they break their own girls. Their girls have never known freedom, but we know what it feels like. We understand what has been taken from us. And the girls who are too young to remember, we older ones remind them, and teach them to resist what they try to teach us.

"But if they start with babies, they can control them from the start. They took the Terrigen from our parents so they can expose as many children as they want to the mists. And it's simple supply and demand—we'd just be brood mares, making more and more slaves. And *every* man on Damaria wants to become a Keeper. It's the ultimate status."

The picture she painted—where young women were used like you'd use a power tool—filled Carol with revulsion and a troubling familiarity. She'd lived on Earth—and elsewhere—long enough to see shades of her own world and society in others, and sometimes not in a good way.

Right now, she was having one of those "not in a good way" moments, because the system that Rhi described was horrifying.

It was also too familiar. Systems like Damaria's existed in Earth's past, present and probably its future. Systems that robbed people of choice, of hope, of freedom. Histories that included slavery and Jim Crow and hundreds of years of struggle for civil rights. Patriarchies and social systems all around the world that crushed women and others who didn't fit into what some man had decreed *normal*. Man vs. woman. Mutant vs. human. Human vs. alien.

Hate was the name of the game for a lot of people. And access to power was what kept that hate alive and made it grow.

Thinking about it, Carol realized she was cracking her knuckles—a preparation habit from flight school that she'd never left behind. Rhi's eyes were drawn to the movement, but then skittered down as soon as Carol noticed. The kid didn't meet people's eyes very much.

"When the ship stopped at our Maiden House for the presidential visit," Rhi went on, "I knew it was my one chance. So I dug the implant out of my arm, stole the ship, and ripped a hole big enough to guide it through. The only thought I had doing it was to find someone who could help. *Please*, are you her? *Did* I find you?" Repeating the first words she'd said to Carol, the girl sounded even more vulnerable and shaky. And this time, knowing her brutal history and her amazing escape, the two questions struck Carol in the heart.

So much horror and despair across the galaxy. Try as she did to tough it out, at times like this, it weighed Carol down. But she had strong shoulders. And it was time to stand up under this load.

Rhi—and all the girls and women of Damaria— needed her help. They needed a heroine, even though they'd been taught there were none. And it was long past time to show them how wrong that was.

Carol reached out and took Rhi's hand gently, mindful of the IV. "Yes, you found me," she said, her own voice breaking as she held the girl's gaze. "And I'm going to see you through this. You, me, and anyone else I can find, we're gonna go save your people."

○────────────○

"THIS IS *outrageous!"*

Carol stepped out of Rhi's room, ready to round on Medusa for shouting at the guards, but all the fight drained out of her when she saw the queen wasn't yelling at security. Instead, she was fuming into a small, disc-shaped communication device, and her red locks were practically standing on end, vibrating in the air like a furious halo.

"She's been going back and forth with the Inhumans for twenty minutes," Mantis muttered.

"Were you out here this whole time?"

Mantis nodded. "I sensed that Rhi would be more open if it was only you in the room. We've been listening on the intercom."

Part of Carol felt relieved. She'd been dreading the task of relaying the grim reality of Damaria's Inhumans to Mantis.

"It's been years," Medusa growled into her comm. "You would think we've grown past such squabbles. Especially when our brother and sister Inhumans are suffering so."

"Talking with the other Inhumans isn't going well, I take it."

Medusa shot Carol an infuriated look before turning her attention back to the comm as a voice intoned, "We register your complaint, Your Majesty. And we ask that you return at once—*without* the traitor."

Medusa jabbed the comm shut, pink staining her cheeks.

"Well," she said. "There it is. No help will be forthcoming from New Attilan."

Sympathy flashed inside her—God, she *really* was getting soft—and Carol stepped forward. "Look—"

"Don't gloat," Medusa interrupted.

"I'm not going to gloat," Carol said. "I understand you wanted to help. And I'm sorry your people aren't interested,"

"Are *you* interested?" Medusa asked, a keen light in her eyes.

"I am," Carol said. "I've just promised Rhi to put together a rescue op. Mantis, are you in?"

"Absolutely," Mantis replied. "Happy to join your team."

"If you do liberate her people, the Genetic Council will not let them come live in New Attilan," Medusa said in a low voice. "I'm sorry. My hands are tied."

"I understand," Carol said, even though she couldn't. Not after she'd heard the story of what Rhi and her people had gone through. Ruler though she was, Medusa was still subject to the Genetic Council's decrees. But Carol had never been one to obey an unjust order, no matter what... though that righteous streak had gotten her into big trouble.

"I must go." But Medusa stood stock still, staring at the hospital-room door. Her hair stirred restlessly in little circles, as if the tendrils themselves were pacing.

"I will tell her that you tried," Mantis said, placing a hand on the queen's arm.

Medusa's head bowed. "I'm sorry."

Without another word, she turned on her heel and stalked down the hall, shoulders hunched, as if the weight of what she'd walked away from was too heavy to bear.

Carol felt for her—but she felt for Rhi more. With no guarantee of refuge, a free life would be challenging for her, her friends, and what was left of her family. But Carol was resolved: She'd find a place for Rhi and her people.

First, they had to get them off Damaria. And to make that happen, Carol and Mantis would need some help. In Damarian society, women were kept under lock and key. Any unchaperoned woman might cause suspicion, maybe widespread alarm. Which meant...

"So, what's our next move?" Mantis asked.

"I can't believe I'm saying this," Carol said. "But I think we need a man."

8

"ARE YOU going to miss your old man while you're gone?" Scott asked, flipping his turn signal and merging onto the highway. Just two more exits before they hit theirs.

"I'll be way too busy," Cassie said blithely. She had inherited more than his lopsided smile and tendency to bite her nails. "Three full weeks of hanging with my friends, and people *encouraging* us to use our powers instead of our parents grounding us because we accidentally melted the blender with our eyes? It's my dream come true!"

"How *is* your friend Amelia?" Scott asked, amused.

"Still grounded," she pouted.

"I think that has to do with the fact that she was making a margarita when said blender-melting happened."

"Would *you* ground me if I destroyed the blender?"

"Do we even have one?"

She pursed her lips, thinking. "Good question. We *should* have a blender. Think of the epic smoothies we could make."

"I'll pick one up while you're gone." He felt a little pang at the thought of not seeing her for three whole weeks. His time with Cassie was always divided with Peggy and limited by his obligations as Ant-Man, but this was different. The thought of these three weeks ahead when she'd be totally out of reach reminded him a bit too much of his prison days, when he had a photo of her, and not much else. But he had to put on a strong dad face, since he didn't want to mar her anticipation.

Cassie was thrilled to be invited to the Rogers Gifted Teen Retreat. It was a chance to spend time with her friends who understood the pressures of having powers and to work with some of the heroes the kids had grown up idolizing. Plus, there were horses—apparently a big draw. And a cute boy Scott wasn't supposed to know about, so he was pretending to be oblivious.

He glanced at her, thinking back to all those years ago when she was sick, and how helpless he'd felt. To save her, he'd done what any father would do—everything he could—and he'd gotten lucky. In his theft of the Pym Particles, he'd been able to rescue the doctor who saved her. Every day, he appreciated that good fortune. Sometimes the thought of all the fathers and mothers who weren't so lucky haunted him.

"You might not miss me," he said, the words coming out a little choked. "But I'm gonna miss you."

"Oh, Dad, come on, don't get emotional on me," she scoffed, but her eyes were a little bright as he took the exit and headed across the bridge toward the island that housed the giant complex of gray stone buildings that made up the Triskelion. He'd never admit it to his kid, but places like the Triskelion always made the thief in him a little nervous. It was all the security and the suits and the agents from alien governments he didn't know about. Even though he no longer had even a finger dipped in the criminal world—okay, maybe *just* a pinky—he couldn't stop his heart's familiar *tap-tap-tap*.

"What can I say? I like having you around," he shrugged.

"You're not such a bad dad," she admitted in a grudging tone that he found quietly adorable. "I know it couldn't have been easy to convince Mom to let me go," she added, with such open appreciation that he felt he had to interject something.

"Your mom just likes to have all the information," he said. "Once she understood how safe this was—and how good it would look on your college applications—she was on board. You know that, right?"

"Maybe. But deep down, she wishes I wasn't like this," Cassie said.

He didn't reply as they pulled up to the security tower in front of the Triskelion. But after he parked, he turned in his seat, fumbling for the right words.

He couldn't evade the truth—she was fifteen, and too old for that. Things were easier when she was five and easily distracted.

"Can I ask you something?" she broke the silence.

He nodded.

"Do *you* wish I wasn't like you?"

"No!" Scott said instantly. "Don't get me wrong—I'm aware that not realizing my daughter exposed herself to Pym Particles for years is a pretty monumental parenting fail…"

"To be fair, you were kind of dead," Cassie said. "But if we're going to be *totally* fair on both sides here, you really shouldn't have taught me how to crack a safe," Cassie said.

"In hindsight, yeah, that wasn't such a great idea," he admitted. "But nevertheless, I am proud of what you've accomplished, and I'm so excited to see what your future holds. As Cassie Lang… and as Stinger."

"It wasn't a parenting fail, Dad. I'm just really wily." He chuckled as she threw her arms around his neck. "I'm gonna miss you, too," she whispered, so quietly that he almost didn't hear.

"Gotcha to say it," he crowed, and she laughed, pulling away and unbuckling her seatbelt.

He got out of the car. Opening the hatch to grab Cassie's suitcase, he smiled when he saw his daughter had continued her bumper-sticker game. She liked to put new magnetic stickers on his car when he least expected it, each more ridiculous than the last. I BRAKE FOR ANTS had been a stand-out—he'd slapped that one on a toolbox in his work shed. And on their last road trip, he hadn't noticed the HONK IF YOU LOVE CHEESE sticker, which resulted in a very confusing drive through Wisconsin.

This time, the sticker read WORLD'S BEST DAD.

o————————o

CASSIE WASN'T due to leave until the morning. They'd spend the night in the apartments on the top floor of the Triskelion, and she'd depart early with her friends.

As soon as they got to the upstairs apartments, Cassie disappeared into a group of her friends at the end of the hall, their voices rising excitedly. So after putting her suitcase away, he headed down to the cafeteria.

He was on his third slice of apple pie when someone set down a tray heaped high with sandwiches across the table from him. He looked up, smiling when he saw short blonde hair and blue eyes and that oh-so-distinctive Hala Star.

Carol Danvers had a way about her. And by that, he meant she looked as if she could crush a person between her fingertips if she wanted. Which was comforting if she was on your side, and terrifying if she wasn't.

"Hey, Carol," he said. "Heard about the ship in the Hudson. I thought you were on leave?"

"You know me," she said, grabbing one of the sandwiches that had at least a half-pound of roast beef pressed between the thick slices of crusty wheat bread. "Always getting into something." She took a huge bite and somehow didn't manage to smear mustard on her mouth. Surely that was some type of witchcraft—he always got mustard everywhere.

"Well, glad you're around to take care of it. We heard about it, driving in."

"We?"

"Cassie's with me. She's going to the Rogers teen retreat tomorrow. She's upstairs right now with her friends, probably plotting to restart the Young Avengers."

"She's a pistol, that one. Like her dad."

"It's clearly my punishment for all the trouble I gave my old man," he joked. "So what was with the ship? Who was in it? We're not being invaded, right? You wouldn't be leisurely eating sandwiches if we were. Or…" he paused. "Are you fueling up?"

She laughed. "We're not being invaded. I'm just hungry. It's been a long day."

"Fill me in."

"The ship that crashed, the pilot survived and is in the med center," Carol said. "She's got a hell of a story."

As Carol laid it out, the whole brutal history—the Inhumans forced to flee Attilan and crashing on a new planet, only to be trapped in a dystopian nightmare— Scott got angrier and angrier. "So, some planet decides *The Handmaid's Tale* is a good model to start with and then takes it to another level of evil," he said.

"You've read Margaret Atwood?" Carol cocked an eyebrow, surprised.

"Cassie's fifteen. She's basically a ball of discovery, rage, and super-powers right now. Of course I read

Margaret Atwood. And Roxane Gay. And bell hooks. I'm trying to keep up with her reading list, but she's a speed-reader. What?"

"Nothing," she said. "You're a good dad, to keep up with her interests."

"I'm trying there, too."

"You're doing a great job," she assured him. "And she's a great kid."

"I can't believe this world... this Damaria. It's sick. The way you describe it, they don't even view these women as people—they're like a... a new cell phone with super-power features. They just choose the right one for the right project and plug them in." He shook his head, a lump growing in his throat at the thought.

"Welcome to my long day." Carol tore into her second sandwich with a little less vigor. She looked tired, but he'd never tell her that. "Mantis is reaching out to some of her friends across the universe to see if anyone's tangled with these people, but it looks like the Damarians have cloaking technology that hides them from most radars and detection systems. They've been tucked away on the dark edges of the galaxy all this time."

"So they're safe to continue their reign of terror?"

"Not anymore," she said, those two words spoken with such conviction that it sent a shiver through him. This is what he liked about Carol. She was a hard-ass, for sure—a hard-ass about the right things.

"You're heading up a rescue mission?"

"Damn right. Like I said, Mantis is on board too. You've met her, right?"

"Yeah, a few times," Scott said. "She's a great person to have in a fight. Or to listen while you sob."

"I'm thinking this trip will involve less sobbing, more punching," Carol said. "Though the way they're running things is making me feel mighty emotional. Is it possible to punch an entire planet?"

"If it were, you'd be the one to do it," Scott smiled. "What about the Inhumans? Are they sending someone to help out?"

Carol shook her head. "Medusa can't do anything. I know she wanted to. But she's beholden to her council, and they're not interested in saving a bunch of people they consider treasonous."

"Some people sure know how to hold onto a grudge," Scott said. "So what are you thinking, attack-wise? Need a hand?"

"Are you interested?"

"Well, Cassie's gone for three weeks, and I thought about pulling an art heist or something so I wouldn't be bored, but this seems a worthier cause."

Carol grinned around a bite of sandwich number three. "Mantis and I would appreciate your help. With the way things are on Damaria, I think we'd stand out even more if we don't have a guy with us."

"So any man would do, I see," Scott joked, unoffended.

"Not just any man. We're pulling a down-and-dirty rescue op, so if you're our dude, our chances are much better," Carol said. "You're good in a tight spot. And you're fantastic undercover."

"If they're a purely pyrotechnic society, I can guarantee you, they haven't seen anything like me before. Or you. Or Mantis. And speaking of Mantis—hey!" He waved at her from across the cafeteria.

Mantis headed over to them, slid her tray across the table, and took a seat next to Carol.

"Did you ask him?"

"She did," Scott said. "I'm happy to be your token male."

Mantis grinned. "You're a good sport. I think Rhi will like you."

"How... how is she?" Scott asked. He couldn't imagine what it took to survive what that young woman had endured and escape it like she did. She was just a few years older than Cassie.

"Determined," Mantis said, before Carol could answer. "Terrified. But not broken. They never could break her, though they tried."

"I can't believe she kept the reach of her powers secret from them," Scott said. "That's..."

"Brilliant," Carol finished, as he nodded. "And must have taken incredible self-discipline, especially for a child."

"It's the ultimate long con," he said. "I think I might have more in common personality-wise with Rhi than you two."

"I can be very rebellious," Mantis put in. "Carol's the one who takes orders."

"I *took* orders. Now I give them," Carol corrected, pointing at Mantis with her final sandwich, a turkey and bacon, to make her point. "But I appreciate you joining our crew, Scott."

"Always happy to help," he smiled. "Plus, if I did case the Louvre like I was tempted to do, it'd take years before I could find a fence for the paintings."

Carol and Mantis exchanged a grin. "I can just picture you carrying the *Mona Lisa* out of there, Ant-Man style," Carol laughed. "It would look like she was walking out on her own."

"The security guards' confusion would be half the reason to do it," Scott said cheerfully, then spotted something in the distance. "Hey, ixnay on the thieving talk. My kid's coming."

Carol looked over her shoulder, waving at Cassie.

"Hi, everybody!" the girl called out, practically skipping over to the table.

"Take my seat, Cassie," Carol said, getting up. "Your dad's been telling me all about you getting into the teen retreat. That's a huge step. Congrats."

"Thanks, Carol. I'm excited."

"Rhi should be released from the med center tomorrow morning at nine," Carol said. "I'll meet you both in the hangar bay after I get her?"

"I'll be there," Mantis said.

"Me too," Scott added.

"Don't give your dad too much trouble tonight," Carol told Cassie. "He's agreed to go on a mission with me while you're off having fun, and I need him well rested."

"Wow, Dad," Cassie said as Carol walked away. "A mission with Captain Marvel? You're moving up in the world."

"It's a good cause," he said, not wanting to get into any nitty-gritty details. "But it's top secret, so don't try to pry it out of me. I'll give you the rundown when I get back." He didn't want to put a nightmare world of misogyny and oppression into his teenager's head when she was about to spend the summer celebrating her special abilities. "Hey, why not go get something to eat before you leave?" he urged her, and she smiled and trotted back to her friends.

When Cassie was out of earshot, he turned back to Mantis.

"This is gonna be a tough one, isn't it?"

"Yes," Mantis said simply.

He supposed that empaths had no use for sugarcoating things.

9

WHEN THE doctors released Rhi that morning, Carol had been waiting with a huge bag of clothes she'd had an assistant round up the day before. For years, Rhi had worn nothing but the gray uniforms they'd been given in the Maiden House. The wool was itchy and sweltering in the summer under the heat of the twin suns, and too thin in the winter when the suns peeked out for only a handful of hours a day.

Now, standing in a side room in the Triskelion, she stared at the huge bag bursting with color, soft and stretchy, delicate and sturdy, for cool weather and warm. For a long moment, alone with the dazzling array before her, she felt almost frozen. How to choose?

She discarded a dress, even though it was a pretty purple. She was done with dresses. Maybe forever. Could she do that—never wear one again? The thought sent a thrill skipping inside her like a stone across a quiet pond.

She pulled on a pair of black pants and buttoned up a shirt with green arrows stamped all over it. When she stepped in front of the mirror, the girl who looked back was like a stranger and an unveiling all at once.

She looked steady. Sure. Finally settled in her skin.

Was this what she would've looked like—*been* like—if they hadn't ended up on Damaria… if they hadn't been forced to leave at all? If she'd grown up a girl free to make her own choices?

There were rules in Attilan, too. She had to remind herself of that. Much of it may have been better than Damaria, and her genetics may have made her Inhuman, but her heart? That was a different story.

There was nowhere to fit and nowhere to go. But she couldn't think about that now. She had to focus on only the first part of her plan: getting everyone out. She'd worry about where they'd go after she got Alestra and Zeke and Umbra and the rest of her friends off Damaria, away from the Keepers.

There was a light knock on the door. Rhi jumped at the strangeness of someone waiting for her permission, and stumbled over the words, "Come in," as if she'd never said them before.

Carol stuck her head in. "Oh, good—you found something that fits."

"I like the green." It reminded her of Umbra's eyes. Just the thought of her sent a pang wrenching through Rhi that she fought to contain. She could almost feel the warmth of Umbra's ID disc resting against the others on the chain around her neck, as if she were calling out to her, *Find me, save me, love me.*

She would if it was the last thing she ever did.

"Are you hungry?" Carol asked. "Last night, I asked a friend to join us on our little mission. I'd like to introduce you to him over breakfast."

"All right," Rhi said cautiously.

"Our engineers have been going through your ship," Carol said as they made their way down the long white corridor of the med center and took an elevator up three floors. "I'm assuming, since the Damarians are all about cloaking their planet, that we should take it rather than one of our own?"

"They shoot any ship that isn't theirs out of the sky," Rhi said. "It was the first standing order for the military after our arrival. They weren't going to make the same mistake of leaving any survivors again."

"Any idea of the size and range of the military?"

Rhi shook her head. "When I was taken places, it was mostly to find water. Half of the planet—most of their farmlands—was suffering from drought. Until Umbra and I came along."

"That's one of your friends?"

Rhi hesitated. Should she say—was it allowed here?

"Yes, one of my friends," she said, even though Umbra was so much more than that. But she had to be careful. One misstep, one wrong revelation, and maybe they wouldn't help her anymore. Then what? She couldn't trust anyone but her friends and Zeke even if she wanted to.

Surprisingly though, Rhi did want to. She'd never dreamed of meeting anyone like Carol Danvers. *Captain Marvel…* that's what one of the doctors had called her. And she *was* a marvel, a woman so powerful she didn't ever flinch, a woman who spoke boldly, who carried herself like she knew all of herself, and was strong enough to learn from her mistakes. A woman of power, moving through the galaxy, unfettered and proud.

What would it be like, to be strong like that? To trust yourself like that?

"Umbra can manipulate water," Rhi explained as Carol held open the elevator door. They walked through the lobby and down a long corridor. "So they'd send us out, me to find the water, Umbra to bring it to the surface for the crops. Now there's an entire continent that's green and fertile because of us—but I wish I'd let them starve." And then, immediately, shame flashing in her, she added, "No, I don't. There are children… they're innocent. And the Damarian women… most of them are innocent, too."

"Societies set up to favor the few—they're always the worst on the innocent," Carol said, stopping at a door marked with a right-pointing arrow and the words HANGAR BAY. She pulled it open to a burst of excited chatter from below. Her footsteps clanging against the metal, adding to the din, Rhi followed her into the vast room onto a metal deck that overlooked the bay. She stared down at the group of teenagers and adults who were talking together. One girl said something to another, who laughed, waggling her fingers, causing her friend's pigtails to fly up like an invisible hand had flicked them.

Rhi's own hands closed around the railing of the deck as she took in the scene, entranced, emboldened, unbearably excited at the sight. It was so carefree. One girl down there who couldn't be older than Mazz was floating, three feet in the air, while her mother rummaged through her bag and tucked some extra snacks inside.

"Where are they going?" She was suddenly nervous, struck by the realization that the last time she'd seen this many families together, half of them, including hers, were slaughtered. She had to dig her nails into the railing to remind herself that it couldn't happen here—could it? She looked up at Carol.

"They're leaving for a retreat where teens go to learn from heroes how to use their powers. I've taught the 'How to properly maneuver around skyscrapers during a high-speed air chase' class a few times myself." She grinned at Rhi, who offered a tentative smile and looked down at the group again, mesmerized.

Their happiness and ease with each other seemed so strange. The adults milling around weren't watching the girls with the keen surveillance she was accustomed to. Instead, they were relaxed—smiling, laughing, and chatting with them, as if the girls were… people.

She couldn't remember anyone on Damaria other than Zeke and her friends who had treated her like a person. That's what living in the Maiden House did to you: It stripped you of yourself and then ground you down until you were only a power. Not a person.

She let the discs on the silver chain looped around her neck slip through her fingers, the clicks of the metal against each other even more comforting than the songs Umbra used to sing to help her sleep after the nightmares woke her up, screaming.

An alarm sounded, bringing her attention back to the present. One of the doors of the hangar bay opened, revealing a waiting bus. The milling parents began the hugging and the goodbyes, and the tightness grew in her chest as the kids lined up, still all smiles, to board.

She wanted to blurt it out, the desperate question on her lips: *They're not going to hurt them, are they?* A knee-jerk reaction, born from a life lived too long under the Keepers' iron grip.

She pushed it down, telling herself to hush. Things were different here. She had hope now, real hope—she couldn't be silly; she couldn't be weak. She was smarter than that... smart and strong. Her mother's last words echoed in her mind, as they had so many times before through the years: She was *someone—something.*

And she was going to go back and she was going to free her friends, even if she had to rip a hole large enough to throw the whole stinking planet in, like garbage.

But that was the needling, terrible thing: She could say she had no home, but what she had told Carol was the truth—she and Umbra had salvaged an entire continent that was now green and fertile. What was once a desert was now flourishing because of what they could do with their powers, together. It had been the first time in her captivity that she'd felt good about what she was forced to do. She could still feel her heels sinking into the once-parched soil, how it turned rich and dark as Umbra pulled water to the surface, and soon after, how the new blades of wheat had brushed against her skin like a greeting. Looking at Umbra across the fallow fields turned fruitful, she had understood not only the pride of what her power could generate, but for the first time, what the word *home* meant.

It was hard not to feel attached to that place, that land gone green because of one girl with a smile brighter than both suns and the other who was too prickly for anyone but her. Because when Rhi thought of home, she thought of that place, of Umbra, and of what could be… if things were different.

She looked down at the hangar door. The last girl was about to board the bus, and Rhi watched as a red-haired man bent down to say something to her, enveloping her in a long hug.

"Come on," Carol said, and Rhi followed her down the deck stairs toward the bus.

"Now, what do we do if there's a crisis?" the man was asking his daughter.

"Stop, drop, and roll?" she answered, flashing a cheeky smile at him.

"C'mon, kid, serious time," he said. "You're gonna be gone for a few weeks. I worry."

"Dad, I'll be fine," she said. "Literally everyone on

the retreat has powers. It's totally safe. Now, I kind of need to get on the bus. They're waiting."

"Oh, sweet summer child," he sighed. "So young… so innocent. The reason I'm concerned is *because* everyone has powers. And teenage hormones. Any practical adult knows that can be a dangerous combination." He gave an exaggerated shudder, making his daughter—and Carol—laugh, while Rhi just stared.

"Give me another hug," she ordered, throwing her arms around her dad and squeezing hard. "Okay. Hug over," she declared, pushing him away gently.

"I love you," he said.

"Love you too. Now I *really* gotta go. Have fun dealing with him, Captain!" she called over her shoulder at Carol, clambering up the steps and disappearing into the bus. With a hiss and grinding gears, the bus took off, rumbling out of the parking area toward the road.

"You tearing up there?" Carol asked the man teasingly.

"I am forever wrapped around that kid's finger," he said, shaking his head. "Don't tell her, though."

"I think she knows, Scott."

He sighed. "Probably." He smiled at Rhi and put out his hand. "You must be Rhi. I'm Scott Lang."

"Also known as Ant-Man," Carol added.

"Ant-Man?" Rhi echoed, shaking his hand gingerly, unused to contact with a friendly male.

"He's got shrinking powers."

"Really, that's all you're gonna offer? Trust me, it's

a lot more complicated than that," Scott said. "What would you say if I said 'She's got laser arms'?"

"You have laser arms?" Rhi's eyes widened, staring at Carol with awe. Was that what she had shown her in the hospital room, when the light crackled along her fingers?

"I do *not* have laser arms," Carol replied. "I just absorb and manipulate energy in ways that a full human cannot."

"Wait—are you not fully human?" Rhi's face lit up in astonishment.

"Have you explained *anything* to the poor girl?" Scott asked. "Rhi, it's clearly my duty to fill you in on the important details, origin stories, and all the good gossip."

"Oh my God," Carol groaned. "It's gonna be like Sweet Valley High."

"I don't know what that is." Rhi was trying to follow their conversation, confused but intrigued at the casual banter.

"Don't worry. I'm sure Scott will have you reading them in no time."

"Jessica and Elizabeth Wakefield have a lot to teach us all," Scott pointed out as Carol laughed, shaking her head.

"Let's go grab some grub."

She led them out of the hangar deck, trading good-natured barbs back and forth with Scott the entire way. Rhi tried not to let it show, how odd it seemed that the two of them, man and woman, were… friends, and even colleagues. And she was frankly stunned at the fact that Carol had apparently fought side by side with Scott as an equal... as a commander.

Mantis was waiting for them in the cafeteria, where the crush of diners made Rhi nervous. There were so many people—talking, walking around, sitting, eating, all unhampered by implants or heat gloves. Here, you could just open the doors. No heat scanners. No places restricted only to those who held the Flame.

"Why don't you sit down with Mantis? I'll bring you a little bit of everything," Carol offered, taking in Rhi's pale face as she scanned their surroundings.

Rhi nodded, relief rising inside her as she chose a chair across the table from Mantis.

"Morning."

"Hi, Rhi. How did you sleep?" Mantis asked.

"Fine. I mean, you were there," the girl pointed out. When she awoke, the first thing she'd seen was Mantis, sitting in the chair across the room. Instead of startling Rhi, her presence was somehow comforting. When you looked in her eyes, you felt like you were stepping into somewhere safe and warm, where nothing would hurt anymore—a very strange feeling for Rhi.

"I didn't want you to wake in the night alone," Mantis said.

"I'm used to being alone."

"But you aren't anymore."

Rhi was absorbing the impact of that statement when Scott's cheerful voice broke through the moment, and Mantis's expression shifted from serious to smiles in a heartbeat.

"Okay," he called out like a carnival barker. "Here comes the smorgasbord: We've got pancakes. We've got eggs. We've got bacon and sausage. We've got fruit salad. And Carol thought it might be a bit wild, but I threw in a cherry Danish, just for our new comrade."

He set the tray down in front of Rhi with a flourish and a grin, and her tiny "Thank you" was just a shadow of the tide of emotion that rushed through her. *Comrade...* she liked the sound of that.

"I did approve of the four kinds of syrup Scott suggested," Carol said, taking a seat next to Rhi while Scott took one next to Mantis.

"It all looks very good," Rhi said, stabbing her fork into the mound of fluffy yellow eggs.

The table fell silent as food became their first concern. Rhi was stunned. The taste of maple syrup was like reaching out on a foggy morning to grab something you knew was there, but couldn't quite grasp. Her tongue remembered it, but her mind couldn't place it—the taste was attached to a memory buried too deep in the past.

"I stopped to check on the ship this morning," Mantis said, after she'd finished her meal. "They've repaired most of the exterior damage already, but they can't seem to get it to turn on to run diagnostics, no matter what they do."

"They won't be able to, not without heat gloves," Rhi explained. "The Keepers—men who hold the Flame— have an elevated body temperature. All Damarian ships are heat-activated. Just like all Damarian buildings. And vehicles. And doors."

"So if you don't have fire powers or these gloves, you can't even open a door?" Scott asked.

"That's right. I had a pair when I crashed. Did—"

"I have the bag with your clothes and gear from the ship," Carol assured her. "We can go through it, get the gloves."

"I bet I can whip up some duplicates for us as soon as I get a better idea of the tech we're dealing with," Scott said.

"You'll have some help on that front," Carol said, pulling out her phone that had just started buzzing. "I thought it'd be a good idea to add another member to our little quartet."

"Am I not enough brains for you, Carol?" Scott joked.

"You can never have too many extra brains on hand," she deadpanned, making him chuckle around a mouthful of waffle. "And the person I've asked isn't just a mega-mind. He's all brawn, too—literally."

10

SMASH.

Amadeus jerked backward just seconds before the robot's arm sank into the wall by his head. Concrete went flying, a small piece striking his cheek.

"Okay, maybe not *precisely* calibrated," he muttered, tapping a new coding sequence into his tablet as the tall silver monstrosity he'd spent the summer creating in his free time tugged its arm free of four feet of reinforced concrete wall and rounded on him, the flat discs at the end of its arms flipping sideways and starting to spin with deadly speed. He'd run enough tests with pumpkins to know that if the robot flung them, Frisbee-style, he'd be bound for Sleepy Hollow.

Exactly *why* had he given the robot deadly Frisbee arms again? It seemed like a good idea at the time. Now he was having second thoughts.

There was an inquisitive rumble in the back of

his head—the big guy was stirring, awakened by his elevated heart rate, but he'd skew his test results by Hulking out right now. This was about outsmarting the robot, not overpowering it.

Each step the bot took toward him shook the floor, but Amadeus stood stock still, waiting until it was only inches away. Then, just as it let one of its death-Frisbees loose, he hit ACTIVATE on his tablet and raised his tablet-free arm. The disc struck the personal force field he'd just engaged; green light rippled around him, but it held. The disc twirled through the air across the lab, ricocheted off a column, and rolled down the floor, stopping at the feet of a group of people.

Oh, right. He'd forgotten he had visitors coming.

Unfortunately, the robot, which he'd built to be much too smart, took that moment of distraction to its advantage.

"Oh, God, not again," he heard Carol say, just as the bot began sending discs of death spinning in all directions.

"Sorrrrrry!" he shouted, but it came out garbled as he began to transform.

Each time, transforming had the same contradictory effects: a confusing mess of opposites when he spun into his new body, not knowing which way was up. His body was his, but it wasn't. He occupied a space alongside Brawn, but he *was* Brawn, all at once. A lot more existential than he preferred, being a man of science, but Brawn? Brawn was the side of him that was all emotion, strength and power.

His muscles rippled, bones growing longer and

stronger, skin stretching and greening as he grew, up, up, up, until the lab equipment looked like toys and the spinning discs were crushed by his massive hands as he swiped them away from their human targets. So tiny… so puny—the discs *and* the humans.

He grabbed the top of the robot's head and twisted it, a pleased smile spreading across his face when he heard the grind and twist of the gears and wires, and then *pop!* goes the robot.

Brawn tossed the head to the ground, and its body drooped like a mechanical flower, creaking as the circuits lost their juice. Only then did he turn his attention back to the humans.

"Hey, Brawn."

He squinted, bending down so he could see her better. The captain. Not Captain America. No, the other captain. The one with the star. Last time Brawn had seen her—it felt like forever ago—he had been angry with her.

"Not that it's not great to see you, but I'm wondering if Amadeus can come out and play?" Captain Marvel asked him. "We had an appointment," she continued. "It's a little urgent."

Brawn sighed, blowing a raspberry so she knew he was doing her a favor even though Amadeus had control. She grinned.

"Thanks, big guy."

Amadeus blinked, slowly getting to his feet and staring down at his now-demolished robot. "I worked so hard on that. You couldn't have helped stop it from getting destroyed?" he asked, looking over his shoulder at Carol.

"I mean, I could have," Carol said. "But I heard about the last metal man someone tried to save from Brawn."

"Tony was fine," Amadeus muttered, cheeks turning pink.

"Stark is *always* fine," Carol said, with very little heat. "Anyway," she straightened her shoulders, all business. "Everyone, this is Amadeus Cho, also known as Brawn."

"Hey." Amadeus stepped over the robot, wiping his greasy hands on his jeans. "Scott, it's nice to see you again, and nice to meet you, Mantis. And you must be Rhi."

"Yes," the girl replied. She couldn't manage much else, still shocked at his sudden transformation from man to Brawn and back again.

"That landing you made was a tricky one," he said. "I watched it live online. I'm glad you're okay. I've got so many questions about the ship—and the Damarians and their technology. Carol sent me the report last night when she floated the idea of me joining the team, but it just made me have more questions."

They'd been spinning in his head all morning, and now that he had the chance of getting some answers, they just spilled forth. "If the society's purely pyrotechnic in abilities, how and why did they have a weapon with the ability to suppress a larger variation of powers? When you crashed on Damaria, your powers were already affected by their technology before the shock bracelets, or even later, the implants, right? If so, we must surmise that they have some sort of power suppressor that's being broadcast somehow. Did they just miniaturize that in the form of an implant? You said the implant was connected to brainwave patterns, right? Do you have the one you took out? If I can figure out how they programmed them, I should be able to find a way to reverse-engineer it. And if it's similar to the larger suppression weapon, maybe I can crack that through learning about the implant."

"Umm…" Rhi licked her lips, her fingers clenching and unclenching under the barrage.

"Maybe not so many questions right now," Mantis said firmly, stepping forward.

"Also, your robot's on fire," Scott said, pointing to the smoking carcass.

"Dear God, it's like herding cats," Carol muttered, hurrying over before Amadeus could even move, grabbing the fire extinguisher and hitting the robot with a few good squirts.

"Just wait until we're all in zero G," Scott said cheerfully, walking over to help her. "Think of the trouble we'll get up to then."

Amadeus seemed to be the only one who noticed how Rhi had stepped back quickly from the fire, her gaze fixed on the flames as if she were afraid they were eyes spying on her.

"Hey, you want to come over here, out of the way?" he suggested, and she followed him to the corner of the lab, where he had a big steel desk covered with stacks of books and piles of papers that would never be organized.

"I didn't scare you, did I?" he asked, even though he had an inkling that the fire frightened her more than his transformation. "People on Earth are used to me greening up, but I know it can be kind of overwhelming."

"I've seen Inhumans who can transform," Rhi answered, reassured by his friendliness. "Not like that, exactly. But similar."

"One of your friends we're going to rescue?" he asked.

Her dark eyes swept down, focusing on the spread of books on the desktop. "No. She's gone now. Not all of us survived those first few years. And not all of us survived our Keepers."

His throat clicked painfully as he swallowed. He'd accidentally stepped in it, and he was afraid he'd be doing that a lot here. He needed to be more aware of her background and the emotional minefields that came with it. Maybe Mantis could give him some tips.

"I'm sorry," he said, feeling awkward, but then she flashed him a quick, reassuring smile, and the awkwardness dissipated a bit.

When he'd gotten the call last night, the last thing he'd expected was Captain Marvel asking him to join a high-stakes rescue op. He never dreamed he'd be even the last name on her list of possible allies to go after the Keepers of Damaria. But life had a way of surprising you... *Carol* had a way of surprising you. And in Amadeus's life, Carol's surprises had been pretty catastrophic. Much of the time, the two of them didn't see eye to eye. Losing Bruce Banner had crushed so many people, and he and Carol had clashed—to put it mildly—a lot during that time.

But when she told him about Damaria, he knew he couldn't say no to her, even if he wanted to be petty—which he didn't. Maybe even more than muscle like Brawn, they'd need a tech expert to navigate this world undetected. And with a mother-to-be and a bunch of other lives on the line, the decision was an easy one—he was in.

Like Rhi and her brother Zeke, Amadeus knew what it was like to lose your parents, and he understood her determination to save the only family she had left. If anything happened to his twin sister Maddy, he'd tear an entire galaxy apart to get her back. So yes, he was all in.

"Is this room all yours?" Rhi asked, as Carol and Scott finished dealing with the fire and Mantis watched the two of them over her shoulder.

"Alpha Flight strongly encouraged me to do some of my more volatile experiments here at the Triskelion instead of my home lab. Something about national security and that one time I accidentally turned my neighbor's cat into a twenty-foot treat-seeking fluff monster. Brawn was really happy to have a decent-sized pet for a few hours, though."

"I would have liked to have seen that," she said, running her finger over the spines of his stack of physics texts.

"See any you like?" Amadeus asked.

Rhi jerked her hand back. "Sorry."

"It's fine," Amadeus said. "Books are meant to be shared and read, right?"

"I—*we...* weren't allowed them," Rhi said. "The only books we had were Damarian histories, and they were kept locked up most of the time."

There he went, stepping in it again.

"Well, that's completely screwed up," Amadeus said, because it was the truth, and he didn't know what else to say. It startled a laugh out of her, one that she clapped her hand to her mouth to stifle, like she was afraid someone would scold her. Which... hell, she was probably afraid of more than that.

His stomach churned. He had enough trouble with most people his age, but he'd need to walk on extra-fine eggshells here. And at least, it seemed, they had books in common. He could work with that.

"You can read, though?"

She nodded.

"Then take whatever you want," he said. "Most of this is science, but I've got fiction on this." He reached over and grabbed his e-reader, tapping it on.

"Fiction? Like mysteries?" she asked. When he nodded, her face lit up like the Aurora Borealis. "I remember mysteries. From before we crashed."

"Check it out," he encouraged her, handing over the e-reader. "Everything from Agatha Christie to Harlan Coben. I've also got the classics and a bunch of new releases, plus all those Inhuman romance novels by

Koli Kane on there. My sister downloaded those," he added quickly.

"Oh, your sister downloaded those?" Mantis asked, grinning over her shoulder as she caught the last bit of their conversation.

"Absolutely," Amadeus said, trying to keep a straight face.

"Such a mystery why everyone denies reading those books, yet they're always topping the bestseller lists."

"Why would you deny reading a book if it's allowed?" Rhi asked.

"It's because it's a romance novel," Mantis explained, walking over to them. "People think they're not as smart as other books, because they're read mostly by women and they're about love. We may not be Damaria, but we still have some major problems with how we treat women here too. And one of those problems involves putting down the things that women like."

"Okay, guilty," Amadeus admitted. "Maddy downloaded the first book, but I got hooked on the series. And now all I want is to find out when Joax will discover she's heir to the Crystal Throne. I'm still torn if the prince really deserves her affection, though."

"So many books," Rhi murmured, paging through a text on robotics. "You really don't mind?"

"We're gonna need something to read on the journey," Amadeus said. "Speaking of that, I should get down to the hangar deck. Will you walk me through how the ship works? It'll be easier with someone who's familiar with the tech. You can bring that with you," he added, when her grip on the tablet tightened.

"All right," she said. "Carol said she had my heat gloves, but they're out of juice. That's one of the reasons I crashed. I can't keep the systems on without the gloves working."

"It's kind of a terrible system to have in place," Amadeus commented. "Especially because not all the Damarian men have pyrotechnic abilities, right? So the ones who don't have the flame need to wear these gloves all the time to get anywhere?"

"Only about forty percent of the men hold the Flame," Rhi said.

"So the other sixty percent and all the women can't even open a damn door or operate a vehicle without the gloves?" Amadeus shook his head. "That's massively ineffective."

"That's the point, Amadeus," Mantis said gently. "If you can't even leave your house or take a bus without a pair of gloves that I assume only the government issues?" Rhi nodded in confirmation. "Then you're going to be really invested in following all the rules required to get—and keep—access to those gloves."

"Pyrotechnic fascism," Amadeus said. "Well, let's go smash it with some science. Give me a few hours, and I'll find a way to keep your gloves energized all the time, Rhi. We're going down to the hangar deck," he called over his shoulder to Carol and Scott, who were standing over the smoking corpse of his robot. "You two ready?"

Carol kicked the robot one last time for good measure. "I think it's been beat."

11

"DO YOU really think he can fix it?" Rhi asked, staring down at the hangar deck, where Amadeus was working on the ship's central command module.

"Amadeus is very skilled," Mantis said.

"And super smart," Carol added. "Don't tell him I said that, though."

Before he and Scott started in on the job, Amadeus had spent the morning scurrying around assembling parts and asking Rhi endless questions. But once he got going, things started moving fast, especially with Scott's help. By the time lunch had rolled around, he'd broken through the heat gloves' security sequencing and rerouted the energy pathways to work in a continuous loop while Scott set to work duplicating the internal heat sensors that warmed the gloves so everyone onboard would have a set and access to all the ship's controls. It would make it a lot easier to infiltrate Damarian buildings this way, as well. Rhi had watched Carol try to use her own powers on the sensors earlier, but that had melted the tech down to a smoking glob within seconds. She couldn't help but wonder how the Damarians would react to a woman who held more power and heat in her body than any of them combined.

Once they figured out how to repair the circuitry and restart the power module, Amadeus became a whirlwind, chatting nonstop, his old-school welding torch sending sparks flying as he soldered the split control-panel screen back together. Rhi retreated to the deck overlooking the hangar bay, far from the sparks. Amadeus noticed, and seemed to understand that she didn't want to be near the fire. He suggested gently that she might like to join Carol and Mantis up on the deck, where they were hammering out battle plans.

She smiled and turned to go, hiding her surprise. Over the years, she had become unused to anyone offering her options or speaking to her without a patronizing tone, as if her brain was too small to understand the question, much less give the answer.

You're smart and strong. Those were the words each girl would whisper to Mazz every night before they fell asleep. A tradition that Rhi had started, her mother's words fresh in her mind back then. Mazz had been so young when they crashed. They'd all been scared that she'd forget what it was like to be more than what the Keepers told them they were. So, as she'd told Carol and the others, the girls had made sure Mazz knew who she was and where she came from. And they'd explained what freedom meant, so that even if she couldn't remember what it felt like, she was taught in secret to reach for it.

That's what she knew Ansel wanted: girls who didn't know better. Girls he could exploit from the cradle. Girls he could train from their first breath to believe they weren't enough, that they were dangerous, that they were too weak to bear the power that was their birthright. But that was going to end—soon.

"If Amadeus keeps up at this rate, we'll be able to leave tomorrow," Mantis said, handing Carol a neat list she'd torn from a notebook. Carol glanced down at it, then up at the empath.

"Do we really need *two* cases of flash grenades?" she asked.

"We will be infiltrating the Maiden House, which sounds like the equivalent of a prison," Mantis pointed out. "And not all of us have..." She flicked her fingers. "You know."

"Laser arms?" Carol rolled her eyes. "You have a good point, though. Rhi, how big is the Maiden House?"

"Ours is the smallest because we were considered the most dangerous," Rhi said. "The building is three stories tall, surrounded by desert and sand dunes— nothing green for miles. There's an electrified fence circling the grounds, and a force field beyond the fence that sets anyone who touches it on fire."

"They really like their fire," Mantis muttered.

"I can take care of the force field," Carol said. "Amadeus can disable the fence. Are the girls kept on one floor?"

"Yes, except for exercise time, we're always on the top floor," Rhi nodded.

"So we've got to get through the other two floors and whoever's guarding them," Carol said. "I could fly up there, but I'd have to take the girls out the windows one by one. It's not fast enough."

"There aren't any windows, anyway," Rhi said. "None anyone could fit through."

"Push comes to shove, I could crash through the walls," Carol said. "But let's make that a last-resort option. What about the tech? Were you locked in rooms? Are there heat sensors or actual keys?"

"There are sensors, but there are also keys, for safety, because of Miss Egrit. She has the keys," Rhi said.

"Who's that?" Carol asked.

"She's the mistress of the Maiden House," Rhi said. "Each one has a mistress running it, to teach us proper Damarian manners."

"That sounds like a terrible job," Carol scowled.

Rhi nodded. "But it's the only job you can hold as an unmarried woman in Damaria."

"So the only way to get yourself some power is by tormenting a bunch of young women." Carol shook her head, her lip curling in disgust. "Traitors."

"Does she keep the keys on her?" Mantis asked.

"Always," Rhi said. "Just in case there's an emergency and she can't get to her gloves in time."

"We'll have to get them," Mantis said, flipping to a second page of her notebook and continuing her list.

"Miss Egrit won't let the girls go without a fight," Rhi said. "None of them will."

"If they want a fight, we'll give them one," Carol said briskly, looking at Rhi with a smile. "And we'll win." The girl stared back, awed by her confidence.

"Rhi, can I ask you something?" Mantis propped her chin on her palm, staring down at her notebook. "Why do they fear women with powers? Their resource problem would be solved if they enslaved the Inhuman men and boys like they do the girls. Why do the men get to stay on the islands in relative freedom?"

"There's a myth," Rhi explained. "They call it history, but I don't think it actually is. It tells of a powered woman who fell from space hundreds of years ago and began bestowing powers on the Damarian women, so that they would know power like the men. But those powers, they destroyed the women. Distracted them to the point of madness and starvation. When this woman was finally defeated, the women remaining— the afflicted, they called them—were rounded up and killed to cleanse Damaria, for the betterment of all."

"All but the ones they killed," Carol muttered, shaking her head in disgust.

"Hey, Carol! I could use your help down here!" Amadeus called out from deep inside the ship's central command module. "I can't get this metal to melt with my torch, but I'm thinking you might be able to."

"Coming," Carol called.

Instead of taking the stairs, she just pushed off the deck and floated down to the ground, landing with such grace that it took Rhi's breath away. To fly like that… it sent a stab of envy through her. She'd spent so much time in the Maiden House, peering out her sliver of a window up at the stars, dreaming about being out there again. And Carol could apparently spin off into space whenever she wished.

Mantis continued making notes in her book while Rhi watched Carol stride off toward central command.

"Umbra is the girl who is being kept by President Ansel?" Mantis asked. Rhi was beginning to realize that she liked to double-check everything.

"Yes. She's been gone for seven months." Seven months, ten days, and a handful of hours, if you were counting—and Rhi was. "And Jella is being kept by Security Secretary Marson. She's been gone for almost two years now. But I know where she is." She withdrew the chain from underneath her shirt, revealing the ID discs strung along it. "I have each girl's old ID disc that they made us wear the first year. If I hold them, I can find them."

"That's useful," Mantis said, making another note. Even as she continued to write, her eyes on the page, she said, "You know, it's all right, Rhi."

"What?" Rhi asked, confused.

"Umbra," Mantis continued. "And how you two feel about each other. Love is a beautiful thing. I'm glad that you found it in a place of such pain."

"I—" Rhi licked her lips. "*Really?*" her voice cracked on the one word, unable to truly believe it, and Mantis looked up, slowly reaching out and grasping Rhi's hand once she turned her palm up in permission.

"Really," she squeezed Rhi's fingers and smiled with such reassurance it made her want to cry. "That's not to say there isn't a minority of people here on Earth who feel differently. I want you to be prepared for that, if you and your friends return here to live, but those people are lost in hate. Pay them no mind. But among us, and most decent folk?" She swept her arm down to encompass the rest of the team. "Nothing to fear."

"It's… it's not allowed in Damaria."

"I figured," Mantis said. "I didn't want you to worry that you had to hide here. I know it must be terrifying, to have the woman you love in such danger."

This time, Rhi squeezed Mantis's hand, a thankful little movement that kept the tears from trickling down her cheeks. She didn't have words that were big enough.

"Hey, are you two paying attention up there?" Scott called, peeking his head out of the module door. "We're up and running!"

"Well done," Mantis clapped her hands together lightly as Amadeus grinned, wiping a streak of soot off his forehead.

Her stomach tight, Rhi got to her feet, staring down at the module—which, sure enough, was rumbling, its outer rings glowing as it began to power up.

"It's going to be okay," Mantis said.

"I know."

There was no other option. She had to be strong, and she had to be smart. For Umbra and their love. For Alestra and Zeke and their baby. For Mazz, who couldn't even remember freedom, and Jella, who had endured a Keeper's control for too long. For Tynise and Tarin, who knew there was a special hell waiting for girls like them, girls who could be used as real weapons.

"I'm ready," Rhi said.

She had to be. She had found Captain Marvel, a hero who held even more power than the star woman the Keepers had feared for centuries, and they had a team and a plan. Now it was time to save her people.

12

OPEN SPACE: vast, mysterious, tantalizing—unlike anything else.

Carol stared out the window of the Damarian ship, her view obscured every few seconds by the dual solar rings constantly spinning to power it. But even interrupted, the view filled her with the kind of peace and surety she'd never experienced anywhere else.

Perhaps it was strange to feel so welcome in the darkness, but Carol knew that space was much more than emptiness. There was good to be cultivated and evil to be vanquished, and in that pursuit she had found her driving purpose in life.

After the smooth takeoff, once she'd gotten used to the ship and the constant heat of the gloves Scott and Amadeus had fashioned for them, her mind turned to the mission at hand.

She could hear Rhi and Amadeus out in the

mess, making what would be dinner. Laughter floated through the ship's curved halls, and that fuzzy feeling rose in her chest again. As the laughter increased, she knew that asking Amadeus to join them was a good idea. When Mantis had suggested that they find someone close to Rhi's age Carol had been wary, but now she was glad she'd listened to the empath. Amadeus seemed to have won a friend for life when he'd given Rhi the tablet full of books.

With some time before dinner, Carol headed back to her bunk, where she'd spread out all the maps and notes and bits of Damarian information Rhi had found and hidden through the years. There were even a few digital recordings of speeches by President Ansel, which Carol had watched twice.

The Damarian bunks were small, and the slanting walls might feel claustrophobic to someone unused to a cockpit, but to Carol the close quarters were comforting.

As she settled down to read through the booklet titled *Your Keeper Duties*, she heard a light knock on her door.

"Come in."

Mantis peeked her head in. "Getting through it all?" she asked.

Carol nodded. "There's a lot of it."

"How did she hide so much of it from them?" Mantis asked, sitting down on the edge of the bed.

"She shoved it all in one of those rips she can make. So this stuff was just floating in the in-between until she needed it."

"Clever."

"She is."

Carol tossed the pamphlet—a load of hateful propaganda—on the bed. "You check out President Patriarchy's speeches yet? They're doozies."

Mantis smirked at the nickname. "*For the betterment of all,*" she said, quoting the Damarian motto.

"What a crock. More like for the betterment of the few privileged dudes," Carol snorted. Ever since Rhi described witnessing her parents' murders, a ball of anger had been growing in her gut. And as she sifted through all the Damarian propaganda, her fury had only grown. President Ansel had his people snowed, that was for sure. But she knew there was an in—there was *always* an in when it came to these restrictive societies; a weakness she could put pressure on until everything shattered.

"He is a charismatic leader," Mantis said.

"But look at this," Carol said excitedly, pulling out a scrap of paper stamped with twin suns above the words "Quench the Flame" in big block letters. "I think there's a resistance movement."

"That makes sense," Mantis said. "There must be people who object to the Inhumans' imprisonment."

"And Rhi said that only forty percent of the men had the flame," Carol said, tapping the paper thoughtfully. "So how does the other sixty percent feel about a society that restricts rights to only the guys who can shoot fire out of their hands?"

"I thought this was a rescue mission, not a revolution," Mantis warned.

"It is," Carol said. "It is!" she insisted, when Mantis shot her a thoroughly unconvinced look.

"You forget who I am," Mantis said. "And you forget I know who *you* are—without even having to read your feelings."

Carol sighed. "My priority is to get Rhi's friends out," she said. "But their Maiden House isn't the only one on Damaria, Mantis. There must be, what, forty of them across the planet? Fifty? Plus all the Inhumans held on those islands. And that's not even factoring in all the Damarian women. If they treat the powered girls like this, how the hell do they treat their own?"

"That question has been gnawing at me as well," Mantis admitted, staring down at the papers spread across the duvet.

"We know at least some of the women buy into the sick system," Carol said, "if they're running the Maiden Houses for the Keepers in exchange for a bit of power." God, every time she thought of another woman betraying those girls like that, she wanted to launch into a sun just so the heat would match the burn inside her. "If Rhi's fears come to pass, they'll probably have more mistress positions available. And if that's the only way to get any independence and power as a Damarian woman... that means the ones who are craven enough will support the president's plans to create more Inhumans."

"He's smart," Mantis said, staring down at the tablet that had the president's speech paused on it. "He covers all his bases, doesn't he?"

"He didn't bargain on Rhi," Carol said, feeling proud. "She got the better of him."

"He's going to be very angry about that. We need to be careful."

She was right. Rhi's escape, if the government had revealed it to the public, would make the president look weak, especially since she stole his own ship from him. It might cause hysteria—if one of the girls could escape, could all of them?

Satisfaction curled inside her. She hoped he was scared. She hoped he was *terrified* that Rhi would be bringing the wrath of the galaxies upon him. Because that's exactly what she was about to do. Because the more Carol learned about this planet, the more pissed off she got. By the end of their four-day journey, she might be so amped up she'd go full Binary on the enslaving dirtbag. She smiled at the thought, feeling cheerful for the first time in a few days.

There was a tap on the door. "What are you grinning about in here?" Scott asked.

"We're just going through the Damarian documents Rhi's pilfered through the years," Mantis said.

"I read that Keeper booklet—it's disturbing," Scott said. "The instructions on what to do when your Inhuman starts crying—apparently you're supposed to ignore them. Or shock them so they learn not to do it. What happened to them that made these people like this? What the hell is wrong with them?"

"What was wrong with us when it took us hundreds of years to give women the vote? And even longer to give women of color the vote?" Mantis asked. "We also didn't allow women to have their own credit cards until the mid-1970s."

"You zoom out, and our history isn't all too different," Carol gestured at the spread of papers and pamphlets across her bed.

"Our *present* isn't necessarily all that different," Mantis said.

She was right, of course. Carol knew that though she was privileged in many ways, her life had been a battle against inequality from the start. Rejected by her father in favor of her brother, she'd gone on to struggle for recognition as a woman pilot in the Air Force. At NASA, she'd hopped from boys' club to boys' club, having to fight her way in every time. Regardless of her talent and expertise, because she was a woman, the deck was still stacked against her—on her own planet as well as others.

And then she became *more*. More than just a human, but with the experiences of a woman who had clawed her way up. You never shook that: the power plays, the disrespect, the insinuations, and sometimes much worse. All of that fueled her: It kept her warm on cold nights, and lit her up on hard ones.

"Getting the girls out doesn't seem like enough," Scott said, his shoulders slumping.

"It has to be our focus," Mantis stressed. "We can make a full report after we get them off the planet, with an appeal to Alpha Flight and some of our allied planets so we can go back to free the rest of the Inhumans and help the Damarian women. And if that doesn't work,

I'll get the Guardians on board and start a revolution myself. But only *after* Alestra and the rest are free."

"We'll get them out," Carol said firmly, just as Amadeus's and Rhi's voices called in unison from the mess, "Dinner's ready!"

○———————○

WITH THE ship on autopilot after the meal, the team broke up to bunk down for the night. Alone in her room, Carol found she couldn't relax. Because the ship was so small, it didn't have a track to run laps on like she did when she had insomnia at Alpha Flight Station. Instead, she found herself pacing the dark, hushed halls until she made a stop on the deck.

"You're up late," she said, venturing farther into the control room upon seeing Rhi standing at the window, looking out into the vast unknown.

"I never needed much sleep," the girl replied. "And this…" She stared out the window, transfixed. "I didn't think I'd ever see it again."

Carol crossed the deck, veering around the vast panel that controlled the ship with its many hand sensors and switches, to stand next to Rhi. "It is a beautiful sight," she said. "I used to wonder if I'd ever get up here to explore the universe like I dreamed."

"They told us we'd never leave the planet," the girl's voice cracked. "Sometimes I believed them."

"People told me that, too," Carol smiled. "We both proved them very wrong, didn't we?"

A ghost of a smile echoed back to her. They never

stayed long. Carol wondered if Rhi had forgotten how to hold a smile with so little happiness about in her life... or if, in her enforced compliance, its brevity was a kind of rebellion.

"I was so scared, getting this thing in the air," Rhi confessed, running her hands along the ship's curved wall. "Zeke, my brother, he works on the old ships. Taking them apart on the Forgotten Islands for scrap. He's the one who taught me how to fly, visit by visit, until I could recite the launch procedure in my sleep. But it was all theory—no practice. The real thing was so different, I still can't believe it worked."

Carol, for once, was speechless. Finally, she said, "That was incredibly brave."

"It was incredibly desperate," Rhi corrected. "In our original plan, Zeke was going to pilot it. I was just backup. And now..." Her mouth clenched, tears gathering in her eyes. "They must have taken him into custody," she said. "Right after I stole the ship."

"Rhi, how exactly *did* you steal the ship?"

Carol had wanted to ask that question from the minute she saw Rhi emerge, dazed, from the hatch, the ship bobbing in the Hudson... but as soon as it was out of her mouth she regretted it, because the girl went so white so quickly, Carol was afraid she was going to crumple.

"President Ansel wanted to see me," she said. "He always wants to see me when he visits."

Carol stayed silent, not wanting to ask why.

"He has Umbra," Rhi continued. "He likes to rub that in my face."

"You two are close," Carol said, understanding filtering through her voice.

Rhi nodded. "Ansel was the only person on the ship. He likes to interrogate me in private. And there was this big metal paperweight on his desk, and he turned around for a moment so his back was to me, and I just... I looked down at it, and I *knew*: This was my chance. So I picked it up and brought it down on his head as hard as I could. And he went down like a sack of rocks." That fleeting smile flickered across her face for a moment. "That *thump* was the most beautiful sound I've ever heard."

"I bet." Carol was fighting a grin thinking about it.

"After I ripped out my implant, I dragged him to the emergency hatch and tossed him out. I was up in the air before his guards even noticed. I didn't think it through—just reacted. And as soon as I was onboard, all I knew for sure was I couldn't get us all free by myself—I had to get help. Just trying to land and take off again would have been the end of it, whether they shot me down or I crashed on my own, like I did in your river..."

"Well, you were right." Carol still marveled at the girl's astonishing courage and skill to have pulled off this solo escape. "And now you have all of us. And we're ready for them."

"What if we can't get Zeke out with the rest?" Rhi asked. "He's in prison for sure, maybe even already sentenced to death..."

"That's not going to happen," Carol soothed.

"You're not going to lose anyone else, Rhi. Especially not your brother. I know what that's like, and I won't see it again."

"*You* lost your brother?" Rhi whispered, eyes wide.

Carol flushed, realizing she'd overshared. Outside of her family, she didn't often talk about Stevie. It had been a long time now.

But despite her silence, she thought of him every day. Her big brother, the golden boy. He'd always believed in her. And what an incorrigible joker he was… *You're smarter than me by miles, Carol. But I'm definitely prettier.*

He'd left this world too soon. War had robbed her of him, teaching her a harsh lesson about loss and battle and soldiering. Sometimes, on days his absence felt especially raw, she wondered what he'd think of who—and what— she had become. How he'd feel about his little sister, spinning across multiple galaxies, altering interplanetary history, transformed into a super hero, all because of two battles—the one he'd lost, and the one she'd won.

"It was one of my brothers," she said. "He was a soldier. He didn't make it home."

"I'm sorry."

Carol inclined her head in thanks. "Zeke's going to come home," she said firmly. "He taught you to fly. He'll be here to see that… to see his and Alestra's baby grow up free. And after all, it's not like they can hide him from you."

Something sparked in Rhi's eyes at Carol's last words. "No, they can't."

"President Ansel will be sorry he ever messed with your people," Carol said, and it sounded like a vow.

When she got back to her room, she looked at the pile of documents on Damarian oppression stacked on her desk, a tightness growing in her belly at the thought of how scared Rhi's friends must be, locked in that Maiden House, not knowing if she'd made it out. The Keepers had likely lied to them and told them she'd crashed or died already.

Carol rifled through the stack on the desk until she pulled out what she'd been looking for—a screencap printout of a news bulletin on the construction of a new Maiden House.

In the photo, the building looked like a prison. Slivers of windows were set high in brick as rusty brown as day-old blood—for ventilation only, not to be looked through. She traced her finger along the edge of the roof, the jagged spikes set along the gutters to... what—discourage birds from landing?

Or girls from throwing themselves off?

Carol's fist clenched, and she tossed the page back on the desk, feeling even more restless. She'd shown an optimistic front for Rhi, but she knew this mission was tough—very tough. There was no quiet way to infiltrate a building like that unless she sent in only Scott as Ant-Man, and that would never work. Not that he wasn't capable, but because the Inhuman girls had no reason to trust him. And if she and Amadeus started smashing in their own special ways, the guards would come running.

She needed to find another angle. Another way in.

She needed discretion. Wiles. Experience.

A smile tugged at the corner of her mouth as a thought struck her. She crossed the room, grabbing her worn canvas go-bag from the back of the closet where she had tucked it. In a hidden pocket at the very bottom, she pulled out a small rectangular comm and flipped it on. She tapped in the coordinates to Damaria, sent them, and then switched the device to record.

"Hey, it's me," she said. "I could use your help. And you do owe me that favor, remember? I sent you coordinates. Let me know if you're in the neighborhood."

She sent the message and tucked the comm back into its secret pocket before settling on the bed. And as she finally drifted off, she didn't hear the muffled *ping* of a response.

13

NEVER IN a million years did Rhi think she'd end up here, sitting in the mess of President Ansel's patched-together ship with a crew of people who had the kind of powers that would make him shake in his boots. Every time she wondered how terrified he'd be if Amadeus transformed in front of him—or if Carol sprang into flight—something grew inside her, something that felt a little like strength.

"Did they inject these into your arms, or did they surgically insert them?" Amadeus asked, peeking out from beneath the giant magnifying glass he had pointed at Rhi's implant.

For the past few hours, he'd been messing with the implant she gave him. They were on the third day of their journey—*just one more day, then it's you against Ansel*, her mind whispered—and Amadeus had been making progress, but she could tell he wasn't satisfied.

After just a few days spent with the genius, she was starting to understand that he liked things done quickly and perfectly—the first time. And as smart as he was, he usually succeeded at that. But she didn't.

"I don't know," she said. "That first year, they sedated us a lot. One day, the second or third week we were in the Maiden House, when we woke up, everyone's arms were bandaged."

"Do the implants hurt when you try to use your powers? Or keep you from using them?"

"Both."

He poked it with a pair of long tweezers. The implant looked like a bullet, something shiny and unnaturally destructive. Ready to rip flesh and mind apart.

"So how do they turn them off when they want to use your powers?"

"The Keepers have implants, too," Rhi explained. "You must be side by side, like this…" She got up and circled around the table to stand next to him. Grasping his right arm with her left hand, she clasped his hand, the inside of their arms in line with each other. "And then the Keeper guides the girl. Physically and mentally. His implant gives him complete control. He can use her power even if she's resisting it, as long as he's touching her."

Amadeus stared down. "So they're touch-activated."

"I guess," Rhi said, letting go of his arm. "But I don't know how they work."

"Lucky for you, that's my job," he said cheerfully,

pressing the tip of his tweezers into the end of the implant. It started blinking red. "Huh, that's new."

"I wish I could help more."

"You can," he said. "I want to know more about your friends and what they can do. We've got Alestra, right? The mama-to-be."

"The Damarian generals want her," Rhi said. "Because her voice... she can make your head explode with a few notes. Or make you fall asleep with her lullabies. Or convince you to walk into a lake and drown yourself with a ballad."

Amadeus pondered the last sentence and shook his head. "People get cool powers like that, and here I am, can't even carry a tune," he joked, twisting the implant's blinking lower panel and pulling it off, exposing the wires and microchip inside. "Was this attached to any wires when you pulled it out?"

She shook her head.

"And how deep was it in your arm?"

She blinked, and for a moment, she was back in Ansel's ship office, frantically rifling through his desk, looking for something sharp to get the implant out. *Hurry, hurry, before he wakes, before they realize.*

She'd dug it out of her arm with his letter opener, then stood looking down at his prone body, the crimson dripping off her arm and staining his white shirt. She wanted nothing more than to sink that dull, bloody blade into his back. She hoped that when he woke and saw the stain, he would understand what she was willing to do to beat him.

"It was deep, at least a half-inch," she said, realizing that Amadeus was still looking at her expectantly.

"Wonder why they didn't put it closer to the brain," he murmured to himself, poking at the device. "So who else is there, friend-wise?"

"Mazz is the youngest. She's only thirteen."

And Rhi didn't know what to do about that. Didn't know how to begin to give Mazz back the childhood that was stolen from her.

"Mazz is... she's very shy. Her parents refused to hand her over to the Keepers, just like mine." And they were murdered, just like Rhi's. But she couldn't bring herself to say it. "So she doesn't have anyone but us now. We tried our best, but it's different for her, because she was so young. Most of us were old enough to remember Attilan and a life where we weren't in the Maiden House. But all Mazz has is our stories."

"Stories are powerful," Amadeus said. "That's why they tried to keep you from reading them."

She smiled, a brief, crooked glimpse. "That's true."

"Okay, so—Alestra, the musical one. Mazz, who's the shy one and the baby. Who else?"

"There... were Vik and Vale. They were twins, the oldest of all of us. They... they were the first ones to leave the Maiden House. It was just a year after we arrived. The Keepers thought they could control them, that the implants would be enough. But they underestimated the twins. Damarian women don't have fighting skills, but the twins did. They didn't need their powers to murder their Keepers—they needed only their bare hands."

The Council had killed them. Made an example of them. And when Amadeus asked, she told him so. And then, "They made us watch." She saw him wince and close his eyes. There was something about Amadeus that made her feel relaxed in a way she'd never experienced from another man except her brother. It was like they could be friends. He listened, he cared, and he showed it. She knew he would understand her mourning for her parents who she never got to grow up with and the girls who became family out of that loss.

"Fighting to protect yourself and others? That's a noble end," he said, the look on his face telling her he knew it wasn't much to offer.

"I know," she said. "But it doesn't make it less hard."

"That's true," he said. "My parents…" he stopped. And for the first time since they'd started talking, his hands stilled. "They were murdered, too. The person who killed them… he did it to hurt me. It took me a long time to let go of the guilt."

"You blamed yourself."

He nodded.

"I did, too."

They sat there, two people connected by the kind of tragedy no one should experience. For a moment they just sat, each breathing, each remembering, because the ones they'd lost could not. And then he smiled, a self-conscious twitch that made her smile in return, and went to work again, as Rhi tucked her feet up on the stool and continued.

"And there's Tynise and Tarin. They're sisters. Tarin

is…" she paused. "Tarin hasn't done well in captivity," she said finally.

Kept from nature for so long, Tarin had suffered, her power and its connection to all growing things warping in strange ways from the prolonged confinement. Their exercise yard was gravel, and there were no trees, no plants, nothing green surrounding the Maiden House. They had chosen the most remote outpost, far from their own girls and their own cities, to keep the Inhuman girls.

A year into their imprisonment, Tarin had a nightmare. The earth rumbled and shook, and when they woke the next morning, a two-hundred-foot oak tree towered over them in the middle of the exercise yard. They had reprogrammed her implant after that and felled the tree. But new growth sprang from the mutilated stump, like a warning that they could not keep Tarin down for long.

"I don't think anyone would do well there," Amadeus said. "So those are the four girls at the Maiden House?"

She nodded. "Jella's next," Rhi said, determined to finish. "She's been with a Keeper for almost two years now. Everyone wanted her—she can't go exactly invisible, but she can blend in anywhere, against any surface, so it's just as good, and so can anyone touching her. And there's nothing the Keepers love more than spying on each other. I don't know who the security secretary bribed to get her, but he got her. He's probably using her to spy on his enemies nonstop."

"But at least you know that at the end of the day, she's got to be somewhere near him, right?" Amadeus asked. "Since her implant can unlock only in the proximity of her Keeper. So once we get there, we'll be able to track her down."

She touched the chain around her neck that carried each girl's ID tag. "Yes, I can find her."

"And then there's Umbra, the… girlfriend," Amadeus shot her a smile, and after a brief hesitation she returned it, secretly thrilled to hear it named, even as a joke.

"It'll be hard to get to her," Rhi said, her mood darkening. "President Ansel won't want to give her up."

"Well, too bad for him," said a voice behind her.

Rhi turned to find Carol standing in the doorway. "How's the work on the implant going?" Carol asked.

"Good," Amadeus replied. "I should be able to pull all the data from the microchips before dinner, and then I can untangle the code and figure out how they really work. They've got to have some sort of failsafe to make them turn off. I figure out what that is, and we won't have to perform a bunch of mini-surgeries on people while we're on the run."

"Thinking ahead—I like it," Carol smiled. "Why don't you two come out on deck? We've been breaking down the operation, and I want your thoughts."

Scott and Mantis were sitting in front of a whiteboard with writing all over it in bright blue marker. Rhi caught sight of her friends' names, and a sketch of the layout of the Maiden House's third floor where they slept, with red Xs marking the security posts she'd painstakingly memorized through the years.

"The plan is simple," Carol said, once she and Amadeus were seated. "Covert and quick is the name of the game. We land at night, shielded so we don't show up on their sensors, half a mile outside the Maiden House. We approach on foot. Ant-Man will go in first, to take out the cameras and deactivate the locks. Then Mantis, Rhi, and I are on. We'll get the girls out, and by the time anybody realizes something's up, we'll already be back on board the ship."

It sounded simple, but Rhi knew it wouldn't be. "Miss Egrit sleeps on the same floor as us," she said. "She'll hear."

"Leave Miss Egrit to me," Mantis said, and the grim note in her voice gave Rhi a frisson of terrifying anticipation. The empath had another side that she hadn't imagined... and didn't want to.

If there was one person Rhi hated almost as much as Ansel, it was Miss Egrit. The idea of her actually receiving some sort of justice...

It was dizzying, she wanted it so much.

"Where do you want me?" Amadeus asked.

"Outside, waiting to smash if need be," Carol said. "If something goes wrong... we're going to need the big guy."

"It's not going to go wrong," Mantis said immediately, shooting Rhi a gentle smile.

"It's a solid plan," Scott added.

"Can you really shrink so small they won't notice you?" she asked.

He grinned. "I think I'll pull my suit out for some

after-dinner pranks to show you. Trust me, they won't notice a thing. I'll get you all inside. Prison is kind of one of my things."

Prison. To have the Maiden House acknowledged as one made her stomach lurch in a sick sort of gratitude. Miss Egrit had made them call it *home.* The Keepers told them it was a palace. A roof over her head, food in her mouth, and the burden of her affliction lifted from her shoulders—what more could a girl ask for?

Freedom. Equality. Truth. Love. Hope. *Power.*

"What about Umbra and Jella? And Zeke?" Rhi asked. "If we get everyone at the Maiden House out, they'll be looking all over for us. Security around them will tighten. Whatever prison they're holding Zeke at will be in lockdown."

"You're right," Carol said. "Once we take the first four girls, we can't avoid tipping off the Keepers that we're there. Same thing if we go after Jella and Umbra first. Or Zeke. Every first move we make lets them know we're here. It's unavoidable.

"We'll take it one step at a time," Carol said, and her expression was so sure, so soothing, that Rhi could feel her worries slipping into confidence. "Split up as soon as we have their locations and make a coordinated attack to grab them, so there's no way the Keepers can warn each other." She looked over her shoulder. "What do you think, Rhi?"

Her mouth dry, she looked at the board—at the scribbles and question marks, her friends' names, the floor plan of the prison she grew up in—and then she looked at the heroes standing in front of it.

There were so many answers she could give. So much worry and so much hope she was feeling. So many people she was trusting.

But instead, she said the thing she wanted most to be true:

"I think we're going to win."

14

PROXIMITY ALERT! *Attention! Proximity alert!*

Carol's eyes snapped open. She was up and out of her bunk and hurrying down the corridor in less than a second. The ship was still dark, the lights flickering in the hall as she raced to the deck.

And there it was, in the distance. She passed the control panels and headed right to the window, where she saw the planet Damaria, shrouded in red mist and circled by two suns.

"A red sky," said Mantis's voice behind her. "Isn't that some sort of sailor's bad omen?"

"Red sky at night, sailor's delight. Red sky in the morning, sailors take warning," Carol recited. "Guess we're the warning."

"The suns are a lot closer to the planet than our sun," Amadeus said, shuffling onto the deck. "I wonder if the gas around the planet is a protective measure against the radiation or something."

"How can we see the planet through their shields?" Mantis asked.

"The ship's sensors penetrate them." He'd brought a few cups of coffee with him from the mess and an array of granola bars. The breakfast of champions. Or in this case, super heroes.

"Oh, you are my savior," Mantis said, picking up a mug and sipping the brew.

"Can they see us approaching?" Carol asked. "We won't be picked up on any radar they've got?"

Amadeus shook his head. "Scott and I disabled all the tracking tech we found on the ship. And we should be able to slide through undetected because of our own cloaking tech that I kludged into the system."

"Fingers crossed it holds." Scott grabbed the final mug of coffee.

"Oh!" Rhi's startled voice made Carol turn. The girl was standing in the doorway of the deck, frozen, staring at the planet in the distance.

"We're here," Carol said, trying to project calm and collected because Rhi was so pale she looked like she might keel over.

The girl took a halting step forward, then another, until she stood by Carol's side, surrounded by the rest of the team.

"It's going to be okay," Mantis said, pressing a reassuring hand between Rhi's shoulder blades.

"We're gonna kick some ass," Amadeus added encouragingly.

Carol remained silent because she knew no words would calm the girl's fears. She could imagine the questions racing in Rhi's head: *What if it's not enough? What if I have to leave someone behind? What if someone gets hurt? What if someone dies? What if I die?*

The questions that ran through anyone's head before they went into a battle.

The control panel started chirping, and Amadeus slipped on the heat glove and headed over to it, pressing his hand onto the sensor to gain access.

"The suns have set over the continent," Amadeus said. "Our window of night has just cracked open."

Carol's stomach didn't leap, and her adrenaline didn't rush. Instead, a calm poured over her, a deep sense of rightness and readiness settling into her bones, a knowing: *This is where I belong. This is what I do. This is who I am.*

"Gear up, team," she said briskly. "We're heading in."

o———o

WITH A flurry of activity behind them as Scott and Mantis secured the equipment not bolted to the floor and Amadeus gathered all the supplies they needed, Carol and Rhi carefully piloted the approach trajectory toward the red haze that surrounded Damaria.

The heat emanating from the gloves that powered the ship was so intense that even Carol's skin prickled with it. Having secured their travel gear, Amadeus stayed glued to the window, making notes on his tablet, probably scribbling down hypotheses on the composition of the gas surrounding the planet, Rhi imagined. She was distracting herself for a moment from the tension of their imminent landing.

Scott stood at the ready behind them in his Ant-Man suit, his helmet tucked under his arm because he complained that it made his forehead sweat. And Mantis was seated in the captain's chair, her mouth set, her fingers digging into its arms, absorbing the team's stress and anticipation.

"So far, so good," Carol said, as Rhi typed in the coordinates for the Maiden House and the ship circled, the solar rings whirring around the perimeter in a blur as it shifted into the landing stage. She checked the screen again. "Nothing on the radar. Let's prep for landing."

As the ship entered the cloud of red that surrounded the planet, the haze engulfed it, and sirens instantly began to blare. Two dots lit up on the radar screen.

"Pull back! Out of the gas!" Carol barked out as Rhi executed the code with shaking fingers. The ship's windows faded from ruddy clouds to the blackness of space.

But even as they spun away from the gas, it was too late. The missiles—they were too small for ships—were racing toward them.

"The mist," Amadeus said. "It's not to protect from the suns' radiation. It must be some sort of security net."

"Did this happen when you escaped?" Carol asked Rhi.

She shook her head, her eyes wide. "I didn't go through the haze," Rhi said. "I tore a rip right after

I got high enough in the air. Oh no. I'm so sorry. I should have…"

"It's okay," Carol said, her eyes fixed on the missiles tracking toward them. *Beep. Beep. Beep. Beep.* With every klick, the missiles were closer.

She stood up. "Rhi, you've got the ship. I've got the missiles."

"But—"

Carol didn't have time to explain or stop. She needed to get those missiles away from the ship—now.

"Mantis, come with me. I need your help."

Carol spun on her heel and sprinted to the end of the deck and the ladder that led up to the escape hatch and down to the lower level of the ship. Carol climbed down, to the guts of the ship, where the engine room lay.

"The missiles are minutes away," Mantis said, following close behind her. "There are evacuation pods—"

"They'll just shoot more missiles at those, and we can't maneuver the pods like we can the ship." Carol shook her head as her feet hit the floor. The clanging engine core took up most of the space, but behind it was a door leading to the airlock. She headed toward it, her mission steady in her mind: *Draw the missiles away.*

Exactly *how* she was going to do that was still up in the air. Soon, she would be, too. She grabbed the wheel that sealed the airlock, clicked the safety latch and spun it counterclockwise. Mantis hopped down from the ladder and joined her.

"Seriously?" she asked when she realized what Carol was doing.

"Any better ideas than launching a decoy to distract the missiles?" Carol asked.

Mantis worried at her bottom lip as the comm above them repeated *Proximity alert! Proximity alert!* "Not really," she admitted.

Carol stepped inside the airlock. "Me neither," she shrugged, and closed the door behind her.

Mantis turned the wheel, sealing the airlock shut from the inside. Through the window, she stared at Carol and said through the comm, "I know you're invulnerable and everything, but this is a scene in basically every good and bad sci-fi movie ever."

Carol grinned. "Come on, haven't you ever wanted to put Rocket in an airlock when he's getting annoying?"

Mantis shot her a half-annoyed, half-amused look, as if she'd have laughed had the situation been different.

"You've got the team?" Carol asked. Even though she knew the answer, a part of her needed to hear it.

"I've got the team," Mantis said, locking eyes with her captain. Carol nodded and held her gaze as Mantis pressed her gloved hand against the sensor that activated the airlock.

The floor beneath Carol's feet slid back like a trap door and she fell into open air, spinning out of the ship and into the cold embrace of the stars.

She flipped and tumbled through the air, moving away from the vessel, and *there*—she could see them, breaking through the mist—two flaming spheres zooming toward her.

Time to generate some heat and light. With the deep cold stinging her cheeks, Carol powered up, her hands beginning to pulse and glow with the energy stored inside her. Lit up like a monumental firework, she streamed her power behind her like a trail of tiny stars as she soared up and away from the ship, a bright streak of heat and light and movement across the sky.

As she'd hoped, the missiles changed course and spun after her, attracted to this sudden new source of energy.

The darkness of space surrounding her and the red haze at her back, Carol gathered speed, her body straining as she pushed forward toward the burning lights ahead.

Those damn suns that circled so close to the planet. She grinned, an idea forming in her head, as she looked over her shoulder to make sure the missiles were still on her trail.

They'd detoured from their course toward the ship completely, drawn to her power signature. It said something about the technology that it wasn't smart enough to tell the difference between a person and a ship. Or maybe it said something about her, about the power inside her, the potential that she'd never been kept from fulfilling, unlike the Inhuman girls who awaited rescue below.

You haven't seen anything like me, she

thought, glancing down at the planet. *Just you wait, President Patriarchy.*

Everything else fell away as she raced past the stars, the missiles following her like ravenous wolves. Her arms thrust forward, legs tight, toes pointed, she jetted through the atmosphere, a bright ray of earthly energy come to bring some hard lessons to Damaria.

The profound, echoing silence associated with free flight in space was something that you got used to, or so she told herself. It was the kind of silence that was spooky to someone raised on Earth. She could remember the first time she stepped into it— back then, she'd needed a spacesuit—but still, even through all the gear, it was the type of vacuum that hit you emotionally almost as much as physically. It wove deep down inside you, into the lonely places, infiltrating them, filling them. In time, she came not just to accept it, but to respect and use it as another tool to hone her power.

The suns were brilliant, burning red and orange in orbit, and she could feel the radiation, the energy, exploding off them. The human part of her, the one that had been just Carol Danvers, warned *Danger*, while the Kree part of her screamed *Opportunity!*

She flew around the twin suns, a dizzying loop-the-loop, changing course and direction, dancing around one, then another as the missiles spun, trying to pin down her heat signature under all the radiation. It was like her training days, when student pilots were run through all sorts of vomit-inducing exercises to test their mettle. The flash of the solar flares was enough to send spots dancing along her line of sight, and the heat was almost unbearable, even for her, radiating down her arms and back, sinking through her suit. She could feel her Hala Star glowing over her heart. And still, the missiles followed, closer and closer to her with each orbit around the suns.

But with each loop she completed, the more energy she drew from the suns' flares and the more searing power raced through her veins, pooling beneath her skin, until she felt stretched too tight, too thin, too full—as if she might go pure Binary, right then and there.

It was time.

She sped off, away from the suns, and the missiles latched on once again, following. Carol flipped, screeching to a halt, turning to greet the glow of the suns in front of her. The missiles were in sight, one fifty feet behind the other, barreling toward their target: her.

She kept still, waiting—the ultimate game of chicken, as her old buddy Monica would call it. Her heart thumped and her world narrowed to the space between her heartbeats, the silence, the waiting, the mounting pressure of the sun's energy and the knowledge that it wanted out. It wanted out *now*.

Even after all these years—even after knowing she was invulnerable, and even after surviving so many epic battles and super villains and such monstrous torture— her fight-or-flight instinct still kicked in during these moments when she pulled off a do-or-die move.

She breathed around it because she knew what that made her. It made her someone who remembered where she came from, who she'd been... and who she had become. Because now she was someone who didn't need to choose between fight or flight. She was someone who flew *toward* the fight.

The first missile was a hundred feet away. Fifty feet. Twenty. Fifteen. Ten. And still, Carol waited.

Five. Four. Three...

Choosing the right split second, she lashed out, her fist striking the missile's nose with all of her might. The impact cracked her knuckles—and crunched the missile's base like paper—and she spun upward, out of range, and watched as the missile caromed and hit the second missile behind it. *Bam.* The collision was a brilliant smash of metal and weaponry, crushed by her timing and strength.

The explosion sent solar flares glittering in all directions as debris went flying toward the suns—and Carol. Dodging the flotsam and jetsam, she barely noticed when a piece of hull plating sliced her arm; she propelled herself forward, away from the blowback, away from the debris and the twin suns, down through the upper atmosphere, down toward her ship and her team, hovering right above the red fog.

The airlock was still open, and she twirled up inside it. Holding herself up by the handrail and slamming a gloved palm against the sensor, she felt the airlock floor snap together beneath her feet and seal in place with a hiss. She echoed it with a sigh of relief, and opened the interior door to duck out of the airlock into the control room, calling up the stairs, "I'm back on board—let's get out of the air before they lob some more missiles after us."

"On it!" Rhi yelled back, her voice upbeat with relief at her safe return.

Carol had just put a foot on the ladder when a sizzling sound filled the air.

She yelled for Rhi, for Mantis, for Scott or Amadeus—*any* of them—but her shouts were drowned out by a deafening metallic screech. Then the ship jerked to the side, knocking her onto the engine-room floor as the lights cut out abruptly.

"The ring!" she heard someone—Amadeus, her mind supplied—yell. "Oh my God, Scott! Watch out!"

The backup lights flickered on weakly, casting everything in a muddy red glow. A slamming sound. Someone moaned; someone else screamed. Carol leaped off the floor, scrambled up the ladder, and dashed toward the bridge as the ship tilted at a steep angle, jerking her off balance. To avoid a fall, she flew upward, her stomach brushing the floor as she half climbed her way up toward the bridge. What had happened—another missile? She should have stayed longer on guard out in space. She'd been careless…

"Are we hit?" she called out. "Report!"

But when she made it up to the bridge, she saw it before anyone could answer. Half of the solar ring had broken off in a jagged semicircle and was spinning off into the red fog.

The red cloud that surrounded the planet wasn't just a warning system, it was a toxic gas—and the further they descended into it, the more toxic it got. It was eating their ship alive, starting with the power rings that kept it in the air.

"The other half's gonna go!" Amadeus yelled. "Grab onto something!"

15

WHEN THE ship lurched like an unruly colt, jerking equipment loose and scattering it across the floor like confetti, Carol knew from too much experience they were nearing midair breakup. The team members scrambled to avoid flying fixtures and keep their footing while the sphere shuddered like a beast trying to shake off a flea—but this flea was one of the solar rings that powered the ship.

The second part of the ring snapped off; the jagged crescent moon of tech and metal floated away into the void, following its other half. The ship convulsed again, and after a few sickening swoops, began to hurtle downward through the darkness. As black faded into the thick red gas of Damaria's outer atmosphere, Carol lost sight of the second ring out the window—was it still hanging on, or had it cleaved off, too?

"Impact in five thousand feet," the warning system

kicked in, echoing through the intercom. *"Correct course immediately."*

There was no time for another fast-and-loose flying feat. The gas surrounding them that served as the Damarians' security shield was too toxic. They had to do this the old-school way: a controlled crash landing.

"Amadeus, slow us down!" she shouted. "I don't care how, just *do* it!"

Struggling to his feet, he grabbed the control panel with one hand, his hacking tablet in the other. "On it, Captain!" he said in a shaky voice.

"Impact in four thousand feet."

"Rhi!" Carol called, trying to spot her in the chaos.

"I've got her!" Scott yelled, waving a hand from behind a pile of crates. "We're okay."

"Mantis?" Carol turned in a careful circle, looking for black hair and finding nothing. Where was she? "Mantis!"

"Impact in three thousand feet."

Carol's stomach tightened. She'd survive the crash. So would Scott because of his suit, and Amadeus, too, because the big guy wouldn't let something like a crash landing get him down, but Mantis? Rhi?

"Mantis!" she called out again, her voice echoing in the silence. No answer. No time to look.

"Impact in two thousand feet. Proceed immediately to evacuation pods."

The lighting panels in the ceiling flickered, and some sparks rained down on their shoulders. She turned to Amadeus. "Figure something out *now*!"

"In progress!" he shouted, dodging the sparks. Then he jerked his head back and stared upward, his face illuminated in the shower. Carol smiled, recognizing his *sudden breakthrough* expression.

Amadeus shook off the sparks and turned back to her. "If we ditch the remaining solar ring, the ship will be forced to reroute any residual backup energy to power—and that'll slow us down, maybe even enough to keep us from smashing up... if it doesn't *blow* us up."

Carol stared at him. "That's our best option?"

"I didn't say it was a *good* idea... but it's the only one I've got," he shrugged.

"Impact in one thousand feet. Evacuate immediately."

Impossible decisions against impossible odds. Amadeus looked at Carol hopefully, awaiting her orders. Because she was the leader here; responsible for them—and for what would happen next, not only to them but to the planet below.

"Do it," she told Amadeus.

His hands flew over the tablet, typing in strings of code. "Better hold onto something."

"Brace for landing!" Carol shouted. She ran over to Scott and Rhi, who were already taking cover in an empty corner. The girl mustered up a strained smile, and Carol smiled back and knelt between them, her arms encircling their shoulders, as Amadeus executed the final line of code and hit the *Send* button.

"Here we go!" he called out, curling up in a recess.

The solar ring released from its housing, clicking free

in one piece. For a few moments, the ship veered into a slow spin, free of the ring. Power ebbing, it swooped haphazardly across the red sky. Then they began to drop, but slower this time. Would it be enough?

In free-fall, a sickening race where your stomach can't quite catch up with the rest of you, Rhi screamed. Carol kept hold of her and Scott, pinning them to the floor, protecting them with her body as the computer counted down:

"Impact in five hundred feet... Impact in four hundred—"

Suddenly, the ship trembled, bucked, slowed, and then—*boom!* It landed, in a bone-rattling—but not breaking—crash, metal crumpling on soil, glass shattering on rock as it bounced and skidded to a stop, smoke and red dust obscuring the view out the windows.

Rhi whimpered softly beneath her, and Carol stood up. "You two okay?"

Scott gave her a thumbs-up and rose to his feet, holding out his other hand to help Rhi up.

"Yes, I think so," the girl said quietly.

Scott peered into her eyes, checking her pupils, flashed her a smile, and shot Carol another thumbs-up.

"Check the perimeter while I find Mantis?" she asked him, turning away.

"On it," he replied. "Rhi, stay right here, all right?"

She nodded, looking dazed, but steady on her feet. Scott went for the ladder, going up it, unsealing the escape hatch and pulling himself out of the ship.

"Mantis!" Carol shouted, spinning around. Where *was* she? "Amadeus!"

"I'm okay," Amadeus called. "Just a little dizzy."

Carol shot him a grateful look and loped off to continue the hunt. "Mantis! *Report!*" She could hear panic rising in her voice. Had the empath been knocked out when the first ring broke free? She'd be damned if she was going to lose a team member, especially when their mission had barely started. She wasn't going to lose *anyone* this time.

But what if she did?

That damn voice nagging at her. So tricky. So hard to silence.

"Mantis, where *are* you?" Carol pulled apart the half-smashed doors leading to the kitchens, her muscles barely straining, and pushed through the gap she'd created. The mess was terrible. One of the pantry cabinets had broken off the wall and lay in pieces on the other side of the room, food strewn across the floor. Furniture was scattered and overturned, and… *there*! Carol caught a glimpse of a hand from beneath the table.

"*Mantis!*" She hurried over and hoisted it off the empath, who coughed as the pressure was released from her chest. Then she rolled to her side, curling into a fetal position as she moaned.

"Are you hurt? Where?"

"No," Mantis whispered. "I'll be okay… It's just all the emotions here… this planet…" Her eyelids fluttered and then squinched tight, trying to gain control.

Carol stared down at her. Rhi had told her the

Damarian weapon increased some people's powers while diminishing others', so she'd worried about Amadeus getting stuck in his Brawn form, but hadn't anticipated what problems the empath might encounter.

"Go tend to your command, Captain," Mantis said, slowly sitting up, her eyes still half shut. "I can get a hold of this... I just need to sit here a few moments to adjust." She winced. "I can *feel* them."

"The girls?" Carol asked. "The computers are down, I'm not sure where we landed. Are we near the Maiden House?"

Mantis shook her head. "We're near a city," she said. "We have to be. There are so many people. So many women. So much hurt. So much pain from the men who understand and fight for better. And the cruelty..." Her horrified eyes, wet and wide, lifted to meet Carol's. "This planet is *hell*."

Carol swallowed, her throat dry. She wanted so badly to reach out and comfort Mantis, but touch intensified an empath's sensations. So instead she just said softly, "That's why we're here."

Mantis gave a short nod and leaned back against the wall, flooding her senses. Reluctantly, Carol turned, strode across the mess, and pushed through the crumpled doors to rejoin the rest of her team on the deck.

"That was smart, losing the second ring," Carol told Amadeus, squeezing his shoulder gently. "If you hadn't come up with it, I'm not sure we'd all be here at all."

"Thanks."

"Where's Mantis?" Rhi asked.

"In the back. She's okay—just needs a few minutes alone. Whatever weapon the Damarians have, it's enhancing her powers instead of suppressing them."

"Oh no." Rhi's hand closed over the spot on her arm where the implant had gone, a compulsive stress habit Carol had noticed. "I didn't think—I'd hoped it wouldn't—is she all right?"

"Well—how bad did it get, with the Inhumans whose powers were enhanced by the weapon, instead of suppressed?" Carol asked.

"I don't know," Rhi said. "They were the first ones the Damarians slaughtered."

"I'll be fine," Mantis's voice rang out across the room and they all turned to the hall, where she was standing. "Especially if you all stop worrying so much—I can feel you clear across the ship." Mantis walked gingerly onto the deck, and Rhi and Amadeus hurried over to help her.

"*Guys!*"

Carol's head whipped upward, where Scott's worried voice emanated from the escape hatch. Then her fingers tingled and her feet itched for air beneath them, confirming her suspicions even before she heard him shout, "We've got incoming!"

16

CAROL SCRAMBLED up the escape-hatch ladder, with Amadeus and Rhi bringing up the rear. Rhi had to help Mantis, who was still sweating and flinching from the onslaught of emotions.

They had landed in a ravine, a narrow crack between two tall, jagged cliffs the color of rubies. The rock glowed and pulsed as if it were alive deep inside, and red dust from the cliffs swirled in the air, dimming the light of the twin suns. The rest of the team scrambled off the ship and onto the ground, kicking up dirt. Carol stood on top of the dented, smoking hull, staring down the end of the ravine that branched into wide-open land. There were dark specks on the horizon—human-sized specks... Damarians, heading right toward them.

She swiveled, catching sight of more troops approaching to their left as she slid down the curved hull and onto the ground in a smooth movement, positioning herself in front of Rhi and Mantis.

"Above you," Rhi whispered.

Carol looked up and saw two more men on the ridge—plus a ship, a smaller version of theirs, in the air just nearby. She estimated maybe three minutes before the seven men on the ground were close enough for combat. Who knew what the two on the ridge could do.

"We're boxed in," Scott said, clenching his fists. "We're gonna have a fight on our hands."

"How's everyone doing power-wise?" Carol asked. She felt a weight in the air... and a low-grade buzz in her head that she couldn't shake. When she wiggled her fingers, energy ran like trickles of water through them. Her head pounded at the simple act, but at least it worked. And her strength... she could feel it, always, rushing through her. She jumped, waiting for the familiar rise within—that giddy, spinning sensation that never failed to hype her up.

Nothing. Her eyes widened. *No!* Not her *flight!*

She jumped again, putting her strength into it, but she fell so fast and hard that dust shot ten feet in the air and her heels sank six inches into the ground.

Her stomach wrenched with a kind of fear she hadn't felt since she was a child, thinking she'd never get to soar through the stars where she *knew* she belonged. The Damarians on the ground were drawing closer. "Amadeus, how about you? We need Brawn—now."

"I'm trying," Amadeus said, the muscles in his neck straining, his eyes shut tight. "He *wants* to come out," he gasped, his whole body starting to shake under the strain. "But something's stopping him... God, what is that *humming*?"

"It must be the weapon," Carol said. "I hear it, too. Scott, is it affecting you or the suit?"

"Let's see." Scott tapped his wrist and suddenly disappeared. Relieved, Carol had to strain to see the red-and-black dot moving on the hull, no larger than the specks of red dirt their landing had scattered everywhere.

The miniature version of Scott jumped off the hull onto Amadeus's foot and began to tug. Carol watched, her heart sinking, as Ant-Man, trying his hardest, finally moved Amadeus's foot—one whole inch.

Scott popped back to normal size, breathing hard.

"My strength's all screwy," he gasped. "Shrinking was like wading through wet cement."

Rhi shot him a worried look. "The longer you're exposed to the weapon's effects, the easier it gets to fight it," she offered.

"How long did it take you to be able to tear a proper rip?" Scott asked.

She flushed. "A few years."

"So not soon enough," Carol said, her eyes fixed on the ridge where a light had just appeared.

"Incoming!" Carol shouted as the fireball was launched, hurtling toward them in a graceful, deadly arc. They scattered, Scott heading left, toward a cluster of boulders, Amadeus following with Mantis. Carol grabbed Rhi by the shoulders and leaped behind the ship, twisting in midair, curling herself around Rhi just before they slammed onto the ground, the ship shielding them. They tumbled in the dust, acrid red puffs swirling into Carol's nose and mouth, just as the spot where they'd been exploded into flame. For a second they lay motionless in the dirt, panting, staring at the line of flame the fireball had ignited in its path, the smoke rising from it.

Carol staggered to her feet, her ears ringing from the fireball's impact. Then she spotted it: the squad of four guards on foot, blocking their way out of the ravine.

"I've got the guys headed toward us on the right— you take the left," she yelled over her shoulder at Scott and Amadeus. "Mantis, stay down."

The guards picked up their speed and began running full-tilt right at them. Carol smiled. She might not have her flight, but she had her speed, her endurance, her invulnerability. The ache increased every time she reached inside herself for one of those powers that made her special, but energy still crackled along her fingers, with heat that made the fire behind her feel like tepid water.

She had the power of the stars and their beloved suns inside her. The photonic energy she could blast from her body was going to beat their fireworks, every time. And it was time to show them who they were messing with.

"You've got my back?" she asked Rhi, holding out a dusty hand.

Rhi took it, letting Carol pull her to her feet. "I've got your back," she promised.

Carol nodded her head in approval, the woman within making room for the soldier that formed her steady, eternal core: *Protect your people. Fulfill your mission. For your unit. For your country. For your planet.*

For the innocents. For the victims of Damaria.

Her sash whipped around her legs as she pelted toward the guards, a warrior cry wrenching from her throat. They were kitted out like riot-control security, with high-necked armor that sparked every few steps like miniature force fields. Her fingers itched to get ahold of one of those vests, pull the energy from it, and use it against them—she just needed to get near enough. Twenty feet away... now fifteen. They were closing in on ten when one of the guards unhooked something from his belt and lobbed it at her.

"Ember bombs!" Rhi yelled. "Watch out!"

But before it could explode on impact, Carol caught it in her hand—a transparent sphere full of a gelatinous blue material that wobbled back and forth. It was burning hot, singeing her palm. She was close enough to see the terror in the guard's sweaty face as she tossed the bomb from hand to hand. His eyes darted back and forth as Carol gazed into it, as if it were a crystal ball holding her fortune.

His companions froze, unsure what to do now that the enemy was armed with their own weapon. Whatever was inside, they'd counted on it hurting her. But now it might help.

"What *are* you?" the guard gasped out.

She smiled—a condescending tilt of the mouth

that he'd likely never seen on a woman's lips before. "I thought you people had a myth you scare children with about me. Don't you know a star woman when you see her?"

Her words sparked an ancient fear. Like a Neanderthal who'd just discovered the sting of flame, the guard stumbled backward and crumpled before the legendary terror, the fulfillment of a horror story he'd heard all his life: a woman with untrammeled power, sent to destroy everything he knew.

She threw the bomb at his feet as the rest of the squad dove for cover. It exploded as soon as it hit the ground, the sphere shattering and spraying the blue gel over the guard's legs and chest. She watched as it burned its way through his armor and then his flesh, the force field flickering as the toxic gel fried its circuitry. He screamed, clawing at it, getting it stuck on his hands, and then he screamed some more.

"On your right!" Rhi dashed past her, pointing at a guard hiding behind a boulder just twenty feet away. At first aimed at Carol, he swiveled toward Rhi as she ran, both arms moving in a strange circular dance, fingers pulling apart time and space, ripping them as if they were fabric.

Then he took a shot, but Rhi dodged, turned, and flung both arms out in a wide gesture.

"Captain, help me!" she shouted, as the gap between then and now stretched nearer to the man. Carol hurtled forward, lashing out in a precise kick to the abdomen that sent him flying… right into the sparkling hole Rhi had just spun into existence. He didn't even have time to yell—or if he did, they couldn't hear it. The sound—and its source—had vanished, like all things snared in the in-between. And then the rip snapped shut, like a predator's mouth on a particularly tasty treat.

"Is he—?" Carol asked.

Rhi shook her head, her eyes wide with shock. "I sent him backwards in time. He's here still. Just… three days ago." She let out a laugh. "I've never done that before. I was worried it wouldn't work."

"First try's always the roughest," Carol said, yanking her out of range as gunfire rained along the ground. The two remaining guards on the ground had taken cover and started shooting. The two above had held off, letting their friends on the ground take charge. She and Rhi needed to get over to the rest of the team.

Just as she was thinking it out, another fireball—this one spitting flames—hurtled toward them from the top of the ridge, driving them back toward the ship for shelter.

"Go, go, *go*!" Carol shoved Rhi ahead of her just as the ball crashed on the ground inches behind them, the flames spreading faster than the girl could run. Heat nipped at Carol's feet as she snatched up and half carried her, ducking behind the smoking hull, where Scott, Mantis, and Amadeus had fashioned a fragile barrier out of some shards of sheets from the damaged shell—and Scott was still his regular size.

Carol released her, and the girl sank down on the ground next to them.

"That was great, Rhi!" Scott tossed her a thumbs-up and Rhi smiled shakily, still breathing hard.

Carol looked at Scott expectantly. "I can't get the suit to hold for more than a few minutes," he answered her silent question with a grimace. "I took out two guards before it fritzed. And Amadeus got that one with his funky electro-net gun." He pointed to a guard on the ground down the ravine, still thrashing in the glowing net. "So we're clear on the left side. But those guys on the ridge aren't letting up."

"There's still two on the right. I don't think they have powers, though. They keep shooting at us and lobbing bombs, instead of hurling fireballs."

"So we get rid of the two on the ridge, we get rid of the fireballs," Rhi said.

"Easier said than done," Amadeus groaned. Mantis was leaning heavily against him, like he was the only thing keeping her upright.

"Amadeus, anything going on with Brawn?" Carol asked.

He sighed, with a tight, frustrated shake of the head. "Mantis?"

She barely nodded her head. Carol's heart twisted at the sight, but she couldn't take the time to do more than squeeze the empath's shoulder.

Searching her mind for a solution, she crowded closer to her team as the heat climbed to sizzling heights around them. Sweat trickled down her cheeks as anger twined inside her like rusty barbed wire.

The ground shook as another ball landed right

behind them, the impact shoving the ship sideways, its crumpled hull groaning at the movement. New flames leaped closer.

They were exposed. Vulnerable. Outgunned.

Protect them.

Carol whirled into action, her hands thrusting out, but it felt like walking through mud. The humming in her head increased as energy crackled up her arms, gathering, poised to blast. The heat of the fire bore down on her, and she plunged her hands into the whirling flames as the ache in her body popped like a cap off a bottle and the flame's energy surged through her, sputtering down to a manageable height. The searing heat and power raced along the meridians of her body and mind gleefully, and suddenly she was drowning in a deluge of power feeding into her essence: part Kree, part human, all Carol. It rose within her cells, heat and flame and fury, swirling and spitting, building to a volcanic eruption.

Through the field of dimming fire, she could see them: the two remaining guards on the ground. Take care of them, and they just had the powered ones on the ridge to deal with. Her hands clenched and then opened. Her breathing slowed, even as that damn buzzing increased. She could do this.

But before she had a chance to start, a fearsome, high-pitched battle cry echoed through the ravine, and its source, a white-and-black figure, launched from the opposite ridge in a perfect swan dive. Landing in a blur of lightning-fast limbs, she dealt out precise kicks and punches that the guards never saw coming. She was a deadly whirl, with no grace spared to her movements. Her laughter filled the smoky air as she charged through the flames as if she didn't feel the burn, leaping from boulder to boulder as if they were lily pads spread across a lake of fire, before disarming the last guard and then clubbing him on the back of the head with his own gun.

Tossing the weapon—and then her magnificent white mane—she turned around to gaze at Carol and the team through the smoke, her tail twitching as if it wasn't ready to stop fighting.

"Did you miss me?" the woman asked Carol with a sly smile.

Carol smiled back, relief singing through every inch of her body.

"Never... and always, Hepzibah," she replied.

17

"DON'T WORRY, she's a friend," Carol called over her shoulder to the team.

"A friend who's made it a habit to save you," Hepzibah added, dashing over to Carol and inspecting her closely. After deciding that she was fine, she turned her head to watch the guards remaining on the ridge. "How many times is this now? At least a dozen? I do love an even number."

"I think you're overestimating," Carol shot back with a grin, shading her eyes against the suns circling in the sky and trying to assess the situation. They needed to get up on the ridge before more fireballs were hurled their way—and more troops arrived. "I didn't think you were gonna show."

"You pulled the favor card," Hepzibah said. "And how could I resist getting even?"

"She has a *tail*!" Carol heard Rhi whisper to Scott in

awe. She hoped Hepzibah wouldn't take offense.

"They're going to hit us again!" Amadeus yelled, pointing to a cluster of lights gathering along the ridge.

"Take cover!" Carol ordered, and the team scrambled behind the ship. She turned to Hepzibah, her eyebrow rising in challenge. "What do you think?" she asked, jerking her head toward the cliff. "You up for a climb?"

The woman frowned. "Why not fly?"

"I can't right now," Carol said, hating to admit it out loud.

Hepzibah had known her long enough to understand. Sympathy flickered in her eyes.

"Let's get to it, then!" she said briskly.

As they began to scale the ravine, the red stone slippery beneath feet and fingers, Carol was glad she'd spent all that time in Yosemite free-climbing— when you were Captain Marvel, you didn't exactly need carabineers and ropes. But now, as she dug her fingertips into a half-inch gap to hoist herself over a deep crevasse, she was acutely aware that if she fell, she wasn't flying out of here.

Scrambling for the next foothold, she launched herself upward onto a small ledge just seconds before a fireball plummeted through the air inches from her head and landed on the spot she'd just jumped from, obliterating it.

The tang of singed hair filled the air. Wedging her knee against the rock to keep her balance, she patted the back of her head to make sure it wasn't smoldering, watching the ball explode on the ground below and spreading lines of flames.

Hepzibah growled, swinging up effortlessly behind her. "These fools don't know when they've been beat, do they?"

"They're not exactly used to women fighting back." Carol reached for a new handhold. "You feeling one hundred percent?" she asked.

"One hundred and ten," Hepzibah replied. "And you?"

She shook her head. "Their weapon—some sort of power suppression—stole my flight. It's messing with Scott and Amadeus, too, so I'm especially grateful you're here."

Hepzibah grimaced in sympathy. "You poor creatures really do need me," she cooed. "Fortunately for us all, I feel nothing."

"Fortunately," Carol echoed.

Crouching on the edge of the cliff, Carol raised her hand and shot several blasts out of it, a *rat-a-tat-tat* of photon energy. Someone screamed as the air lit so brightly it made the Damarian fireballs look like children's toys. She heard another shout and footfalls—the guards retreating from the edge of the ridge, leaving a trail of fire in their wake. She and Hepzibah locked eyes and spoke aloud, in unison, to each other and the universe.

"*Now!*"

The pair leapt out onto the smoldering ridge as one, honed into a synchronized dance of death from their years as a fighting unit. Her shoulders pressed against Carol's as they lined up, back to back, turning in a slow circle to survey the surrounding terrain. The guards were nowhere in sight—but their ship was just ahead, set down on a flat shard of rock ten feet away.

Carol moved, Hepzibah at her back, quickly and silently toward the ship, hopping over charred and melted bits of rock.

"There." Carol nudged Hepzibah gently. She could see the tips of muddy boots just behind the ship. The men were cowering in the wake of Carol's show of power.

Good. About time they got a taste of their own medicine.

Carol pointed, signifying that she'd circle around the right, Hepzibah to the left. Her friend nodded, mouthing, *One, two, three.*

They broke apart, heading in opposite directions, Carol soft-footed and sure, and Hepzibah? Well, she had her own style. It involved yelling like a banshee and using her tail to swipe at the feet in those muddy boots, knocking the guard to the ground.

"Don't even think about it," Carol said, extending a crackling palm in front of his partner, who was reaching for one of those damn ember bombs. She pushed him against the hull of his ship so hard that it creaked. Her arm pressed against his neck like a steel band and his eyes widened in horror at Carol's glowing fingers, the photonic energy pulsing around them like a pyrotech's would, and then looked at Hepzibah, who'd already finished binding his unconscious partner's hands behind his back. She caught him staring at her, and her tail twitched, her smile mocking as she rose to her feet.

"You've never seen anyone like me, have you?" she asked. He gasped as she drew closer. "What foolish men. You cannot contain a Mephitisoid's powers, not even for a short time. We are an ancient species. Your planet was barely a speck in the stars when my people rose."

"Liar!" His outburst seemed to startle even himself, sweat trickling off his face as Carol's arm tightened against his neck.

Hepzibah chuckled. "Bold words for one who stinks of fear. Now, we can do this the easy way, or we can do it the hard way." She smiled, a menacing crescent blooming across her pale face.

"We need to get moving," Carol interrupted Hepzibah's game. They had no idea how long it would be until more guards showed up—these two might have called for backup already.

Hepzibah sighed. "Very well. Step aside."

Carol did as she asked, and she grasped the guard's head between her hands, passing her wrist along his mouth, under his nose. He jerked backward, his head striking the side of the ship, trying to resist, but there was nowhere to go. He couldn't help but breathe them in, the powerful pheromones that Hepzibah—and all Mephitisoids—could use to manipulate others.

Though Carol had seen her do this before, it was always fascinating. As soon as the pheromones hit the man's system, the change was almost instantaneous: His body slumped against the hull and his shoulders relaxed, his hands falling aimlessly to his sides. His eyes grew hooded, and a trusting smile bloomed across his face.

"Doesn't that feel better?" she asked.

He nodded.

"Now, tell me, where's the weapon?"

He blinked. Once. Twice. "It's guarded day and night, inside Fort Olvar."

"And how do we turn it off?"

He hesitated, his mouth opening and closing like a fish's. Hepzibah waved her wrist under his nose again, painting his skin with pheromones.

"I... I don't know," he said. "It's beyond my security clearance."

She rolled her eyes, annoyed. "Too bad." She punched him on the cheek—a fast, vicious slug that snapped his head backward—and stepped aside as he dropped to the ground, unconscious.

"So," Hepzibah said, tail thrashing. "What do we do now?"

"Gotta clean up this mess and get out of here quick." Carol gestured at the guards, and Hepzibah picked her way over the prone bodies to follow her.

o———o

THEY ENDED up piloting the guards' ship down to the bottom of the ravine and piling the remaining guards, still unconscious, inside. Carol sealed the escape hatch shut, the heat from her hands melting the metal with the kind of seal that could secure a submarine. They wouldn't be getting out anytime soon, and whoever came to find them would have a hard time setting them free.

"I've collected everything we need from our ship," Amadeus said, pointing to the pile of crates and bags he'd stacked outside of what was left of the ship they'd arrived on. "Did you take their comms?"

"Of course," Carol said.

"And I have their weapons," Hepzibah said, lovingly stroking the gun she'd brought. Her pockets were bulging with ember bombs.

"Here," Carol called out, tossing Amadeus one of the bright-red comm balls that each guard had worn strapped to their chests.

"Is everything a sphere here?" Amadeus muttered, catching it.

"Seems to be," Scott said. "So, Carol, who's your friend?"

"This is Hepzibah," Carol said. "We used to run a crew together back in the day."

"We were feared far and wide across the galaxy," Hepzibah added. "But we can talk history later. Your friend there—Mantis, isn't it? We know the same people—is not looking good."

She was right. Mantis was slumped against the charred remains of the hull with her eyes half closed and her legs twitching every few seconds, as if her entire body was trying to reject the overload of emotion. Rhi crouched next to her, dabbing at her sweaty forehead with the sleeve of her jacket.

"My ship's just beyond the ravine," Hepzibah said.

"Let's get out of here before more guards show up," Carol said, striding over and picking Mantis up in her arms. The empath didn't protest, which sent a spear of worry through Carol.

The ravine opened up to a swath of ancient rock formations shining scarlet against the horizon, jagged and fierce, like crooked fingers reaching for the twin suns. Behind them, the red gas swirled through the black sky, obscuring the stars. With Carol carefully carrying Mantis, they made good time traveling through the rough terrain and soon came upon Hepzibah's small ship—a sleek, bullet-shaped shuttle—wedged between two towers of red rock, their shadows falling over them, cooling the evening air.

"I can't believe you got through their shields and sensors undetected," Amadeus said, all eyes as they piled inside. The vessel was a one-woman show, designed to be flown solo or with one co-pilot, so it was short on elbow room. It reminded Carol of a swallow, designed for speed and agility. Which, considering the welcome they'd just received, they were going to need.

"I left my main ship two moons away," Hepzibah explained. "My long-range shuttle's stealth technology is clearly superior, and the Damarians were also distracted by your arrival, so I was able to slip under any radar they had."

"I'd love to talk to you about what you're running

in here," Amadeus said. "You know, after we get everyone rescued."

"I'm better at flying ships than building them," Hepzibah smiled, turning to go. "Come with me to the cockpit if you like. I'll show you the setup."

"Where are we heading?" Rhi asked her.

"My scanners say there's a cave about two klicks from here," Hepzibah said. "It'll be a secure spot to lie low and make a plan."

Carol nodded her assent and gently laid Mantis down on a bench in the tiny kitchen, Rhi following close behind her as Hepzibah disappeared into the cockpit, Amadeus at her heels. Soon, a soft rumble from the engine filled the air, and the shuttle took off gently, straight upward.

The kitchen was neat and orderly, with a set of metal cabinets full of food and supplies bolted to the wall, a polished stove, and a toaster oven that Carol recognized as the one that had gone mysteriously missing the last time Hepzibah had visited her in New York.

Mantis whimpered, her eyes drifting shut. Rhi shot Carol a concerned look. "What can I do?"

"I'm not sure," Carol said. Rhi looked even more worried, but stayed silent.

Scott walked up to stand with them, worrying his lower lip. Before she turned back to Rhi, Carol noticed a shiny ember-bomb burn on his arm that would need some treatment. "You did an amazing job out there, Rhi."

The girl let out a shaky breath. "We're not anywhere

near the Maiden House. The Field of Fire—that's what these stone formations are called—is hundreds of miles away. We're closer to the capital than to my Maiden House. And your powers…" She looked up at Carol, panic in her eyes.

"I know," Carol said, trying to sound reassuring. "It's a rough start. But that doesn't mean we can't get control of the situation."

"We kicked their asses even without most of our powers, albeit with Hepzibah's help," Scott pointed out, holding a coaxing smile until Rhi returned it for a moment. "And maybe we'll get used to the weapon faster because we're all different, in terms of how we got our powers. The Damarians will be running scared in no time."

Minutes later, Hepzibah called out from the cockpit, "Secure for landing!" Guiding the ship into a graceful descent, she tucked the shuttle into a narrow hollow in the stone at the base of a crooked rock that speared toward the sky.

Carol could feel it in the air, how the adrenaline surge from the fight was starting to fade from her team's bodies while the Damarian weapon still buzzed in their heads, obscuring their powers. As the ship powered down, she rooted around in the set of cupboards in the kitchen to find a first aid kit.

"Here, let me," Rhi said. She found the burn cream and spread it across Scott's arm as he winced.

"What's in that burning blue gel?" he asked, tucking in the end of the gauze Rhi had just wrapped around his arm.

"A caustic mineral that's mined in the Tukan mountains," Rhi said. "When it's exposed to a Keeper's flame, it turns into the gel."

Amadeus and Hepzibah entered: Amadeus looked thoughtful. "That could be interesting... Maybe I can reprogram the flame trigger to be something we could use," he said. Mantis had fallen into a fitful sleep on the bench; concerned about her fragile state, Carol let her doze on. "Is there a bunk for Mantis?" Maybe some space away from the team would calm things down in her mind.

Hepzibah nodded, and Carol followed her down the shuttle's narrow hall. There were a few paintings along the walls, skunks and stars and even a flying figure that looked a *little* like Carol. There was definitely a figure who had to be Corsair, Hepzibah's partner in crime and life. It looked like he was ripping off someone's head, but maybe Carol was reading into the rough sketches.

Hepzibah stopped behind her as she crouched down to slide open a door leading to the empty bunk. Carol set Mantis down on the bed built into the wall, and she didn't stir, even when Carol covered her with a blanket.

"Hopefully some rest will help," Carol said, looking grim. "I'm worried about her."

"This weapon of theirs, it must be destroyed," Hepzibah said. "We—" She frowned, her head whipping toward the mess. Carol heard it, too, and she hurried out into the hall, following the muffled voice.

A voice that didn't belong to any of her team. A voice that she suddenly recognized, with a sick feeling in the pit of her stomach.

The guard's comm, the one that she'd given Amadeus to examine, was on the kitchen table. Rhi had sunk onto the floor against the wall, staring at the comm like it was broadcasting every nightmare she'd ever had.

The speaker crackled, and a haughty voice filled the air. President Ansel's voice.

"I know you've returned, Rhi," he said, his words sharpened with static and cruelty. "I must admit, I am surprised. I didn't think you had the mental capacity to pilot such an advanced craft."

"It's okay," Amadeus muttered to Rhi. "He can't find us through this. He doesn't even know you're listening."

"He knows," the girl said, rocking back and forth, her knees drawing up to her chest as Amadeus stared helplessly at her. "He knows. He knows."

Rhi was on the edge of a meltdown. Carol decided she had to show her, right then and there, how someone—a *woman*—could stand up to this man who had made her an orphan, tortured her, and stolen the woman she loved.

"Umbra wept when I told her you'd escaped," Ansel continued. "She was punished for it, of course. But I can never stay angry at her for long. What do you think she'll do when I tell her you were stupid enough to return? Did you think you could take her from me?

Foolish thing—she's *mine*."

Carol reached for the comm, thumbing the switch from *Off* to *On*. Rhi's gaze shifted to her, startled.

"Hey," Carol began, her voice lowered to an unnatural growl as a disguise. "Finished with your ridiculous villain monologue yet? 'Cause I've got a few things to tell you."

There was a pause—a prolonged one.

Rhi gasped. Amadeus patted her hand gingerly, an awkward moment made sweet when she squeezed his fingers back tightly.

"Who is this?" Ansel's voice changed, growing deeper, less mocking.

She thought about how the Damarians had reacted when she'd claimed their mythic star woman. The fear it had inspired in them. "Ask the guards you sent after my ship," she said. "What's left of them, at least. They have an interesting story for you. Believe every word, because I'm coming for you and that precious weapon of yours."

Without even waiting for his answer, she slammed the comm against the wall with all her strength. It shattered in her palm, the bits of plastic and metal ground to dust under her grip.

"That was either really smart… or really reckless," called Scott from the hallway.

"I vote for smart," Hepzibah said, thrashing her tail. "Now they're scared. And they should be."

Carol raised an eyebrow, smiling.

"But now they're going to have even *more* security

surrounding the president and the fort where the weapon's kept," Scott countered.

"They will," Carol replied, a new plan already unfolding in her mind. "But it won't matter. Because we're going to walk right through the front gate."

18

SCOTT DID a classic double take. "What are you talking about?" he asked. "I told you, I can't get my suit to hold for more than a few minutes. And I'm not sure I can dismantle tech like that on my own. I kind of need Amadeus."

"We don't need you… I mean, we *do*," Carol said. "But to get in, we won't need Ant-Man. The guard Hepzibah questioned said the suppression weapon is at Fort Olvar." She turned to Rhi. "And you said that your friend Jella and whoever she's touching can just blend into any surface, so she's as good as invisible, right?"

Rhi nodded. Her eyes widened as she caught on to Carol's thinking. "Yes!"

"Okay, so Jella can get Scott and Amadeus into the fort to dismantle the weapon while the rest of us get Umbra. After that, the Damarians won't stand a chance."

"Jella would be a game-changer," Scott agreed.

Hepzibah nodded in approval, rose, and disappeared in the kitchen while they tossed ideas about timing back and forth. A few minutes later, she returned with a large plate of flatbread, olives, and a slightly dusty jar of a spicy relish Carol recognized as a Shi'ar recipe Hepzibah had learned to make while growing up under their rule. For a second, the team lost themselves in the restorative crunch of salty bread and the zing of the relish, then returned to the task at hand.

Amadeus set his tablet on the table and hit a key that displayed a holographic calendar with dates scribbled on it. "If we do it right, I think there's a way we can rescue Jella *and* Umbra at the same time. Before we crashed, I managed to download some of Ansel's files—look." He circled a date on the hologram. "If my calculations on the Damarian calendar are correct, this fundraising event is tomorrow. Which means the president and all his underlings will be at this Damarian museum in the capital, Edias."

"So what do you suggest, Amadeus?" Carol asked, curious about how he'd lay out a plan like this.

"We go in undercover," Amadeus said. "I can whip up some counterfeit invitations and ID. You, Scott and I... we look the most like the Damarians. No offense, Hepzibah."

"The Damarians couldn't dream of being as glorious as me," Hepzibah waved his apology away. "But I understand—they do not possess such magnificent ears or tails, or antennae like Mantis. It's their loss."

Carol looked over her shoulder at the bench where Mantis was sleeping. She hoped the empath's dreams were good ones. Tomorrow, she'd be waking up again to a nightmare.

"Tails and antennae are cool," Amadeus said, ducking his head a little to hide a smile. "So, if the three of us go in, posing as donors from, I dunno, what's a really far-off place in Damaria that the president doesn't visit a lot?"

"The Isle of Tuke," Rhi suggested. "It's remote, but the ember-bomb minerals come from there—which makes the landowners very wealthy... and very protective of their island. They don't leave often."

"Sounds perfect," Amadeus said. "Scott's likely the guy they'd take most seriously, so he'd go as the landowner, Carol as his wife, and me as the assistant?"

Carol ran down the pros and cons in her mind. It was risky, especially since she'd confronted the president over the comm. But she had a feeling that Damarian women didn't talk much at these events, anyway—so with the right clothes and demure attitude, she had a good chance of getting away with it. There was power in being underestimated.

"I like it," she said to Amadeus. "What does everyone else think?"

"Seems solid to me," Scott said.

"The big question to answer: how to get the girls away from their Keepers?" Hepzibah asked. "They keep them close, no?"

"They're within arm's length at all times," Rhi said. "Just in case the Keepers need to use their powers."

"Physical contact is required to turn off their implants and for the Keeper to maintain control," Carol explained to Hepzibah in an undertone.

"I think I've figured out how to disrupt that," Amadeus piped up. "At least temporarily, until we can remove Jella and Umbra's implants. I made some mini EMP patches. Placed over the implant on their arms, it should scramble the sensor long enough for me to perform some quick extractions. I had to crank the pulse up really high to disable Rhi's implant. They are powerful. And they have kill switches. We need to be careful so the Keepers don't suspect us."

"I'd suggest a showy distraction," Scott said. "But as long as they have contact with the girls, they could use their powers against us, right, Rhi?"

She nodded. "They will not hesitate to use our powers, or our bodies as human shields."

Scott's mouth clicked closed, clearly fighting his reaction to Rhi's matter-of-fact statement. "Okay, so we've got to be discreet."

"Rhi and I can wait somewhere in the shadows in case you need us," Hepzibah suggested.

But Rhi shook her head. "If I can't be seen at or near the fundraiser, and I know I can't, I should be focused on Zeke. I still have to find out where they're keeping my brother."

Carol frowned. "You can't find Zeke?"

"I haven't honed in on him since we got here," she said. "They must be keeping him on the move. If they don't stop, it's much harder to get a hold on his location."

"Can't you just spin one of your rips and pull Zeke through it?" Scott asked.

"It's too risky. The in-between is a tricky place and often you end up leaving things behind the longer you linger inside it. Sometimes it's memories. Sometimes it's your eyes or your teeth. Or even vital organs. There's a reason I flew a spaceship instead of just walking through the rip. It's a tear through time and space—it won't kill you, but it's not exactly a friendly environment."

Carol didn't even want to touch on how Rhi had discovered all this. She was just going to trust the girl knew her stuff.

"They can't keep him on the move forever," Carol said, propping her chin on her hands as she thought it through. They might have set up some sort of mobile prison for Zeke, and if the technology she'd seen so far was any indication, the whole planet was powered mainly by their precious twin suns rather than fossil fuels or other sources. Who knew how long they could keep the boy moving without stopping? What if they had him on a boat or underground?

Her lack of flight was hampering her at every turn, and it itched under her skin, the frustration, the pure *fury* at being limited like this. Then she felt a flash of guilt, because Mantis was truly suffering right now. Carol's issues paled by comparison.

"Ansel might have the details on Zeke in his home office," Rhi said. "He lives on an island outside of Edias. I know his house will be empty because he'll be at the fundraiser. I want to break in and search for it."

"The president's home will be heavily guarded," Scott warned.

"That's why she'll have me with her," Hepzibah said instantly, smiling at Rhi. "I will accompany you, Rhi. We'll find where they're keeping your brother while Carol and the others get your friends."

"If we dismantle their weapon after we get Jella and Umbra, and Rhi finds out where Zeke is, all we need to do is grab him and then free the girls at the Maiden House," Amadeus said. "I guess the big worry is if they'll move the girls now that they know Rhi is back?"

"I don't think so," Rhi said. "It would be a risky move, and Ansel doesn't like to take risks. My Maiden House already has extra security because we were considered the most dangerous. And it's in the most isolated spot."

Scott bit back a yawn. "Should we move now?"

"No," Carol said. "The Damarians are going to be up and down the Field of Fire all night, searching for us. It's better to stay cloaked and powered down as much as possible, so they can't detect any energy signatures, and then head out with the sunrise."

"Then I'm gonna spend some time hacking into the Damarian network so I can cook up some fake invites and ID, snoop around a little," Amadeus said, getting to his feet and stretching his arms above his head. "Where should I set up so I'm out of your way, Hepzibah?"

"I shall show you." She got up, and then looked at Rhi. "Do not worry," she told the girl. "We will crush them."

"She certainly has a way with words," Scott commented, getting to his feet as well. "I'm going to go sit with Mantis for a while and try to… I dunno, project calm, good thoughts at her. Maybe it'll help."

"I'm sure she'd appreciate that," Carol said.

Then it was just her and Rhi, sitting in the tiny shuttle kitchen in the middle of the night, plotting to overthrow a planet whose security forces were mobilizing to kill them.

Carol folded her hands and leaned on the table. "Let's talk about Umbra and Jella," she said. "And how I can let them know I'm there to save them in a discreet way. Is there a code word or something you set up?"

"Oh, it's simple," Rhi said, reaching inside her dirty jacket and pulling out the necklace she usually wore. This was the first time Carol had seen it up close, the series of silver discs sliding on a silver chain. With them laid out across her palm, Carol could see the etchings: numbers.

"The first year they put us in the Maiden House, they tried to take our names."

A chill twined around Carol's spine, but she kept silent, waiting, hoping Rhi would continue.

"Miss Egrit assigned us numbers and we had to wear these discs as ID." She traced a finger around the one that had a five stamped on it. "Miss Egrit made me number five. Or she tried."

"You fought back." Carol didn't need to make it a question. She understood the determination it took to rise in a world designed at every turn to reduce you to a tool, not a person.

Rhi nodded and went on. "So we started switching numbers. It was my idea. That first year, a lot of different people were there, observing us, apart from Miss Egrit. They started getting confused—*I thought Number Five had the water powers, not the finding powers?*—you know, that sort of thing."

"So you annoyed them into giving you back your names."

"Yes. And after they gave up on the numbers, I kept the discs, even the twins'," Rhi said. "It's like I knew even then that I'd end up being the one who ran, and I'd need these so it'd be easy to find them all again."

"You ran to get help," Carol stressed.

"But I still left them behind," Rhi whispered. "No warning. He said—he said on the comm that Umbra cried when he told her. They must all think I abandoned them. Or died."

"They don't," Carol said firmly. "Umbra doesn't. She knows you. And when I give her and Jella the discs, they'll know for sure. They'll know you came back to free them, just like you always promised."

Rhi pulled the chain from her hand, sorting through the discs—at least a dozen, and Carol knew they weren't rescuing a dozen girls. Remembering Rhi's story about the twins, she didn't ask what had happened to the others, as Rhi slipped two discs off the chain, numbers 11 and 12.

"These belonged to Vale and Vik," Rhi said,

pressing them into Carol's palm. "If you show them to Jella and Umbra, they'll know I sent you."

Carol stared down at the discs, recognition rising inside her. She knew what it was like to have nothing much left of someone other than memories and an ID tag.

"You look sad," Rhi said. "I—did I say something wrong?"

"No," Carol said quickly, her voice growing hoarse. "I just…" She let out a laugh, an uncomfortable sound that had her shifting in her seat as her hands closed around the silver circles. Sometimes, she was no good at emotions. "We have something similar to this back home, in the military. Ours aren't dehumanizing like this, more for ID purposes, if you get lost in a war zone or your body is discovered in a…" she trailed off, clearing her throat, thinking of Stevie's smile, of her brother, frozen in her mind in his twenties. "We call them dog tags."

"Did you have them?"

"I did," Carol said. "And so did my brother… the one who didn't make it back home. His dog tags did, though. For a long time, I wore them around my neck next to mine, even though it was against regulation. When I took my job with NASA—that's one of our space-exploration agencies—I gave them back to my mother. I knew I'd never hear the end of it if I lost Stevie's tags in space."

"That wouldn't be ideal," Rhi said with a hint of a smile.

"I think space might have been safer for them than

Earth," Carol said. "Few years back, my mom lost a bunch of stuff in a flood. Including Stevie's tags. Mother Nature can be nasty sometimes."

Sometimes Carol had pictured them, carried far from home, probably buried in mud or at the bottom of a river, and she felt a little heartbroken.

Some things were just objects. But some things... they became talismans. Symbols. She knew that all too well, Hala Star on her chest and all.

Rhi's head tilted, and then she smiled, a brilliant smile that was full of a kind of joy Carol had thought she didn't know how to feel. She held out her palm. "Take my hand," she said. "And think about the tags."

Carol clasped Rhi's hand in hers, and the steel tags—with the stamped letters of his name, blood type, and ID number—formed in her mind's eye.

Carol watched as Rhi spun her other hand in a counter-clockwise motion, the air above the table rippling and spitting in a tiny whirlwind. The blue-and-white sparks gathered into a tiny hole, which Rhi air-massaged and stretched into a glittering six-inch rip.

Then Rhi leaned forward and reached into the tear, her hand disappearing into the light. Carol tasted moist earth and ozone on her tongue, and gasped as the girl yanked out a muddy chain, dirty tags swinging in the open air between them. The rip snapped shut, and Rhi let go of Carol's hand, dropping the tags into her open palm.

Carol couldn't stop the choked breath she let out as she wiped the still-moist soil away, rubbing the indentations compulsively, as if to reassure herself the tags were really there.

Steven J. Danvers. Blood Type O+. ID 5421964.

The last piece of Stevie, finally back with her. When she met Rhi's eyes, her voice cracked with emotion.

"Rhi, I—"

But the girl just smiled. "I know."

She got up, leaving Carol alone with the necklace. As she watched Rhi walk down the hall to find a corner to bunk down in for the night, her fingers curled around the tags and the two discs that had belonged to the dead twins. And she swore on her brother's memory, on Rhi's lost sisters, that even if it was the last thing she ever did, she was going to free these girls.

19

MORNING CREPT toward them while Carol was on watch. Stevie's tags were again around her neck, tucked under her shirt, but she couldn't begin to describe how this made her feel.

Rhi had given her a tremendous gift.

She sipped the flowery herbal tea Hepzibah was fond of and watched the twin suns rise along the horizon, the dawn light shining through the crooked red-stone spires that stretched across the distance.

"You made a whole pot," Hepzibah said, climbing into the cockpit and slipping into the co-pilot seat next to Carol to pour herself a cup.

"I missed the taste. You can't get this on Earth. And I knew you'd be up soon," Carol said, still staring out the shuttle window. "What do you think, Hepzibah?"

She turned to look at the horizon. She didn't need to ask Carol to clarify. "Amadeus showed me the blueprints he found of this Maiden House. It's ridiculous they call it that—it's a prison. Nothing else." She shook her head, as if she was trying to ward off bad memories. Carol understood—prisons made Hepzibah uncomfortable. Her skill at breaking out of—and into—them had saved her life and put her on the path to help form the Starjammers. But Hepzibah had spent her childhood on a planet under an invader's rule, and then as an adult was kept on a prison planet and sentenced to be eaten alive. The thought of that particular punishment still made Carol shudder.

She'd escaped that fate, but some memories lingered.

"If we can shut off the weapon, I think we have a good chance," Hepzibah finally answered her question directly. "If not, I guess I'll just have to do all the heavy lifting for you."

Carol snorted. "Just because I can't fly doesn't mean I can't break into a prison."

Hepzibah reached over, squeezing her knee affectionately. "I know how much flying means to you," she said quietly. "But it's not gone forever. And you know I'm joking—you've assembled an excellent team. But then, you always did have a gift for joining up with talented people."

"You know, the term *humble-bragging* was invented for you," Carol told her.

"I do not need to be humble," Hepzibah said, her brows drawn together fiercely. "That is what they teach the women here on this miserable planet—to make themselves small. I refuse to fall into such a trap. There is strength in pride… in a woman knowing her worth and proclaiming it for all to hear."

Carol had missed her. Even when they both had lived on Earth, Hepzibah had been busy with the X-Men much of the time, and it had been even longer since they'd worked side by side like this, liberating people in their rough-and-tumble Starjammers way: no paperwork. No higher-ups. No politicians breathing down her neck.

"Sometimes I wish I had your confidence."

"Just sometimes?" Hepzibah teased.

They heard some rustling and clinking sounds coming from the kitchen—the rest of the team was up. Carol needed to check on Mantis. She took the pot of tea and poured another cup before she ducked out of the cockpit and took a left down the corridor, her feet making echoing metallic *tings* with each step. She tapped on the bunk door before sliding it up and peeking her head in.

Mantis was sitting up, eyes swollen, with half-moons of deep blue-green shadows beneath them. Carol handed her the cup of tea, and she took it, breathing in the fragrant steam between sips.

"You worried us there," Carol said gently. "But I guess you know that."

Mantis let out a weak laugh. "I'm sorry."

"Don't say that." Carol shook her head. "You have nothing to apologize for."

"I think I can handle it now that I've gotten a bit

acclimated. I just had no idea it'd be this bad," Mantis said, her voice hushed, as if she could barely admit it to herself, let alone Carol. "I—I can feel every single person within a hundred miles, Carol. And the pain… There's one woman, thirty miles away—she wakes up every morning reaching for her daughter, who was executed years ago. The Keepers like that… the public executions. They're in so many people's minds. The images, playing on repeat, because you can't run from it once you see it."

Carol kept her face blank, but inside, a storm was raging. Her knuckles itched to sink into someone's face. They had to do something about this planet once they had rescued Rhi's friends.

"What can we do?" she asked.

Mantis met her eyes, and her own seemed to almost glow with fury. "Make them pay."

o——————o

BEFORE THE dawn had finally broken, Hepzibah had set the course for Edias, the capital city just eighty miles across the Field of Fire. She wove the shuttle skillfully through the pillars of red rock, confident that its cloaking mechanism would foil any searchers below. Amadeus had zeroed in on an abandoned warehouse that would make the perfect hideout. They just needed to get there undetected.

The twin suns were just starting to peek up against the reddening sky when the capital came into sight, a sprawling city set along the coast of a blue-green ocean.

Thousands of domes rose from the red soil, glowing softly in the pre-dawn light, packed along the coastline for miles. Some were the size of a small town, others a modest home.

"We're here," Carol announced as they flew over the outskirts of the city, heading toward the water. "Hold on, everybody."

Scott grabbed the doorway when the shuttle made a sharp turn, and Hepzibah called Amadeus's name.

Carol followed him, peeking into the cockpit as Amadeus sat down next to the Mephitisoid. They were at an abandoned dock, hovering a few feet above the water in front of a dingy white dome that looked like it was about to deflate like a sad balloon. There were cracks in the white walls, and a few splashes of bright paint in symbols Carol didn't recognize—Damarian graffiti.

"This is it?" Hepzibah asked as Amadeus tapped code into his tablet, his eyes on the dome.

"Yep, give me a second."

"Hurry," Hepzibah urged, jerking her head to the side. "There's a boat coming in to dock over to our left."

He finished tapping. "Done."

When the top of the dome broke open like the petals on a flower, Carol felt like cheering. Hepzibah steered the ship into the building, setting down on the main level, where several abandoned hover-cars and not much else had been left behind by the dome's previous owners.

"I'm going to do a quick sweep of the place,"

Carol said, turning around as Hepzibah made sure all the thrusters were locked.

The delivery warehouse was dark and gutted, water dripping from the pipes in one of the small bathrooms—God, you couldn't even flush the toilet without a heat sensor on this damn planet, Carol thought as she surveyed the stripped expanse. The office on the second level just had a desk and a few chairs left, but she located a generator in the back and pressed her gloved palm against the censor. Their luck held: It buzzed to life.

"All clear," she called as she loped back to the main level, turning on just one interior light to avoid drawing any attention. One by one, her team climbed out of the shuttle, looking around.

"I've got to get to work right away," Amadeus said. His backpack bulging, he also carried a crate full of equipment tucked under one arm. "And we need to go over our cover stories."

"Let's find an office and do that now," Carol responded. "Come on, Scott."

"Rhi and I are going to review our plan to break into the president's inner sanctum," Hepzibah said. "I shall enjoy shattering his sense of safety when he returns home."

"That would be…" For a moment, Carol thought Rhi was horrified by Hepzibah's bravado, but instead, a smile spread across her face—part mischief, part revenge, and all wonder. "That would be *amazing*," she said eagerly.

"Make sure you're at least a little discreet," Carol suggested, ignoring Hepzibah's raised eyebrow.

She led Amadeus and Scott into an office and turned on the light. Amadeus set down the crate and spread out equipment from his backpack on a dusty desk.

"I've got to finish this second EMP," he said as he carefully sliced a rectangle out of a swatch of black material.

"I'll go over our background for tonight while you do," Carol said. She nodded at Amadeus's tablet on the desk, and Scott set it at an angle all could see. It displayed a Damarian alert issued a few months ago on their network: *KHAL MINING PATRIARCH DIES.*

"This guy left his company to his son, Davian. Scott, that'll be you; I'll be the wife. The Khal miners have serious money, and 'Davian' should be a big enough fish to wiggle close to the inner circle—which means proximity to Jella and Umbra."

"Sounds good," Scott nodded. "But what if somebody at the fundraiser knows Davian?"

"The island miners are infamously insular, and you bear a passing resemblance," Carol said, "so chances are good that might get us through. On top of that, a little snooping in his personal correspondence showed he's on a family cruise around the Southern Islands for the next week, so you won't have an unexpected doppelganger tonight. Amadeus can pass as an assistant to the owner of the company, so he'll be able to move through the museum without suspicion."

Following the story, Amadeus nodded and

picked up a bottle of glue, squeezing it along the edges of the material he'd just cut out. Then he grabbed a pair of tweezers and began to spiral a set of magnetic wires carefully into the glue. "I'm hoping I can get to the generator room to set the charges to wipe out the power pretty fast. But you guys might need to mingle for a while."

"And we need to find the girls and let them know we're safe before the power goes out," Scott said. "We can't just try to snatch them in the dark, no explanation."

Carol nodded in agreement. "I've got the tokens to show them we're connected to Rhi, but getting the discs to them might prove tricky. That's where I'll need your help to run interference, Scott."

"I will be as distracting and charming as possible," Scott promised.

"Any questions?" Carol asked.

"I'm good," Amadeus said. "I do think Rhi wanted to teach you some Damarian 101, though. Especially you, Carol. She seemed worried you were going to stand out."

"That's my next stop," Carol replied. "Let me know if you need anything, Amadeus."

She and Scott made their way back to the delivery floor, where Mantis was going through the equipment. Rhi and Hepzibah were sitting, their heads bent together as they went over their own plan for the night.

"We need to dig out the clothes we had made before we left," Scott said, heading over to help Mantis. "Did they give us Damarian formal wear?"

Carol nodded. "Funny, I never thought I'd be

using Alpha Flight's team of costume designers."

"You do have a pretty classic look," Scott said.

"Clothes over here," Mantis said, pointing to the red-topped crate. "Weapons are in the blue crate. I made Hepzibah give up the ember bombs."

"Not all of them," Hepzibah sang out over her shoulder.

Outside, Carol could hear the city waking up as the twin suns rose in the sky. The splash of water lapping against the shore, the *whompa-whompa* of ships in the harbor, the voices of the dock workers calling to each other as they began their day—always the voices of men, not women.

She closed her eyes, thinking of her mother's voice, of the songs she used to hear her singing softly, late at night. She hummed one of the tunes to herself, some old Gershwin that she didn't even know half the words to, her own voice blending with the noise she heard outside—adding a female thread to it. Even if no one could hear it but her.

Carol sighed, trying to shake her sadness. She needed to walk. To burn off some energy.

"I'll be back," she said. "Just gonna look around."

She could feel Mantis watching her as she left, heading to the back of the warehouse, where it smelled musty. Letting out a long breath, she leaned against the curved, damp wall and closed her eyes, picturing President Ansel's face. And then she pictured herself punching that face. Repeatedly.

She'd spent a good hour in her room last night

trying and failing to hover even an inch in the air—and feeling ridiculous each time. But that hadn't stopped her.

She couldn't shake how vulnerable she felt, flightless; then she'd laugh at herself—she'd been here less than twenty-four hours, and already the limitations had gotten under her skin. How privileged was she, both here and on Earth, that she couldn't stand the loss of even *one* of her powers for a day or two? Rhi and her friends—all the Inhumans—had suffered a decade of it, and under monstrous oppression. It was just that she knew something she wouldn't admit to the team: To pull off this risky plan, they needed all the help they could get.

Her fingers curled around the dog tags that had been returned to her from the void. They were warm from her skin, and they pulsed with her own heartbeat, reminding her of her promise.

She'd been a soldier; she'd been a spy. She knew how to play a role. How to stick to that role, no matter what happened. But still, it hurt to walk into a den of wolves and rescue only some of their prey, leaving the rest behind.

20

RHI TAPPED on the door of the bunk in the shuttle, where Carol was changing.

"Come on in," Carol called.

She was sitting on the edge of the bed, wearing the long dark-blue dress with the skirt reaching near the shuttle floor. "What do you think?" Carol asked, getting up and spinning around. "Do I look the part?"

"Almost," Rhi said. "But your hair…"

Carol touched it. "What? Do they not wear their hair short here?"

"No women do."

"Hmm, good to know. I'll figure out some excuse."

Rhi hesitated, not knowing how to start. She'd spent the whole day with a tight ball of anxiety and dread growing in her stomach. How could she allow them to do this? Crashing in the ravine and fighting the Damarian Guard when they didn't even have full access to their powers was bad enough, but now she was encouraging them to walk right into a building that had every member of the Council in it. She was asking Hepzibah to accompany her in breaking into Ansel's *home*. How could she ask this of them? It was all so dangerous.

But you're so close, said a voice inside her.

She was... *so* close. She had gone all the way to the end of the galaxy to get help and had come back with it—and now she could almost see it all: her friends' joyful smiles, the relief in Alestra's eyes as she realized she wouldn't have to raise her child here, Mazz's face when she experienced freedom for the first time, Umbra's kiss when they were finally reunited. She wanted all those things so badly, but she couldn't shake the feeling that she was sending her new friends into a death trap.

"I wanted to talk to you," Rhi said. "Not just about the hair, but about... how it is here. I don't want you to... I don't want them to find you out."

Carol's head tilted, and for a moment, Rhi was afraid she'd offended her, but then she sat back on the edge of the bed, patting the spot next to her.

"Why don't you tell me about the rules?" Carol prompted.

Rhi sat down, studying her hands, focusing on the torn cuticles, how they were bitten to the quick. How could she impart this in the right way? She'd learned the important lessons that very first day she'd met Ansel. They'd been imprinted on her soul in her parents' blood. Then, later, Miss Egrit had drilled the rest into all of them through repetition, deprivation, and abuse, physical and mental.

"There's a way to act," she said. "Keeping sweet, that's what they call it. You're supposed to be demure and unbothered and gentle. Never angry; always cheerful and obedient, no matter what they do to you. You can't meet any man's eyes. If you speak before one speaks to you, they'll think you're a radical bent on shaming her husband."

"Fantastic," Carol smirked. "What else?"

"You'll stand out no matter what," Rhi went on. "The way you hold yourself, how you move, you're going to draw attention. But if you play it right, you can use it to your advantage. He will notice you."

"The president?"

Rhi nodded.

"How much time have you spent with him?"

She twisted her fingers together. "Enough. He came to the Maiden House often when we were young, but he fixed on Umbra early because she can manipulate water. His perfect counterpart, he used to say. Her father encouraged it."

"He *what*?" Carol's voice sharpened to a knife's edge in one word, her head whipping toward her.

"What?" Rhi asked. "Did you think all the Inhumans remained noble and stalwart on the islands, heroically plotting their daughters' rescues?"

"I'd… hoped," Carol said quietly.

Sometimes, Carol's optimism surprised Rhi. How did you get like that? To be so powerful, to experience so much—because there was pain running deep in Carol, Rhi could see it, especially the night she gave her back the dog tags—but to still have so much hope? Rhi wanted to be like that. She wondered whether she was capable anymore.

"Umbra's father realized quickly that having a Council member so intrigued by his daughter could get him special perks, and then when Ansel became president, well…" Rhi said. "Now he's the presidential liaison between the Council and the Forgotten Island Inhumans. The job was a reward for signing over his visitation rights to Umbra. Ansel wanted her to himself."

"I don't know if I've said before," Carol gritted out. "But I really, really hate these people."

"Me too." There was no violence in Rhi's voice—just unvarnished truth.

"When it comes to Ansel, we do have one advantage," Carol said. "He's scared of you."

Rhi's stomach lurched, and she almost laughed because the idea was so absurd. "No, he's not."

"Of course he is," and Carol said it so much like it was fact, like it was the most obvious thing in the world, that Rhi was taken aback, wondering whether she might possibly be right. "You have things that he will never have."

"What?" she asked, because she desperately wanted to know, because she wanted to believe it. She wanted to believe Carol, this woman who was fiercer and freer than anyone she'd ever known.

"Your people believe in you. Umbra believes in you. And you believe in them. You came back. You didn't have to. If he was in your place, Ansel would never return. He'd never come back to fight. Because a person like that? They can't inspire loyalty, because they have none of it themselves. And loyalty on both sides is one of the keys to a great leader."

"I don't know how to lead," Rhi said, her voice small, her stomach twisting.

Carol flashed an encouraging smile. "Yes you do, Rhi—that's how you found me. And you'll learn even more as you go. Now, it's time. Are you ready?"

Taking a deep breath, Rhi met her eyes. This was the moment she had dreamed of for years: She had found help out in the galaxy and returned to free her people. She stood up straighter, holding Carol's gaze.

"Yes, Captain," she responded. I'm ready."

○————————○

NIGHT FELL quickly over Edias, the sounds from the dock waning as the boats settled in for the evening and the rest of the city began to buzz with the energy of the nightlife. When Rhi and Carol reached the lower levels, they found the rest of the team readying to leave.

Watching them drive the delivery truck out of the warehouse was almost as hard as the moment Rhi fled the Maiden House to reach for the stars. Hepzibah clapped a hand on her shoulder when Rhi sniffed, trying to hold back tears as the truck made the final turn and disappeared into the city.

"Do not fear, Rhi," she told her. "Carol is almost as wily as I. And don't tell her I said this, because she doesn't need a bigger head. Even without her ability to fly, she is a most challenging opponent to defeat in a battle."

"I know," Rhi said. "I just…" She licked her lips, trying to voice it. "I just don't want to get my hopes up. Because if everything goes right, then in a few hours, Umbra and Jella might be standing right here… but if it goes wrong—"

"If it goes wrong, we will find a way to make it go right," Hepzibah insisted. "Now you and I have a mission as well."

Rhi looked over her shoulder at Hepzibah's shuttle. "Does it really go underwater?"

Hepzibah grinned. "Let's find out, shall we?"

21

"EVERYONE'S COMM working?" Amadeus asked as he pulled the delivery truck into the alley behind an abandoned lot. All around them, the squat, curved domes of the city rose like little warts on the landscape.

Carol wiggled the comm tucked in her ear. "Check. Alpha. Bravo. Charlie."

"Coming in clear," Scott said.

"Me too," Mantis added from the front seat.

Driving through the winding streets of Edias had been interesting—and a little dizzying. The streets operated on a spiral pattern, instead of a grid like she was used to, and by the time they parked a few blocks away from the museum, Carol was wondering how the Damarians got *anywhere* on time.

Everywhere they looked, on every screen and electronic billboard they passed, Rhi's face was plastered with the words DANGEROUS FUGITIVE emblazoned above it.

The president was running scared, and it was a sight to see.

Carol checked the clock. "Rhi and Hepzibah should be reaching the president's office soon," Carol said, nerves sparking, though she knew Rhi was in safe hands with Hepzibah.

She tugged at her tight, itchy cuffs. The long skirt was confining, not her normal style. She liked a good dress now and then, but hated all this fabric swishing around her ankles. Though she supposed she could use the excess to choke someone out if needed. She'd done that with her sash a few times. The thought cheered her slightly.

"Fundraiser started twenty minutes ago," Scott said, gesturing to the clock. "So we'll make a fashionably late entrance. That way the right people will notice the wealthy new donors."

"You two got your backstories straight?" Carol asked Scott and Amadeus.

"Yep," Scott said, grimacing as he ran a finger along the high neck of his starched shirt. "Old man died, leaving big bucks… and I'm looking for a fresh target to toss cash at."

"Carol, here, take one of the EMP patches." Amadeus handed it over, a small oval blue sticker.

"How does it turn on?" she asked, flipping it over.

"It'll activate as soon as you put it over the girl's implant," Amadeus explained. "It took me forever to squish enough power into something this small, so I've only made these two so far. Make sure you stick it on directly over the implant on the first try. If you pull it off and try to slap it on again, it won't work. It's a one-shot thing."

Carol nodded, taking the patch from him and digging in her purse to pull out the compact Mantis had given her. She popped it open, slipping the patch underneath the powder puff while Amadeus tucked the second patch into his pocket.

"We're all agreed on the distraction?" Carol asked.

They nodded.

"And you've got the night-vision contacts in?" Amadeus checked.

"They feel like sewer grates on my eyes," Scott said grumpily.

"Sorry," Amadeus said. "I couldn't make them as thin as regular contacts."

"I'll deal," Scott said, straightening up and hooking his fingers in the door handle. "We ready?"

"Ready to roll," Carol said, with more confidence than she felt.

Scott hopped out of the truck, and Carol followed him, smoothing her skirt and taking his arm when he offered it.

"Ready to play the submissive Damarian lady?" he asked, trying not to grimace.

"I'll hold my tongue, but it's gonna be a challenge." She meant it as a joke, but Scott didn't laugh; instead, he squeezed her arm lightly, reassuringly.

"The best thing about you, Carol, is that you *never* hold your tongue. You always speak up. Especially for the folks who can't."

She smiled, touched by the compliment.

"I've got your back in there," he promised. "After all, that's what a good 'husband' does."

She laughed. "Luckily, our fake marriage is going to last only a few hours. I don't think we'd be able to convince anyone for much longer than that."

"Absolutely not. I could never land such a fabulous prize," he said, his eyes sparkling in jest.

Carol smacked him lightly on the chest with her little purse and he staggered against the truck exaggeratedly, making Mantis laugh as she shut the truck door behind him, remaining in the cab.

"You're okay?" Carol asked her.

"I will be fine," the empath said, but her mouth was pinched and her eyes were glassy under the continued onslaught of Damaria's emotions.

Carol hesitated, looking back at her, but the empath went on. "Get Jella and Umbra, so we can turn off that wretched weapon. Then we'll all be fine."

Carol pressed her lips together. "Stay safe."

"You as well, all of you."

Carol let Scott lead her out of the alley and onto the open streets of Edias, Amadeus bringing up the rear as they made their way three blocks down to the Damarian Museum of History.

Carol kept her gaze lowered as they walked, her arm tight in Scott's as she concentrated on the rules

Rhi had given her. *Don't raise your gaze. Don't speak until spoken to. Defer to Scott in all things.*

With every step she took, it grated like someone running a paring knife along her skin. The people on the street were almost all couples or the occasional lone man, but no women alone. Each one they passed had her head bowed like Carol's, her hand tucked in her chaperone's arm, meek and subservient. As they passed a domed building, the glass triangles lit up with advertisements, all directed at men—because, of course, a Damarian woman wouldn't have access to money.

"You doing okay?" Scott muttered. "Because you're digging your nails into my arm."

"Sorry." She loosened her grip, trying to focus on her feet instead of the people passing them. It was hard to do—against every instinct she had as a woman, as a person, as a soldier. Was it like this for them, the women she passed on the street? Or were they all so used to it that they accepted it as normal?

No. Oppression built resisters. Women and men and non-binary people who dared to stand up and say, "This is wrong." She'd seen it on Earth and on countless other planets: Eventually the oppressed rise up under the fist that dared to grind them down.

Carol breathed in and out, drumming her fingers against Scott's arm until he placed his other hand over it to calm her, shooting her a reassuring smile as they approached the elaborate iron gates of the Museum of History.

The building was a marvel of architecture—she

had to give the Damarians that. The huge glass dome was set in the middle of a sprawling outdoor arboretum filled with a riot of alien trees and plants that would give the botanists at Alpha Flight Station the vapors—some literally. Suspended above the dome on cables so thin even Carol could barely see them were two smaller spheres made of the same red rock as the ravine where the team had crash-landed. The smaller domes spun constantly as they orbited around the large dome, symbols of the dual suns that the Damarians believed had blessed them with their powers.

"Spheres, spheres, everywhere," Amadeus tutted like a cranky old man, and Carol had to duck her head even lower to hide her smile. "Though I will give them some credit: Geodesic domes, built from triangles…" he sketched the shape in the air, "…*are* the strongest structures. The fixed angles—"

"Okay, let's get in character," Scott interrupted as they stepped into the short line at the gates. In front of them stood a man in the standard Damarian black high-necked suit, grasping the shoulder of a young woman with long violet hair. The brilliant color and her slightly curled ears, like spiral seashells, were definitely not human. Carol stiffened, realizing she was seeing her first Keeper in person. She and Scott exchanged a brief, knowing glance. Her fingers itched. She could blast him right here, right now. His back was to her. He'd drop before he realized what was happening. But that would destroy their plan—which was a long shot, she admitted to herself, but it was all they had. She had to stick to it.

Without a word, Scott handed their invitations and ID cards to the guard at the gates, and he scanned them under the blue beam shining from the tip of his small light pen. "The president welcomes you, sirs," he said, pointedly ignoring Carol and handing the cards back to the men as the gates swung open.

Scott nodded brusquely, and in they walked, just like they owned the place. The criminal in him shone here, she could see it. And they needed that tonight. Confidence was the universal essential ingredient to working undercover.

The gravel path through the grounds to the museum—more of the ubiquitous red stone—was lined with huge willow-like trees draped with mottled vines. Beneath them grew a variety of strange plants—from snake-like purple ground-covers to plump, spiky brown succulents—the entire grounds giving off pungent aromas reminiscent of cinnamon and vinegar. These assaulted their noses, and they held back sneezes as they made their way up to the museum, the domed walls curving high above them, blotting out the light.

Entering through the huge marble doors, they craned their necks looking up at the walls. On just about any other planet, it would feel peaceful and inspiring to be in such a beautiful building.

But the grand entry hall's showpiece in the center of the huge space was a pure-white marble statue, twenty feet tall. It was a woman engulfed in flames, her face twisted into an eternal scream of torment, with three men bent at her feet, feeding the fire. Carol stumbled when she caught sight of what was etched above the woman's heart.

An eight-pointed star. Just like the one on Carol's chest.

This was the woman who fell from the stars— the woman of myth that Rhi had told her about... the supposed reason why the Damarians hated powered women.

Carol chanced a glance to her left and caught sight of a long line of paintings suspended in midair in rows across the dome's vast expanse. Then she realized they were all portraits of women in pain... of the "afflicted" who had to be "put down." A monument to misogyny and torture, *this* was the history the Damarians displayed so proudly. *This* was their idea of art and beauty.

Carol turned away and lowered her gaze again, only to catch the inscription on the statue's base: *What the flame wants, the flame will have.*

"This is sick," she muttered, shaking her head as if to drive away the morbid images. "We need to get on the move. Ready, Amadeus?"

He nodded. "I'll find the room with the solar generators and plant the charges to wipe out the power. I'll be on the comm if you need me."

He grabbed a glass of bright green liquid from a passing waiter and headed off. Scott took a glass as well, sipping it and then grimacing.

"A beautiful piece, isn't it?" asked a voice as Amadeus disappeared into the crowd.

Carol had to fight every instinct she had not to turn around. She waited for Scott, then followed his lead, her hand still tucked in the crook of his arm, keeping her eyes lowered so all she could see was feet—a man's and a woman's.

"A tremendous depiction of our ancestors' triumph," Scott said, extending his free hand to grasp the other man's forearm in the Damarian version of a handshake Rhi had taught him. "I am—"

"Davian Khal," the man finished for him. "I was informed you had honored us with your presence. I must say, it's a rare sight for one of the landowners from the Isle of Tuke to come inland."

Scott nodded warmly in assent. "I thought it past time."

"I am Security Secretary Marson, of course."

Carol's glance shifted—not to Marson, but to the woman standing next to him. *Jella*. She was right there, just inches away, her jet-black hair falling down her back, the telltale bump of the implant on her forearm, her eyes lowered. Carol stared just a beat too long, and Jella seemed to feel it—she looked up, her brilliantly violet eyes meeting Carol's, and Carol found she couldn't look away. How many times had a Damarian woman's gaze just slid over Jella like she was nothing more than a lamp or a table in the room; an object to be used when needed, and nothing else? Carol fought down a sudden urge to grab her, then and there, and run. She had the ID discs tucked in the outer pocket of her little bag, ready to slip out and press into someone's palm. She just had to do it without the security secretary noticing.

"Of course," Scott said. "It's wonderful to meet you, Secretary Marson."

"I was sorry to hear about your father's passing."

Scott inclined his head in thanks. "I appreciate that. My father was a great man. But I must admit, he was a man anchored in the past. That's one of the reasons I chose to make the journey here with my lovely wife. I'd like to strengthen Khal Mining's relationship with the government—and ensure our president is able to lead our planet into its bright future."

The security secretary nodded and turned to Carol. "It is a delight to meet such a lovely specimen of Damarian womanhood, Madame Khal," Marson said, giving a little flourishing bow.

Carol barely held back the snarl as she inclined her head and then finally raised her eyes to meet his. "Thank you, Secretary Marson. And I must apologize for my appearance." She touched the edges of her hair with a rueful smile. "When I was spending time with my nephew, I turned my back for a moment and the little rascal got hold of the scissors. The next thing I knew, my braid was in his hand!"

"She's going to have to pay more attention when we have our own little ones," Scott said, his voice laced with a fond condescension that made her want to slug him, even though she knew it was feigned.

"It took a dramatic chop to fix the mess," Carol continued. "I didn't want to come, afraid I might embarrass my dear husband…"

"Nonsense," Marson assured her with a paternal smile. "A woman like you would look lovely even with all your hair shorn. And I know how young boys can be—full of mischief. It's not a bad idea to indulge that boisterousness... leads to a strong man who won't take *no* for an answer."

"You are too kind," Carol simpered, thinking about how beautiful the crunch of cartilage would sound as she broke his nose.

"What do you think of the statue, Madame Khal?"

She smiled, and it took considerable effort to make it sweet instead of sharp and smirky. "It makes one grateful for the safety and order that was ushered into our world afterward," she said, her eyes sliding over to Jella.

"Have no fear," the secretary said almost jovially. "She may be afflicted, but I'm in complete control."

Not for long, Carol thought, smiling as a server swept by with a tray of the green drinks. Carol reached for a glass, and as she did, she fumbled the stem, letting it fall to the ground. It shattered, and the emerald liquid splashed onto the tile floor.

"Oh dear, I'm so clumsy!" Carol said, bending over and setting her purse on the floor as Marson barked, "Jella, help Madame Khal!"—just as Carol had hoped.

When the girl crouched down next to her and picked up a large shard of glass, Carol slipped the ID disc free of her bag's outer pocket and palmed it. Reaching out, she took the shard from Jella's hand and slipped the disc into it with the same smooth movement. The girl glanced down, confused; when she saw the disc, she almost dropped it, her eyes wide with shock.

"Be ready," Carol whispered in her ear, closing Jella's fingers around the disc. Then she raised her voice. "Careful! Silly thing, you'll cut yourself!" she scolded, as if Jella were a naughty puppy. "They're so childlike," she commented, rising to her feet and handing the shard of glass to a server who had hurried to clean up the remaining mess.

"Part of the affliction, I suspect," Marson agreed. "Their abilities eat away whatever sense they were born with. It's really a blessing for them, that men like me are willing to take on their burdens."

"Such a blessing," Scott said, a muscle in his jaw twitching.

Someone called out Marson's name, and he turned, raising a hand in the air before turning back to them. "Master Khal, Madame Khal, it's been an absolute pleasure, and I anticipate a fruitful association in the future. I will be sure to let the president know you're here."

"Please do," Scott said with a forced smile. "I hope to discuss how I can help his campaign."

"I know he'll be most interested," Marson smiled enthusiastically before turning to go. "Come along, Jella."

She hesitated. Just for a split second. But it was enough to make Marson frown and raise his fingers as if he was going to snap them. Jella sprang up at the gesture, hurrying to him, but he didn't lower his hand until she was by his side.

"Did you give it to her?" Scott asked, as they watched them walk away, Jella's shoulders stiff and hunched with fear.

Carol nodded, raising her hand to her ear to activate her comm. "Amadeus—status report?" she whispered.

"Found the generator room, right here under the rear of the dome," Amadeus said. "Should be done in a few."

"Good. We can get out of here soon," Scott muttered. "This place gives me the creeps."

"The paintings are making me sick, too," Carol whispered as they ventured farther into the museum. The crowd was buzzing and jovial, with deep waves of men's laughter and conversation echoing through the high-domed ceilings—punctuated only occasionally by a woman's voice uttering some pleasantry. The overly sweet drinks were flowing freely, and Carol had a feeling that Ansel would be getting a lot of donations from tonight's party. He'd picked the perfect place for it.

The paintings hung in rows throughout the dome created pathways. They stopped right in front of one as an elderly woman and her husband crossed the way, and Carol had to bite the inside of her lip to keep from punching a hole straight through the canvas. It depicted a woman on her knees in front of a man shown in profile. Blood was pouring from her face—and her eyes, which were sitting in her beseeching palms, held out to the man who glared down at her. The placard below gave its title: *The Affliction of Prescience.*

As Carol stared at it, another painting came to mind—Artemisia Gentileschi's *Judith Slaying*

Holofernes. She'd seen it in Florence once. It depicted Judith beheading Holofernes to save her city, with her maidservant's assistance. It had been a bloody and brutal testament to sisterhood, to teamwork, and to survival. Carol had spent an entire day sitting in front of it, staring at lines of paint, at the story it told, absorbing it, as if she could draw Judith's strength from it. And standing there in the Damarian museum, in that maze of painful monstrous history portrayed proudly, like badges of honor instead of shame, she found that strength again.

Everywhere she looked, when she dared, she saw silent Damarian women at their husbands' sides, heads bowed, speaking only a word or two, rarely raising their eyes.

"Heading back up in a second," Amadeus's voice came over the comm.

"Jella knows we're here for her," Carol whispered to him as they moved forward. "But we still need to find Umbra."

They stopped again, but the elderly couple had already made off. Scott had frozen, his eyes widening, every bit of color draining from his face.

"What?" Carol hissed, looking up, and then she stilled. Right ahead of them, perched on the ledge of the red-stone fountain, was a little girl who couldn't be more than ten. Her blonde hair was done in an elaborate crown of braids wound around her head and her ears, but the style couldn't hide the sharp points that marked her as different.

Another Inhuman girl. But this one was a *child*.

A man came up to her, his gray coat flapping at his knees as he walked. Scott stepped forward, his face intent.

"Don't," Carol gritted out, her hand clamping down on Scott's elbow, trying to make it look submissive instead of controlling.

"She's a preteen," he hissed. "What is she? Nine? Ten? What's she doing here? I thought Rhi said they weren't given to Keepers until they're twenty."

"I—" A horrible thought occurred to her, and her heart skipped a wretched beat as that realization was confirmed when the man stooped down, handing the girl a plate of canapés.

"Thanks, Daddy!"

"You're welcome, sweetie."

"Oh my God." Scott's arm tensed under her grip.

"Easy." He was almost to the point of pulling away from her, he was so worked up. "Pretend to be looking at the painting," she directed, turning them slightly, so the little girl and her father were still in their line of sight. The painting was a gruesome depiction of a woman covered in bloody sores, surrounded by piles of dead bodies with the same malady. The placard read: *The Affliction of Healing*.

"This is…" he hissed. "That guy…"

"Is an Inhuman." She glanced down at the girl's wrist. There was a ribbon tied around it, similar to the ones that Carol's own mom used to put on Christmas presents back on Earth, painstakingly curling each strand by zipping them along the blade of her scissors. An explosion of pastel curls cascaded down the child's arm, hiding the telltale bump of the implant on her wrist.

"Rhi told me they'd turned some of the parents," she said. "But I hadn't realized there'd be one here."

"You shouldn't be able to turn a father," Scott hissed.

The flash of warmth in her chest at his conviction made her glad for Cassie. Scott was the kind of father who'd burn down the world before letting his daughter be used like the Inhuman girls in Damaria. It was one of the reasons she'd asked him to come on board—that extra fire in the belly was important on missions like this. But it also made things riskier when you were undercover—because he wanted to whisk that little girl away just as much as she did.

"Where's her mother?" Scott asked, looking over the heads of the milling crowd.

"That's probably how they got him to turn," Carol whispered. "We know they killed Rhi's parents when they refused to hand her over."

A murmur broke through the crowd, and Carol's eyes snapped back to the floor, wondering whether they'd been too suspicious.

"Master Khal, it's a genuine pleasure to see someone from the Isle of Tuke come to our little fundraiser."

Carol didn't look up. She didn't have to—she recognized Ansel's voice. She'd watched his speeches, studied his face and his inflection, noted which words made his eyes gleam and his tone change. *Know thine enemy.* She took that adage seriously.

She knew him. Knew the cruelty and fear in his heart, and how it fueled him. She knew why he'd chosen this place to hold his fundraiser, this hall of hell, a reminder of the power of their men and the supposed weakness of their women.

By the time she was done with him, he would understand he was the weak one in every inch of his being. He was going to *feel* it.

"President Ansel, it's an honor to be in your presence," Scott said.

"I had to come by and say hello after my dear friend Marson mentioned you were here," Ansel said. "I see you've noticed our little Fern."

"I'm sorry?"

"The Inhuman girl."

"Oh, I must admit I've never seen one so young before," Scott said, half-tripping over his words.

"They are usually kept in the Maiden House at this age," Ansel said. "But Fern is a special exception, since her father is such a friend to the cause. And I will say," he leaned forward, almost conspiratorially, "the younger they are, the better."

Carol's fingers curled around Scott's elbow, her hand shaking, all the might inside her keeping her from clenching her fists and accidentally breaking poor Scott's arm. *Breathe. No punching. Later. There will be so much punching later*.

"It's so much easier to educate them when they're that age," Ansel continued. "The ones who are older…" He raised his hand in the air, as Marson had done earlier to Jella, and snapped his fingers.

Almost instantly, a girl hurried out of the nearby

crowd to stand next to Ansel. Her skin was tinged a light blue, and her hair shone a deep black that glowed almost green under the light. Her eyes swept down, and Carol could see darker blue marks peeking out from her dress's high neck—bruises.

"The older ones are harder to train," Ansel said. "I had to keep sharp things away from this one for the first few months so she wouldn't hurt herself, didn't I?" He gave her shoulder a scolding little shake, and Carol's heart ached as Umbra's cheeks darkened in humiliation.

"Yes, sir," she said, her voice barely a whisper.

"Perhaps you should have been more afraid of her hurting you," Carol said.

For the first time, his eyes snapped to her as if he'd just realized she was there, and she didn't look down or away, even though she half wished she'd kept her mouth shut, for their plan to *work*. Rhi's advice was running through her head, but deep down, at her core, Carol was a soldier.

And a soldier looks her enemy in the eye.

"After all," Carol continued, with a graceful wave of her hand, "we're surrounded by such historic reminders of just how dangerous a woman with power can be."

A moment—poised on a razor-sharp edge; it could go either way—passed, his eyes on hers, searching. Did he recognize her voice somehow? Did he suspect?

But then a wide smile broke across his face. "Well said!" He clasped Scott's shoulder briefly. "I see you've found a patriotic woman to marry, Master Khal."

"She is one of a kind," Scott said, swirling the

melting ice spheres in his glass. The president's eyes flickered down to it, and then, casually, he grabbed Umbra's hand like it was his own and pressed her fingers against Scott's glass. It instantly frosted over, the contents chilling from Umbra's ability to manipulate liquids.

Scott swallowed with a click, though Carol could tell he wanted to smash the glass in Ansel's smirking face. He raised the glass to his lips and took a sip. "Neat trick," he said as he lowered it.

"They have their uses," Ansel said. "In fact, if you're willing to leave your lovely wife for a few moments, I can elaborate on that. I wouldn't want to bore Madame Khal with the details, but I know a businessman like you prefers to know all you can before making an investment. And that's what a donation to my campaign is—an investment in the future, in yourself, and in the betterment of all."

"That sounds good to me," Scott said heartily. "Darling, stay here, will you?" He brushed a perfunctory kiss across Carol's cheek, and Ansel snapped his fingers at Umbra.

"Keep Madame Khal company. Fetch her whatever she wishes," he ordered.

Carol kept her gaze lowered as the president led Scott away, not realizing he'd just given her the moment she needed. Umbra stood next to her, hands folded together, head bowed. Carol glanced around them—the throng of people had passed through the Gallery of Afflictions and were heading up the spiral staircase to the conservatory level of the dome, where dinner would be served. They didn't have much time—Amadeus's EMP bomb was designed to go off when the first course was brought out.

She was about to pull the last ID disc out of her purse when a voice broke through the crowd. "Umbra, Umbra!"

It was the Inhuman father, holding his daughter's hand. This close, Carol could see her face. She was nine or ten, which meant... God, had she been *born* here? She supposed one of the Inhuman women could have been pregnant during their journey and then given birth on Damaria. Did that mean this little girl had never known freedom?

Carol realized she was staring into the future Ansel was building. A little girl raised in a society that taught her from birth that she existed to serve, to be used, to be exploited. That she didn't deserve to hurt or heal or want or rage. That she was lesser when she was really much, much more.

"Yes, Master Sylas?" Umbra asked.

"Take her for me," he shoved his daughter's hand into Umbra's. "The president needs me."

Before Umbra could even answer, he hurried off.

"I have to use the washroom, Umbra," the little girl said, tugging at her arm.

Umbra's eyes darted to Carol, worrying her lower lip.

"It's all right," Carol said. "Go ahead."

"I'll return, Madame Khal."

Carol turned back to the painting, her throat tight with anticipation. Now or never. She counted to five in her head, until Umbra and the little girl had disappeared in the crowd, and then she followed.

22

RHI'S NOSE was glued to the cockpit window as Hepzibah navigated her shuttle underwater with the skill of a submarine captain of old. Fish swam by, flashes of orange and purple darting in and out of the floating seaweed through water that turned a deep, brilliant emerald as Hepzibah dove deeper.

Rhi's ears popped as they cut through the chilly depths of the bay, the shuttle groaning under the pressure. Above them, some huge creature swam past, its shadow darkening the waters above, making Rhi shiver and even Hepzibah tense up.

It was an astonishing view of the world, but Rhi remained acutely aware, even with the wonders surrounding her, that what she was about to do was beyond reckless. And every time she closed her eyes and reached for the inner strength that got her to Earth and back, her thoughts turned to Zeke.

She wasn't leaving without him, and she knew Alestra wouldn't either. They *had* to find information about his whereabouts somewhere in Ansel's mansion. Without it…

"You know," Hepzibah said, as the radar on her screen beeped, signifying their approach to the island outside of Edias where Ansel made his home, "there's a place like this on Earth, a small island right off a major coastal city. The humans made it into a prison instead of a palatial estate, though. And then after they closed it, they turned that prison into a museum."

Rhi's eyebrows scrunched up. "They turned a prison into a museum?"

"I always thought it was ghoulish, but humans can be."

"You were in prison," Rhi said tentatively. "Carol mentioned it."

"I was, for a long time," Hepzibah replied, and Rhi wondered whether she even knew how long—or whether the days, months, and years bled together, as they had for her.

"Your worries—the future the president wants, the children he will force the girls to bear—it is smart for you to fear this and fight it. To be born into a world under rulers who treat you like commodities…" Her head bowed, the light bouncing off her pointed ears. "It is hard to break free, even with help."

"Did *you* have help?"

A fond smile spread across the Mephitisoid's face. "I had the Starjammers. With them by my side, I felt as if I could do anything. I think that must be how you feel about your friends?"

"Yes, I do…" Rhi said, wondering if she'd ever get used to being so easily understood by women like Hepzibah and Carol and Mantis. She'd held onto the memory of her mother, her memory of the Inhuman women she'd grown up with before they left, but as the years passed, those memories fuzzed over like mold on a piece of fruit. Miss Egrit had been the most consistent woman in her life for a decade, stealing the moments that belonged to their mothers: Miss Egrit had been the one to hand out pads when they started menstruating, the one who'd fitted them for new clothes as their bodies changed, the one who'd scolded them instead of comforted them when cramps or headaches or sickness stole over them. *Bear your womanly burdens with grace, girls. Just like the Keepers bear the burdens you heap on them with strength.*

"Look, right ahead." Hepzibah pointed to the island rising out of the shimmering water before them. A wicked smile spread across her face as she flipped a latch, revealing a red button. "Carol has urged discretion," she said. "But at times, one must improvise."

She pressed the button and the ship jolted, a four-pronged claw shooting out of its prow through the water and hooking into the force field that surrounded the island hidden in the clouds behind it, vibrating at a frequency higher than the field's energy output. Rhi watched bubbles streaming up in the water all around them as the field buzzed and sparked, lighting up the water with a brilliant flash before sputtering out. "And they think their tech is so advanced," Hepzibah scoffed. "That's a child's security system."

"On the ground, they light you on fire," Rhi felt compelled to point out, just in case Hepzibah came across any others, but it just made her snort derisively.

The shuttle moved past the now-fried force field and began to rise. She swallowed to counteract the popping in her ears and watched the seaweed sliding off the little ship's windows as it bobbed to the surface. Then she saw it: The island emerged from the fog, and the president's domed mansion loomed before them like a giant red warning.

Hepzibah hit a few more buttons on the console to drop a sonic anchor to keep the shuttle in place, and a hissing sound filled Rhi's ears as it began to depressurize.

"We'll use the secondary exit on top," Hepzibah said, rising and heading out of the cockpit. Rhi followed her down the narrow hall to a pressurized airlock hatch leading out of the ship that she slid up and open. Then she turned back to Rhi, digging in her pockets to produce two spheres full of blue gel—the ember bombs she hadn't handed over to Mantis.

"Just in case," Hepzibah said, trying to give them to her, but Rhi shook her head.

"No."

Hepzibah frowned. "They're useful, Rhi. And you have not been taught to fight. You need to be armed."

"Give me one of the guns you pulled off them. I'm

not gonna use that stuff. Not on anyone. Not even them."

She could still remember the twins' screams as they were lowered into the gel; the smell of their burned flesh. She looked up at Hepzibah, begging her to understand without an explanation, and to her relief, Hepzibah tucked the bombs back in her jacket and handed her the gun instead.

"Do you know how to use this?"

Rhi nodded, the gun heavy and unfamiliar in her hand. "I'll manage."

Hepzibah put a finger to her lips. "Remember," she said. "Discretion."

HEPZIBAH'S IDEA of discretion was not like other people's. As soon as her feet were on the island, she became a streak of deadly black and white. The first guard along the shore where they'd dropped anchor was down before he could call for help, Hepzibah choking him into unconsciousness with her tail. Rhi stumbled in the sand, her hand sweaty on the gun as they moved forward in the dark, up the beach path and through the lush jungle that Ansel's gardeners painstakingly maintained on his island retreat. She was so focused on keeping up with Hepzibah and getting into the mansion that she almost didn't hear the crunch of someone stepping on a shell behind her.

She whirled, her finger squeezing the trigger before she could think. The gun kicked back in her hand, and there was a gasp—from the guard she'd just shot. Blood bloomed on the man's shoulder, and Rhi stared as he fell to his knees, clutching his arm.

Hepzibah leapt forward, kicking the man hard in the jaw as he reached toward Rhi. He slumped forward, unconscious; she bent over, plucked his comm from his belt, and tossed it into the shrubbery. "If you're going to shoot them, make sure it's bad enough that they can't call for help," she directed gently.

Rhi stood there, her hands shaking, but she couldn't fall apart. Closing her eyes, she took a deep breath, reminding herself that she had to do what she must, to survive, get out, and take everyone with her.

Hepzibah grabbed Rhi's hand and tugged her up the path, the thick press of trees and vines closing in on them as they ran toward the mansion. Light blazed through the trees, and Rhi yanked Hepzibah down behind a tree heavy with fronds just as a fireball from near the dome soared over their heads, crashed onto the path, and burned out as soon as it hit the ground.

Rhi frowned as another fireball arced over them and crashed two feet away, the flames dissipating instantly. Was the Keeper shooting at them senile, not in full control of his powers, or just a bad shot?

But as another fireball arced over their heads, swiping a patch of ferns and sputtering out, she realized what it was.

The Keeper was trying to fight them *and* keep the fire from destroying any part of Ansel's precious garden. A hysterical giggle rose in Rhi's throat, and Hepzibah shot her a concerned look.

"The Keeper doesn't want us to hurt the plants," Rhi explained. "Ansel will be furious if his garden gets burned up."

The scorn dripping from Hepzibah's next words was priceless: "Oh, will he?" she asked.

She leapt out from behind a tree, tilting her head back and letting out a fearsome yell before launching an ember bomb in the direction of the fireballs. Rhi heard a crash, then a shout as smoke and flames sparked up the path near the mansion.

"Run!" Hepzibah yelled. Rhi didn't have to be told twice. She leapt to her feet, and tore up the path after Hepzibah, the guards positioned along the perimeter distracted by the fire as the domed mansion came into sight. Two guards were posted at the entrance, and as they approached, Hepzibah chucked another bomb at them, sending them flying in opposite directions to avoid the toxic, burning gel. But Hepzibah's aim was sharper than their reflexes, and their yells of pain mingled with the smoke and desperation in the air.

"Use the guard's glove," Rhi hissed before Hepzibah could reach to open the door. "Ours might not work. His will have the extra security chips in them."

Hepzibah nodded, grabbing the nearest guard's still-smoking hand as he struggled against her. She pressed his palm against the sensor on the door, and it slid open with an obedient click. The women rushed inside, leaving the singed guards behind. Hepzibah whipped a strip of metal from her belt, slapping it against the door, and it began to smoke and sizzle as soon as it touched the stone and metal that made up the dome, frying the door's circuitry—and making it impossible to open.

"So they can't get in," Hepzibah explained.

"But now *we* can't get *out*," Rhi said, alarmed, the feeling of being trapped closing in on her. What would Ansel do if he arrived back here to find his guards out of commission, his garden destroyed, and her sitting there?

She knew, of course. He'd kill her.

The moment she and Ansel were face to face again, only one would survive. She knew that. She'd been preparing for it. Praying that she was strong enough... and smart enough. That she could finally make him pay.

"Don't worry," Hepzibah said, pulling out a black baton and brandishing it. "I have that covered." She twisted the handle, and a bright green laser sprang out. "This cuts through anything. You have to put some muscle into it, but it's gotten me out of more than a few scrapes." She patted her pockets as they saw smoke billowing. "I have three more ember bombs—how are you on ammo?"

Rhi looked down at the charger cells on her gun. "I'm still pretty much full." She took a second to look around the vast entryway and up at the winding red marble staircase. "His office is on the second floor."

They raced up the stairs and pelted down the long hallway at the landing, Hepzibah following Rhi until the girl stopped at a door—then holding her arm out, blocking Rhi before she could reach for the knob. "Wait."

With her little laser cutter, Hepzibah prodded the

door. It sparked. Rhi's stomach dropped, a horrible sense of defeat filling her. "Not a force field?" she asked.

"I'm afraid so. But don't worry." Hepzibah began to jab along the door jamb, and when that sparked, she moved farther down the wall, tapping around and smiling triumphantly when she found the right spot. She thrust the laser into the wall, her muscles taut as she dragged it down through the layers of wood and plaster and stone.

"They always count on you going through a door or window," she explained to Rhi as she cut another line and then a third at the top to form a door of her own. "So they guard those spaces more fiercely. But I much prefer a good wall." She spun, a whirlwind of power and confidence, her foot striking the seam she'd carved. Half the wall broke to pieces that burst into the room, plaster dust and stone fragments flying, and Rhi let out a delighted laugh. Their own door!

They ducked inside the office; when Rhi saw the picture on the president's desk, everything else faded away. It was a photograph of him with Umbra, framed in red stone. He was seated in one of the Council chairs—she recognized it from that day he killed her parents, the elaborate carved flames sprouting behind him like a crown. And Umbra... oh, Umbra... it had been so long since she'd seen her face. The light blue of her skin that reminded Rhi of a sky she hadn't seen for years until she'd crashed on Earth. The tilt of her head, the glint in her eyes that even *he* couldn't dim.

In the photo, Umbra was kneeling at his feet, and his arm rested on hers, right above the implant, like a warning. A reminder: *I own you.*

His words on the comm echoed in her head: *She is mine.*

But she wasn't. She *wasn't.* Rhi had to keep reminding herself of that. Umbra belonged to herself—she would never be Ansel's. He could never know her or understand her or even care for her. He just wanted to control her.

She grabbed the photograph and threw it across the room so it crashed into the bookcase lining the farthest wall and fell on the floor in pieces. For a moment, there was just silence, Hepzibah quiet and watchful. Blood rushed to Rhi's cheeks, but when she met the Mephitisoid's eyes, Hepzibah smiled and kicked over the antique globe by the fireplace. It rolled lopsidedly across the ground, a large dent in it.

"Feel better?" she asked.

Rhi nodded.

"We can smash more things later. Now we need to find the information on your brother and get out of here."

The desk had multiple screens set into it. After inserting the first of two drives that Amadeus had given her into the bottom of the desk, Rhi touched the screens with her heat-gloved hands. With Amadeus's hacking drive working its magic, the desk sprang to life. The main screen in the center that gave her access to Ansel's personal network was surrounded by a dozen smaller screens—the security feeds. On one, she could see the guards that Hepzibah had hit with the ember bombs, still writhing on the steps outside.

"I'll keep an eye on the feeds," Hepzibah said, coming to stand next to her, peering at the screen stationed in the garden. There were guards moving around the house—trying to figure out a way through Hepzibah's seal on the door.

Rhi focused on the neatly labeled folders on the main screen. Ansel even had them color-coded. So tidy… so neat. She wanted to mess them all up. The virus drive that Amadeus had given her was burning a hole in her pocket, but first she needed to find where Zeke was. The information had to be somewhere on this computer in a document, image, or message.

Rhi searched Zeke's name and transport schedules, but nothing came up. In a desperate bid, she searched *Inhuman*, and dozens of folders and hundreds of files showed up. Though she added more keywords to narrow down the search, she found nothing and was about to try a new search when she noticed a folder labeled *Heritage House*. She touched the screen and opened the folder, which had dozens of files inside— Ansel's plans for the future.

Dread—a familiar enemy—grew thick in her throat as she tapped open the first file, labeled *Initial Stats*.

357 girls post-menarche
80 girls pre-menarche
First-Year Goals: 100 live births

Second-Year Goals: 200 live births, begin process of multiple implantations to increase percentage of female twins and triplets in half the breeding population
Third-Year Goals: 500 live births, cycle to second half of breeding population for multiple implantations

The screen swam in front of her as she leaned against the desk, frantically tapping through the rest of the file. There were blueprints for nurseries to hold the babies, a plan that detailed how to convert a Maiden House into a maternity ward, and page after page of rules and regulations on how to properly brainwash an Inhuman girl from birth.

"Hepzibah," she gasped out the name. As if from a great distance, she heard Hepzibah call out, but she couldn't respond as a kind of resignation settled over her.

It wasn't going to matter. Even if she got Alestra out. Even if she got all her friends out. Even if she got Umbra away from Ansel.

He had decided on this long ago. He was already building his sick breeding factory, ready to be stocked with Inhuman girls. She might be able to save her friends, but she'd be leaving the rest of her people behind—all the other girls in all the other Maiden Houses—with no way out. This would be their future.

She'd told herself that if she got Alestra away, it would somehow stop the future she had feared. But she'd been lying to herself so that the guilt wouldn't crush her.

Now, here it was, in front of her, laid out in a detailed, precise plan: How to turn an entire species into breeding stock in three short years.

"He's going to do it," she whispered to herself. "He's already building it."

Hepzibah peered at the computer and tapped the screen, her lip curling as one arm enveloped Rhi's shoulders. "It's just a plan," she said dismissively. "Plans can be destroyed. So can buildings. And tyrants. Fire is very helpful in such cases... also explosives."

"I failed," Rhi whispered. "I hadn't even gotten started, and already—"

"No!" Hepzibah gave her a not-so-gentle shake. "Don't think like that, Rhi. And don't talk like that. Failure is not an option. Remember?"

The words broke through her panic. *Failure is not an option.*

Hepzibah was right—it couldn't be. The stakes were too high.

You are strong, and you are smart. Her mother's words echoed inside her.

So start acting like it, she told herself.

Zeke's location wasn't in the computer—that would be too easy. Ansel, considering it a game, would have hidden it, just in case she got this far. Another way to mock her... *I have what you want.*

She straightened in Hepzibah's grip, and her fear fell away as she stood up. "The bookcase," she said, her eyes settling on it across the room. "I bet he didn't put Zeke's transport routes on the computer. He went old-school."

"You can't hack a notebook," Hepzibah said, getting the idea and hurrying over to it. Hepzibah began pulling the books off the shelves and leafing through the pages, just in case he'd tucked something between the covers. The rare volumes, with their gilt edges and ancient words, fell to the carpet with dusty thumps. But Rhi had her own method. She closed her eyes, her hands held out, concentrating her entire self on Zeke, on his warm eyes, on his smile that turned sweeter every time he saw Alestra. *I need to find him.*

Something tickled her fingers, tugging at them, urging her forward to the shelves.

Normally, being able to touch all these books—to smell that special dry, ageless scent that clung to her fingers for hours after—would fill her with delight. But right now, she was methodical. She didn't know what she was looking for. A notebook? A hard drive? Ansel must have recorded Zeke's location *somewhere.*

Her fingers brushed against something crumply and plastic; something inside her lit up, singing like a choir as she pulled out an old book, tucked in a protective bag, shoved behind three volumes on the War of the Wastelands. She paused, a prickle of recognition breaking through the cobwebs of her memory as she brushed dust off it and stared at it through the plastic sleeve.

She remembered it—a leather book with blue embossed stars on the cover. She'd seen this before, somewhere… she'd *found* it before. The details started to come back to her as she reached deeper into her memory.

The second year they were at the Maiden House, Ansel had come to fetch her one day; it was the first time she'd been allowed off the grounds. Miss Egrit had called it *a very special mission* in that fake-chirpy way that made Rhi nervous.

Rhi had thought he was going to kill her. But instead, Ansel showed her a crude sketch of a book with stars on the cover, and then he'd reached out to unlock her implant—with that same hand that shot the gun that killed her parents—and said, *It's about time you made yourself useful.*

The flashes had filled her mind instantly, as soon as he touched her, releasing one facet of her power—the only one they thought she had. The rough sketch of the book blurred in her vision, images of the lost filling her instead: grass racing up a hill; bark a deep, cracked brown; branches thrusting so high she had to crane her neck to see the top; and a whisper in the air: *I'm here, find me, dig, dig, dig.*

So she did—she found this book. It had been buried under a tree that was so old its trunk was split three ways, the base so thick that six people would be needed to circle it. He had made her dig the hole, and the longer she dug without finding something, the more impatient he got. When the shovel hit something that went *tang*, he'd let out a breath—a covetous, triumphant sound she'd never forget.

He'd wanted this book more than anything. His

hands shook as he yanked the metal box it rested in out of the hole. He opened it then and there, and he cradled the book in his arms like a kinder man would hold a child. She knew better than to ask what it was about.

Two weeks later, President Lee suddenly resigned, naming Ansel as his successor. She'd always wondered whether the book had something to do with that.

She had the chance to find out now. She could take it, and he'd know she'd done it, this little piece of possible power he'd wrested from someone who'd kept it hidden.

Nothing stays hidden forever. Not even you. Not from me.

The first thing she ever said to him—a warning he should have listened to.

Rhi tucked the star book under her arm, but before she could continue searching, she heard distant footsteps and shouts down below. Hepzibah whirled, tail twitching, eyes narrowed as she focused on the door and the hallway beyond. "We need to go."

"But—" Rhi protested.

"Now!" Hepzibah barked, rushing to the hole she'd cut in the wall and peering around the edge of it. Her heart pounding, Rhi dashed over to Ansel's desk, pulled the virus drive Amadeus had given her out of her pocket, and plugged it into the network control panel. The main screen instantly started fritzing out, splitting the files for Ansel's breeding factory into thousands of bits and then disintegrating them into a random mass of ones and zeroes—a tiny triumph in

a night full of too many things that could go wrong.

She looked up just as Hepzibah's hand closed around her wrist.

"We can't take the corridor," Hepzibah said, brandishing her laser knife again and moving to the outer wall. "The guards broke through the front door and are coming up the stairs."

"What can we do?" Rhi asked, watching the answer: Hepzibah swiftly sliced a hole in the wall that overlooked the water, then kicked the fragments of plaster and wood and glass free.

Rhi stared at the jagged hole and then at Hepzibah's expectant face. The shouts and footsteps grew to a crescendo.

Rhi looked at Hepzibah, eyes wide with fear.

"Can you swim?" Hepzibah asked her.

"Swim? No, I—"

"Don't worry, I can."

"I can't—" Rhi began, but her words disappeared into a startled gasp as Hepzibah looped an arm around her waist and jumped out of the hole she'd just cut in the wall, the two women sailing through the night sky into the dark sea below.

23

"I THINK I can get to Umbra," Carol whispered into her comm, moving through the museum crowd as fast as she could without arousing suspicion. She could see flashes of Umbra's long green-black hair moving through the people milling around the staircase. "Scott's with the president, so he's radio silent for a while. Amadeus, where are you? I need eyes on Jella. Marson doesn't let her out of his sight."

"I'm heading up through the kitchens," Amadeus said. "I'll find her."

Mantis chimed in next. "Quiet here," she reported. "Not so much as a security detail down this street."

"That's what I like to hear," Carol said. "Making contact with Umbra next. Stand by."

The deeper she ventured into the museum, keeping Umbra in sight as she headed into the back hall where the bathrooms were tucked away, the tighter the knot in her stomach grew. She passed an entire room dedicated to the different ways they executed the afflicted, and another filled to the brim with different artists' interpretations of the final battle between the woman who fell from the stars and the Flame Keepers; by the time she reached the end of the hall, her ire was up and her fists were clenched.

"I've got eyes on Jella," Amadeus said in her ear. "She's on the move with Marson, toward the archive rooms. I'm following."

"Scott, you free yet?" Carol asked, knowing he wouldn't answer until he was. Silence on his end. She didn't like that Amadeus had no backup, but she needed to make contact with Umbra immediately.

"Let me know when Jella and Marson stop, but don't engage yet," Carol whispered.

"Got it."

Looking around to make sure she wasn't observed, Carol didn't take the time to pull on the heat glove to open the door leading to the ladies' room. Instead, she pressed her bare palm against it, sending energy sizzling through the sensor. The pad sparked and smoked, and Carol fanned away the acrid smell of burning plastic and metal as the door swung open. They wouldn't need the damn gloves anymore.

She stepped inside. It was a dank, dark little room with just a handful of stalls, and deep-blue tiles covering the walls and floor. It didn't look like it got cleaned or used often. Were women even allowed in the museum when it wasn't being used for big events? Probably not.

Umbra was standing alone, waiting for Fern in the stall. Carol kicked the door shut behind her, and Umbra jumped at the noise, frowning when she saw Carol. Instantly, she straightened up, tension snapping back into her body.

"Madame Khal, did you need something?"

Carol didn't answer. Instead, she let her abilities do the talking. She laid her palm against the crack in the door, and her skin lit up, heat fusing the door shut against intruders. Umbra's eyes widened to saucers, gasping in the silence of the bathroom.

"Wait, what? I—"

"I'm not Madame Khal. My name is Carol Danvers. Rhi sent me." Carol pulled out the disc and pinched it between her fingers. Umbra rushed forward, snatching it from her.

"Is she—" She couldn't seem to say any more, her eyes begging for an answer.

"She's fine."

"Really?" Umbra let out a sob, her hands covering her mouth, stifling the sound. "He—he said she wouldn't be able to pilot the ship on her own. That she must have steered it straight into the suns."

"He lied," Carol said. "She flew that ship all the way to my planet and found me. Our team's here now, working to free you and Jella and the rest of the girls at the Maiden House. But we need to move fast."

Umbra sagged against the stall door, sucking air in and out in deep breaths as she tried to calm herself. "She's really okay? She's *here*? She shouldn't have come back. He'll kill her."

"I won't let him," Carol said.

"He gets what he wants," Umbra replied, so hopelessly that Carol's heart broke for her. What kind of hell had she endured with Ansel?

"Not anymore," she said—and it was a vow, an oath. A feeling that went so deep it must become a reality, no matter the cost. "Rhi is safe. She's waiting for you, but you need to do what I say now."

Carol pulled her compact out of her purse, flipping it open to expose the EMP patch tucked inside, and held it out to her. "Put this on right over your implant. It'll render it inert."

Umbra took the patch from her, holding it up to the light. "How can that be?"

"The Damarians might have better tech than you had when you crashed here, but I've got a friend who can't be beat in the brains or brawn department. The Damarians don't have a chance."

The toilet flushed, the sound making Umbra jump, like she'd forgotten Fern was still inside the room with them. Umbra was still clutching the patch between her fingers, her eyebrows drawn together. "It makes the tracker useless? And the kill switch?" she asked, like she couldn't quite believe it. "Not just the power blockers?"

"Put it on, and it will be like the implant isn't even there," Carol said, her voice lowering as Fern came out of the stall.

"All done!"

Umbra smiled at her, a false, cheerful grimace that made Carol's stomach ache even as her head turned toward the door, the voices outside growing louder, but then fading as they passed. They were safe. For now… but they needed to hurry.

"Marson took Jella into an archive room, third on the left," Amadeus's voice came over the comm. "I'm positioned right outside."

Fern looked up at Carol. "Hello."

"Hi," Carol said, with a gentle smile that she couldn't hold for long.

"Why is your hair short?"

"Because I like it that way," Carol answered, and Fern frowned, touching her own hair, so tightly wound to hide her pointed ears.

Carol looked down at the child's innocent face, thinking of the grim future awaiting her and all the girls from the Maiden Houses. How could she let this kind of injustice stand?

"Go wash your hands," Umbra directed Fern gently.

She hurried to obey, humming to herself as she washed. Umbra walked over to the stack of red towels on the counter and crouched down to help the child dry her hands, then cupped her face.

"You're a good girl, Fern."

"I know," Fern replied, making Umbra laugh softly. She looked back up at Carol, something burning in the young woman's eyes that she didn't recognize.

"*Like the implant isn't even there*," Umbra whispered, repeating the words as if they were a magic spell.

A second too late, Carol realized what she was going to do. One moment, the EMP patch was in Umbra's hand, and in the time it took Carol to reach forward—*No!* on her lips—the patch was on Fern's arm, covering her implant.

And just like that, the whole damn plan went out the window.

"Ow!" Fern flinched as the patch activated, fusing with her skin. She tried to pick at it, but Umbra swatted her hand away.

"Don't do that! Keep it on, Fern. It's important."

"It stings!" Fern complained.

"It won't soon."

Carol stared at Umbra, pride wrapped in a shroud of horrific awe filling her body. The girl had just sacrificed her only chance at freedom. Rhi would be destroyed when they came back without her. And for now, President Ansel would win. Would they even get another chance to free her? They'd have to find one. She'd made Rhi a promise.

"Umbra…"

The girl straightened, her chin tilting up, pure stubbornness. "She is a *child*. And her father is… weak, like mine. You don't understand; you can't. Please…" Her voice broke, her whole body tense.

"We'll cut yours out—" Carol started to say, looking around for something sharp.

Umbra shook her head. "He reprogrammed my

implant personally the day Rhi escaped. The kill switch will activate the second you make the first cut."

God, if there was a man who deserved to be punched... it was Ansel. Carol's fingers curled.

"You have to go without me," Umbra begged.

Change of plans, then. Carol bit the inside of her lip, scenarios racing inside her head as she worked through it with the split-second instincts she always fell back on. *Assess. Decide. Execute.*

"Amadeus, you there?" she said, activating her radio.

"I'm here."

"We need to revise and expedite. Scott, get ready to run. Things are about to go dark. Amadeus, on my word, get Jella and defuse her implant. Mantis, as soon as the power goes, get in position near the museum's gate with the truck. I have a feeling we'll be making a hasty exit. Stand by."

As her team's affirmatives filtered in, Carol looked down at Umbra.

"What do you want me to say to Rhi?"

Umbra couldn't meet her eyes, but her voice was steady. "Tell her: *We do what we must.* She'll understand."

She wouldn't—Carol knew that, and so did Umbra. The only person who didn't understand the pain that lay ahead was sweet little Fern, swishing back and forth so that her skirt would dance around her ankles.

"You have to go," Umbra said quietly. "He'll be done wooing his donors and want me back soon." She bent down again, so she was eye level with Fern.

"Fern, you trust me, don't you?" she asked, smoothing the little girl's braids back with a shaky hand.

"Of course, Umbra. You're my friend."

"We'll always be friends," Umbra said, tears shimmering in her green eyes. "But right now, I want you to go with the nice lady. Go quickly. And don't make a sound, no matter what happens. Your daddy asked her to take you."

"Where are we going?"

"Somewhere special," Umbra said. "Somewhere wonderful. It's a surprise." She placed Fern's hand in Carol's, caressing the girl's hair briefly before breaking away.

Go, she mouthed.

Carol wanted to say something. Because Umbra looked so desperate. Because she was giving up everything, right then and there, without a thought for the horrors ahead. But what words could acknowledge a sacrifice of this magnitude?

She led Fern to the door, and on the landing, she turned, the message on her lips.

"I see why she loves you."

○────────○

CAROL RAN. She swept up a protesting Fern and sprinted down the empty hall in the opposite direction that she had come, away from Umbra and the staircase and the crowds beginning to form on the observation deck. The archive rooms were on the second floor; she needed a different way to get up there.

"Amadeus, time to blow the power," she said into the comm.

No answer.

"Amadeus?"

Nothing again. Carol bit back a curse.

"Scott?"

Nothing there, either.

"Mantis?"

"On my way."

"Who are you talking to?" Fern asked.

"Nobody," Carol told her, her grip on the child tightening as she raced down the deserted hall, finally opening a door marked SERVICE to find a small staircase leading to the second level of the dome. With a sigh of relief, she took them three at a time as Fern let out a shriek of delight at their speed.

"Amadeus!" Carol hissed into the comm again, her worry growing with each step. She shifted Fern so the child was on her hip, freeing one of her hands. Galloping up the stairs, she quietly opened the door an inch and looked out.

The dusty Hall of Archives was empty, its curved walls punctuated on both sides by doors bolstered with thick metal brackets and ancient heat sensors. There were dozens of rooms down the hall, and the corridor reached back so far Carol couldn't see where it ended—perhaps it curled all around the dome in a spiral. Amadeus was nowhere to be seen.

He must have gone after Jella, she told herself, hoping she was right.

Stopping at the third door on her left, she tried the knob—it was locked. "Tuck your head against my shoulder," she told Fern, who obeyed instantly.

Her hand glowing with the brilliant energy of the stars, Carol kicked at the door with the force of her frustration and her heartbreak about Umbra's sacrifice. Flying off its hinges and skidding across the floor, it slammed into the opposite wall, narrowly missing Amadeus.

Now Carol knew why he wasn't answering— Marson had him pinned by the throat against a bookcase. Amadeus's arms—delivering blows to Marson's head—kept rippling from human to hulk, unable to stick the transformation as Brawn struggled against the suppression weapon's effects.

Carol blasted Marson; he screamed as he reared back and hit the ground hard, his jacket smoking from the beam, his eyes terrified and stunned. Carol kept one eye on the secretary as she stepped over his prone body to get to Amadeus. He coughed, spitting out blood as his body continued bulging in varying spots, green streaking up his neck as Brawn struggled to get out.

When she chanced a look over Carol's shoulder and saw him, Fern screamed, so Carol just clutched her tighter. "It's okay, sweetie," she whispered, even though it was anything but.

"You all right?" she asked Amadeus.

"He wants out," Amadeus gasped. "And he can't. It's making him angry."

Behind her, Carol heard footsteps. She whirled, her

hand raised to blast, and then immediately lowered it when she saw Mantis standing in the broken doorframe.

"I sensed Amadeus…" She hurried over to him and pressed both hands on his head, smiling in relief when Amadeus's entire body relaxed. The green faded from his skin as Brawn receded, Mantis lulling him into a temporary peace.

Finally back in control, Amadeus spat out another mouthful of blood. "I had to stop Marson—he was hitting her. Jella… how are you doing?"

Carol looked over to where he was staring. Jella was crouched in the corner, her knees drawn to her chest, her eye puffy and just starting to turn purple.

"Jella!" Fern wiggled out of Carol's arms, and Jella rose to her feet and rushed over to her. Fern's eyes closed in relief as they cuddled close, and Carol thought about how Rhi had said that Jella had been under Marson's control for almost two years now. Jella and Umbra must have spent a lot of time with Fern.

"Umbra?" Jella asked Carol.

She shook her head, and Jella choked back a sound, stroking the back of Fern's head.

"Who's the little girl?" Amadeus whispered.

"I'll explain later," Carol said, hearing an unmistakable rustle of cloth behind her. She pivoted. "You—*stay down.*" Carol stomped Marson's chest just as he tried to rise. His eyes widened as he tried to push against her weight, his hands wrapping around her shoe, trying to knock her off-balance with what he thought was his superior strength and weight.

"Oh, look, he thinks he can throw you," Mantis's voice was sharp enough to cut, the mockery dripping off it like blood. She bent down, staring into Marson's face. He shrank back, his eyes fixed on Mantis's antennae as if they were poisonous.

Carol moved away, curious to see what Mantis would do.

"I heard what you said about the art downstairs," Mantis said. "How beautiful you thought it was. Would you like to know how the women feel about it?"

Mantis's hands closed around both sides of his head. She cradled his skull in a grip that looked gentle— until you saw the blood trickling from her nails down his cheeks. He gasped in fear, caught in her gaze, and his lip began to wobble.

"That's right," Mantis said, her voice deceptively soothing, even as her fingers—and her power—dug deeper into his skin. "Can you feel it? The revulsion? The fear? How your skin crawls? That pit growing in your stomach with each image? How you can't shake it from your head, even hours after?"

He whimpered, his eyes skittering to Jella, who was holding Fern close.

"Can you feel *her*?" Mantis asked, and Carol could almost taste her power pulsing through the room, magnified by the Damarians' weapon. She could feel Mantis peeling back the layers that made Marson *him*, replacing them with every shred of Jella's fear and pain, fusing them into her captor's psyche, never to leave. "That's what you did to her," Mantis whispered. His face rippled, almost crumpling in on itself like a scrap of foil crushed in a fist. Crushed under *her* fist.

His eyes rolled back in his head, and she slapped his face with one hand, never breaking the contact with the other.

"No," he moaned, his hands scrabbling up to bat at hers. "Make it stop. Make it…"

"You didn't listen when *she* said no. You never listened. But now you will."

He screamed, his fingers coming up to claw at his eyes. She batted them away, so he wouldn't harm himself. "You don't get off that easy!"

"Mantis," Carol said. "We need to go. We still have to blow the power. Before they realize something's wrong."

Mantis jerked back, as if she'd forgotten Carol was in the room. Her eyes were wild with angry tears when they met Carol's, and then slid to Jella.

"What do you want, Jella?" Mantis asked. "I could kill him right now—make him feel it until he scratches his eyes raw. Until he tears his heart out just so it'll stop beating."

"No! Jella, please! Everything I did was to protect you." Marson trembled at Mantis's feet, but his eyes slid to Jella, calculating.

"That's enough." Mantis pulled a knife out of a sheath strapped to her ankle, and Marson shrank back as she covered his mouth with one hand and grabbed his arm with the other, sinking the tip into it. His screams were muffled against her palm as crimson bubbled up, traveling in little rivers down his wrist as she carved out his implant, yanking it free with a vigorous flick of the knife. She handed it over to Amadeus, who pulled out a baggie from his pocket to slip it into.

"Is that all you need?" Mantis asked.

Amadeus nodded. "I'm good to go."

Mantis laid the knife against Marson's neck. "I know you understood what you were doing. You knew Jella's pain. The agony of your beatings. The degradation of being used like your own personal spy camera. You didn't just not care—you *liked* it."

He began to shake his head, but she pressed the knife deeper against his neck, stilling him. "You can't lie to me. I see you. And I will kill you right here, right now, if Jella wishes me to."

Jella handed Fern back to Carol and walked forward until she was standing next to Mantis. Looking in her eyes and reaching out, she took the knife from Mantis's hand.

Marson's entire body sagged in relief against the floorboards, tears trickling out of the corner of his eyes as he sobbed, "Mercy! Thank you, Jella, mercy! I always knew you were a good girl. I always—"

Jella's fingers clenched around the knife.

"*No.*"

As the word echoed between them, she sank the blade deep into her Keeper's throat. And there it stayed, until he was still.

24

MARSON CRUMPLED, crimson spurting from his neck, his eyes going blank in seconds. Carol reached for Fern, only to find Amadeus had already swept her up in the chaos, keeping the child from seeing the bloody scene.

Jella dropped the knife, and her eyes—eyes that had been dead, now sparking back to life—met Carol's. "Are you going to punish me?"

"No," Mantis said, glaring at Carol as if she thought she'd object. She clasped the girl's shoulder for a moment as Amadeus handed Fern back to her. "He would've hurt more girls if he'd lived, I could feel it."

Jella's eyes widened in surprise at Mantis's implicit approval, but she said nothing else, pressing her lips to one of the child's pointed ears and whispering into it.

"Amadeus, time to blow the power," Carol directed.

"On it."

She touched the comm in her ear. "Scott, the power's

going. You need to get away from the president; meet us in the botanical gardens out front."

Scott didn't answer, but she knew—or rather hoped— it was only because he wanted to avoid suspicion.

"Take my hand," Mantis directed, reaching for Jella's. "I can guide you in the dark."

"Here we go," Amadeus said, pulling out a remote detonator and flicking open the tab to expose the keypad. "Lights out."

The air rippled as the electromagnetic pulse shot through the dome, shorting out the building's circuitry and making the fillings in Carol's teeth ache. They were plunged into darkness—but only for a second. A whimper broke through the silence—and then, to Carol's horror, green light sparked and crackled behind her.

"Jella!" Fern's voice spiked with panic as lightning danced between her little fingers, spreading up her arms and shoulders. The girl's eyes widened, terrified. "What's happening? I don't like this!"

"Fern, it's okay," Jella set her down, crouching down next to her. "I need you to breathe. Just breathe."

"Oh no," Amadeus said. "Her implant's deactivated. The stress and her powers…"

"The weapon?" Carol asked, but Amadeus shook his head in the flickering light.

"Rhi built up an immunity to it. Fern and the other girls must have, too. Only the implants would keep them powerless at this point."

Jella grabbed Fern by the arms, wincing as the

lightning sparked over her skin, red welts striping her hands. "Watch me, Fern," she directed, breathing in and out slowly. Tears trickled down the little girl's face as she tried her hardest to imitate Jella; in less than a minute, the lightning flickered and then subsided.

"Good job!" Jella's voice was full of false cheer as her shoulders sagged in pure relief.

"We need to go *now*," Carol said urgently. She could hear shouting downstairs and on the conservatory deck. People were panicking in the dark. Flame Keepers would be reckless with their powers, suspicious of the cause. Maybe they'd light the whole damn museum on fire—that'd be ironic. "They'll be looking for Marson."

They raced out of the archive room, the night-vision contacts helping them guide Jella and Fern through the darkness. They'd almost reached the end of the corridor when Carol's comm switched on.

"Two guards coming up the stairs!" Scott was out of breath. "If you haven't got out yet, you're gonna need to go another way!"

Carol skidded to a halt, the rest of them stopping behind her. "Back up," she hissed. "Get Fern in one of the rooms—now!"

Amadeus pressed a heat-gloved hand to the sensor, and the door clicked open. They hurried Fern and Mantis inside while Carol remained on watch in the corridor. "Amadeus, go inside with them," she said. "Jella—" She held her hand out. "Can you use your power? Will you hide us?"

Jella looked down at her palm as if the idea of being asked instead of ordered was alien. Then she placed her hand in Carol's as the guards' footsteps pounded onto the second floor.

They winked out of sight just moments before the guards rounded the corner at the end of the hall. It was a strange feeling to be present, but not visibly. Carol's skin felt wobbly, as if her very cells were a little scrambled by the transformation.

"Check the rooms," one of the guards ordered.

"Wait for it," Carol muttered in an undertone to Jella. The guards began sweeps of the rooms, methodically criss-crossing the hall, door by door, clearing each one. Carol raised the hand that wasn't holding Jella's, and her palm began to glow red hot. As the guards crossed the hall, she aimed at the string of ember bombs strapped to their belts. Two short blasts and the gel inside splattered all over the guards' skin, sizzling and smoking as they screamed, rolling on the ground.

"Go!" Carol yelled, and the door burst open, her team scrambling out. They raced away from the stairs, knowing more guards would be heading up the stairwell. They couldn't get lost in the panicked crowd that filled the gallery below—they'd stand out and Jella couldn't hide *all* of them—but there had to be another way out. Carol searched ahead of her as she galloped through the corridor, her being narrowed down to *find*, *protect*, and *escape*—her heart thrumming with it as Fern's panicked breathing and Jella's rushed, soothing words punctuated their footsteps along the red-stone floor.

Making a sharp right at the end of the archives corridor, Carol almost let out a cheer of relief when she saw the stairwell. Amadeus opened the door, and they dashed down the empty stairs and through a door marked EXIT at the landing that led out of the building into the night.

"The gardens!" Mantis said, pulling up the hood on her jacket to hide her antennae. "Scott's waiting for us."

Suspended in the air by Keepers below, fireballs hovered in the sky above the trees to illuminate the darkened courtyard and gardens. Guards were trying to keep the guests controlled—and failing. People were stalking through the courtyard, men yanking women by the arms behind them, yelling, shouting orders to their own personal security. Others were pushing at the now-locked gates, demanding to be let out as guards held them back. More guards streamed into the courtyard, pushing through the crowd, trying to part them for questioning. Their uniforms glinted in the firelight as more charged inside the dome to search further and others began to hotly confront the various politicians' private security details.

"We're going to head into the gardens. Hide Fern and yourself," Carol whispered to Jella, who disappeared before her eyes as someone clipped Carol's shoulder hard as they ran past her. The edge of the gardens were just fifty feet ahead, but that felt like a mile in this crowd, the angry voices of privileged men not used to hearing *no* rising. She could feel it in the air, almost taste it—one wrong move, one wrong word, and they were going to spill into a full-blown riot.

A scream rang out, shrill and female, followed by another voice—*How dare you touch my wife!*—and that was all it took. Chaos erupted behind them, cresting like a wave toward them as fire raced along the ground near the gates and the president's guests turned on the museum guards.

"Run!" Carol shouted, her hand hooking under Mantis's elbow in case she needed to pick her up and run. In front of them, the air wavered just a little if you knew where to look. Jella's power manipulated the atmosphere around her as she and Fern hurried ahead.

Move them forward. Keep the team together. Get to the rendezvous point.

Carol had never expected their mission tonight would end up with a kid on someone's hip. And, God, Umbra. Her chest tightened every time she thought of the monumental sacrifice the girl had made, without a moment's hesitation. And how was she going to tell Rhi?

"Hey!"

Yep… someone was definitely shouting at them. Carol's skin prickled in anticipation as she hustled everyone ahead, darting around a few older women grouped together, looking anxious and lost. But Carol couldn't stop to help them. They needed to get to the gardens, where there were more places to hide… and attack.

"Keep going," Carol directed, as they plunged

into the thick foliage of the botanical gardens. The temperature was oppressive, a sticky heat that had sweat rolling down her cheeks in seconds. The alien plants—some gray and stinking of rot, others brightly colored like birds—cast shadows all around them, their leaves and fronds rustling in the heated breeze and the smoke billowing off the fireballs in the sky.

Boom. An ember bomb flew over their heads, smashing in the dirt just feet away, igniting the thick bed of bright orange ferns in front of them. Carol spun around, rushing to cover her team's back, just as another bomb arced through the air. This one struck her chest, the sphere shattering in bits, the gel singeing the fabric of her dress, exposing the Hala Star on the suit she wore beneath it. But the flames couldn't burn her, and she brushed the specks of gel and charred fabric away.

There was movement in the trees ahead; she blasted energy across the thicket, slicing through the trunks so fast and neat they fell like dominos against each other, making the ground shudder as they landed. She heard muffled yelling in the distance—like someone had gotten pinned by a falling branch. Good.

"Hurry," Carol urged as Jella and Fern flickered back into view. Even with the implant deactivated, the girl's face was sweating from the effort of fighting the weapon's effects.

"Guys!"

Carol whirled, her hands at the ready, relaxing when she realized it was Scott emerging from the spiky swath of brush ahead.

"Everyone okay?" he asked, scanning the group, doing a double take when he saw Fern. "Where's Umbra?"

"She's still under Keeper control," Carol said. "We need to move. There are guards on our tail."

"I did a loop of the gardens, and I can't find a way out." His eyes narrowed as he peered into the distance, and Carol heard it, too—voices… a whole squad. Light darted between the trees, seeking, searching, *growing*. The air tightened, a strange whistling filling their ears, the moisture in the younger trees sizzling out. Carol backed up, the team following her lead.

"*Run!*" Carol ordered, just as a tunnel of fire soared above even the tallest trees, heading directly for them.

"Is that… that's a freaking fire tornado!" Scott yelled, scrambling backward and grabbing Jella's arm in the process, dragging her and Fern with him. "Amadeus! Get out of the way!"

Amadeus tried, but the warning came a moment too late. The spinning column of fire sped toward him, rising higher and growing stronger with each second. Suddenly, there was fire at his back and his sides, with no way out. Carol darted forward, plunging into the flames as the team scattered. A roar was wrenched from Amadeus's lungs as he was engulfed and carried upward in the flames. Carol grabbed his hand at the last second, bracing herself in the center of the fire, trying to tug him downward and out. Amadeus's body rippled, his right arm streaking a mottled green, muscles bulging in the wrong places as three of his fingers went Brawn-sized and the rest stayed human. Carol almost lost hold of him as he changed and then snapped back to human, but she twisted at the last second, locking her fingers around two of his Brawn-sized ones.

"Hold on!"

What the flame wants, the flame will have. The inscription beneath that awful statue.

But not this time.

Carol's muscles strained, and her joints popped against the powerful upward draft of the flames as she reached out and yanked Amadeus downward. They both fell to earth and tumbled through the undergrowth. The column of fire was still speeding toward them, expanding with each spin, setting the gardens alight everywhere it touched.

"Time to go!" Mantis grabbed Amadeus, and Carol heaved herself up, doing a quick check—*yep, all here, all okay*—before they raced through the deepening gardens. The fire was spreading almost as fast as they could run.

"What are we going to do?" Jella coughed as waves of heat rolled over their backs, each more intense than the last. Smoke filled the air, acrid and bitter from all the plant matter reduced to ash in seconds.

Before Carol could answer, a group of spheres—at least a dozen—arced over their heads: more ember bombs.

"Take cover!" she yelled. But when the bombs smashed to the ground behind them, instead of the explosive blue gel, the area was blanketed in an expanding purple foam that rose to form a wall against the fire. Though Carol could see the heat and light through it, it was holding back the fire, now slowing its deadly centrifugal tornado.

"What the—" Amadeus said.

"Hey! Over here!"

Carol spun, searching for the source of the voice but not finding it—until she looked down. A woman's head, goggles pushed up onto her forehead, peeked out of the ground like a gopher just ten feet ahead of her. Perched half inside what looked like an irrigation grate overgrown with ferns and debris, she was watching them warily, a gun—the one she'd used to shoot the retardant balls at the fire—in her hand.

"Who are you?" Carol demanded.

"The person who's here to rescue you," she said. "Come on—the foam won't hold for long, and they've got you surrounded."

"Mantis?" Carol questioned.

Eyes narrowing, Mantis stared at the woman, who held her gaze steadily, as if she knew the empath was reading her emotions and thoughts for truth. Then Mantis nodded.

Carol barked, "Quick!"

Set in a fern bed, the irrigation grate was covered with a pile of dead plants and fallen branches. Carol waited until Scott shouted the all-clear from below before she let Jella and Fern climb inside, followed by Mantis and Amadeus. Looking over her shoulder as she hurried below ground, Carol saw the purple foam crumbling and the fire roaring toward them.

Carol quickly ducked into the safety of the irrigation

shaft and slammed the grate over her head. It was a tight squeeze, her shoulders scraping the edges as she climbed down into the dimly lit tunnel in the earth, her feet splashing into a pool of murky water.

"This way," the woman said, flipping on a torch and lifting it to show the tunnel stretching as far as the beam of light.

"Wait a second," Carol held out a hand. "Who are you?"

The woman looked over her shoulder. In this light, Carol realized she was younger than she'd thought—nearer Rhi's age, but with the same eyes that had seen too much. Her red hair was like the fading suns, her skin so pale Carol wondered whether she'd ever seen them.

"My name is Sona," she said, placing her right hand on her heart and extending her arm toward Carol, palm open. "I'm the leader of the Resistance."

25

RHI'S FALL from the president's office into the sea was a shocking drop through the air followed by a freezing impact when she plunged into the bay. Thrashing in the water, she kicked out, desperate for air. Hepzibah's arms tightened around her waist as they surged up to the choppy surface. Rhi gasped, coughing up bitter water as Hepzibah tugged her toward the shuttle bobbing in the waves.

"I cannot believe you did that!" Rhi shouted as soon as Hepzibah helped her out of the water and unceremoniously dumped her onto the shuttle floor outside the cockpit.

"I wouldn't have let you drown," Hepzibah scoffed, disengaging the sonic anchor and powering up the shuttle's thrusters. Within a minute, they were soaring out of the water and into the sky. But instead of flying away from the island, Hepzibah circled up and around it, so they were hovering right above the dome.

"What are you doing?" Rhi rose to her feet and climbed into the cockpit to take the co-pilot's chair.

Hepzibah flipped open the top of the bag of ember bombs that Mantis had apparently *not* hidden well enough from her. "Sending a message." She pressed a button on her control panel, and the window to Rhi's right slid open, cold air whipping inside.

"Would you like to do the honors?" Hepzibah asked. "We don't have to hit the guards. Just the house. And his beloved garden."

Rhi's gloved hand closed over the handle of the bag of ember bombs. She could feel the heat, even from here. She stared into their blue depths and thought of the twins, of the screaming and the smell... and of how the Damarians had cheered.

She didn't even throw the bag—they weren't *worth* her strength—she just loosened her fingers, the bag dropping from her hand and the bombs scattering downward until they shattered on the surface, where the gel ignited and raced along the mansion's roof with such force that the Keepers and guards below had no hope of controlling it. The fire consumed the dome within minutes, the ember gel eating through it as flames whipped through Ansel's belongings, his library, all his precious artifacts.

Well, not *all*. The book was still tucked in Rhi's jacket, still safe.

Still something to use against him.

As they flew off, the guards suitably too distracted

by the fires to mount a search for them, laughter filled the air, and it took Rhi a moment before she realized it was hers.

○━━━━━━━○

THEY WERE almost back to the warehouse by the docks when Hepzibah's pocket started beeping. She frowned, fished a comm out of it and read something on the screen. "It's a message from Carol," she said. "The rendezvous point's changed."

Rhi's heart skipped a beat. "Is everyone okay? Did they rescue Umbra and Jella?"

"She doesn't say." Hepzibah typed a set of coordinates into her computer, and a map appeared onscreen. Rhi recognized the rocky spires that made up the Field of Fire.

"How did they get so far out of the city?" Rhi asked, confused.

"We'll ask them when we arrive." Hepzibah made a hard turn over the bay, heading north instead of south, and the city receded beneath them as they left it behind. The night felt oppressive, closing in on them as the city faded in their wake. Hepzibah flew without lights, trusting her radar to guide her through the labyrinths of stone.

By the time they approached the new rendezvous point, Rhi was on the edge of her seat, gripping the armrests tightly, her mind racing. She hadn't seen Jella in *years,* and she hadn't spoken to Umbra in months. She didn't know what to say… how to act. She was terrified she might burst into tears. She was even more terrified something might have happened, and that they wouldn't be there.

Hepzibah sent her radar scanning the area, squinting at the screen and searching for signs of life. "Ah, there!" She pointed to the formation dead ahead. "There's an opening in the rock."

She flipped on the lights and flew the ship through a narrow crevice that opened up into a deep cavern bolstered by metal brackets that looked like ancient mining equipment. Hepzibah set down the shuttle at the bottom of the cavern, and Rhi leapt to her feet, paying Hepzibah no heed when she yelled after her to wait. She slammed through the shuttle door without even waiting for the stairs to unfold and leaped down to the ground with a painful jolt, Hepzibah following her at a slower pace.

The cavern was enormous, the red-stone walls shining crystalline far above their heads. The air was so cold this deep beneath the planet's surface it made Rhi shiver in her still-damp clothes. She squinted in the dim light, looking at the shadowy figures emerging into the cavern from a tunnel to greet them. She saw Carol first, and then Amadeus, whose arm was smeared with a bright green chalky substance that healed burns.

"Rhi!"

One of the sweetest sounds she'd ever heard, Jella's voice—had she forgotten it until now?—echoed through the cavern. Her friends parted, and Rhi raced across the cavern floor, splashing through puddles and dodging stalagmites as Jella rushed toward her. Meeting in the middle, each reached out for an enveloping embrace.

Rhi sagged in Jella's arms, relief surging through her in synch with her pounding heartbeat.

"It's been so long! You did it, you really did it!" Jella murmured, clutching Rhi as if she wasn't sure she was real. "Rhi, how is Mazz? Tarin? Do you—"

"They're fine. We'll free them next," Rhi assured her, though she could not be sure, pulling back, staring into her beloved face. "I missed you so much," she choked out.

"I knew you'd come!" Jella said, tears trickling down her cheeks as she pressed her forehead against Rhi's. Jella, who had always been so strong... so defiant. Rhi pulled back, looking over Jella's shoulder expectantly, searching the group of people approaching for her distinctive hair. But then, her stomach sinking, she realized.

Her eyes flew to Jella, who looked down. "Rhi—" she began.

"She's not here," Rhi said flatly, because she had to say it out loud.

She is mine. It echoed in her head, the utter confidence in Ansel's tone. She tried to shake it out, but she couldn't.

"Do not worry," Hepzibah began, but Rhi shook her head, refusing to believe what she could see in their faces.

"Rhi, I'm so sorry," Carol came forward, soot still smeared across her forehead. Gone was the evening gown, replaced by the red-and-blue suit that was like a beacon of hope, the Hala Star shining there on her chest.

"She sacrificed her freedom for Fern's," Jella said softly, gesturing behind her, where the little girl was standing next to Mantis.

"She put the EMP patch on her instead of using it herself," Carol explained, her expression so gentle it made Rhi's stomach seize up.

Rhi looked at the little girl... Fern. She was talking excitedly to Mantis, gesturing with her hands; when she moved them, lightning sprouted from her fingertips, a tiny flicker of power that made her start in surprise. Catching sight of the distinctive blue EMP patch on the little girl's arm sent a bittersweet agony surging through Rhi.

But she wasn't surprised—she couldn't be. She knew who Umbra was. Umbra had always disagreed when Rhi insisted they had to be selfish, to look out for each other, not for everyone, because they could never rescue everyone. Rhi was practical, but Umbra was hopeful. And so their different points of view had played out: Rhi was here, and Fern was safe, but Umbra...

Umbra was still in Ansel's grasp. Still under his control. Still *his*.

She wanted to sag against Jella, to give up the struggle, to finally let these burdens fall on someone else who truly understood them. She wanted to melt into a puddle of nothing, to tear a hole through time and space and leap inside, letting the vacuum overtake her until her body finally stopped fighting.

But she couldn't. She had to be strong, and she had to be smart... now more than ever.

"We'll find her," Carol promised Rhi, her blue eyes blazing.

"Carol!" Scott called, and Carol looked over.

"One second," she said, walking over to him.

Jella looked over her shoulder at the team, then back to Rhi, tugging her closer to the shuttle. "Rhi, we have a problem," Jella said, her voice lowering, her hands tightening around her elbows.

"What?" Rhi asked.

"Look who brought us here." Jella dipped her head to the side.

Rhi's gaze followed Jella's. When she'd scanned the people earlier, she'd been so focused on looking for Umbra's distinctive hair she hadn't noticed much else. When her eyes fell on the "problem" standing right next to Carol and Scott, Rhi's heart frosted over, and her legs shook as she bolted forward toward the woman.

"Hey!" Her shout echoed through the cavern, bouncing off the high walls. There was something artificial and smooth about this cave, like it'd been hewn by hands, not by nature.

Carol shifted when Rhi clipped right past her and grabbed the other woman's hand.

Sona shook her off, her face a calm mask, even now. Oh, that face—Rhi remembered a younger version of it so well, and it infuriated her, sparking an anger she hadn't been allowed to show for years.

"Here we go," Sona muttered. "Hello, Rhi."

"*You,*" Rhi growled.

"Me."

Rhi lunged, hissing between her teeth, her fingers aching to close around Sona's neck.

"Whoa!" Scott said, reaching for her and missing as she dodged him.

"Stop that!" Someone yanked her back just as her fingernails grazed Sona's skin, and she fought against them for a second—until she realized the hands restraining her were green. Mantis.

The fight left her immediately—not because Mantis was manipulating her emotions, but because she didn't want to hurt the damaged empath. She could barely imagine carrying Jella's pain, let alone all of Damaria's.

"What the hell is going on?" Carol demanded, stalking up to the girls. Rhi's stomach plummeted at her harsh tone, but then she realized that Carol was staring at Sona. In fact, all of them—her *team*—had grouped around her, tense and poised at the ready. They had her back. They had her trust. They had *her*.

"Rhi?" Amadeus asked, the syllable holding many questions. He'd immediately gone to Jella and Fern, as if he knew Rhi would want them protected. She felt a wave of gratitude toward her teammate.

"This is Sona Lee," Rhi said, and Amadeus's eyes widened when he recognized the name. "She's the former president's daughter," she continued, for the rest of the team.

"That's true," Sona said.

"She's a monster," Rhi snarled.

Sona looked down, fighting to keep her face calm. How many times had Miss Egrit shown them the official presidential portrait with Sona perched at her father's feet, so much like that sick picture Ansel had of Umbra in his office? Sometimes Rhi thought she knew the planes of Sona's face better than her own. She'd certainly spent more time looking at her picture than at herself.

For years at the Maiden House, Sona Lee had been held up as an ideal of Damarian girlhood. Rhi used to feel sorry for her when Miss Egrit spoke of her—a girl who had never known freedom. Who was as trapped as they were, though she didn't know it.

But then, the twins murdered their Keepers, and Miss Egrit took the girls to watch their execution. The president had insisted they attend—and he'd brought his daughter.

"I remember you, too, Rhi," Sona said.

"Then you know why I'm going to rip your throat out." *Why* had she lobbed all the ember bombs at Ansel's home? If only she'd kept just one, she'd be able to…

"Maybe someone should explain what's going on before we proceed to the throat-ripping?" Scott piped up.

"I'll tell you," Rhi said, her teeth grinding in the effort to keep from punching Sona. Every second the girl avoided her eyes, the fury rose in her until it felt like the only way it could come out was to scream. "I've mentioned the twins who murdered their Keepers and were executed for it. Sona's father ordered it. He made us attend."

"He made *me* attend, too," Sona interjected.

"Do you think I don't know that?" Rhi hissed at Sona. The only thing keeping her from going for her again was the fact that the team—the people at her back, the ones who would be there even without answers—deserved to understand. "You've all seen what the ember bombs do with just a cup of the stuff. President Lee lowered the twins into a pool of it. We had to watch. We had to listen as the crowd cheered. As *Sona* cheered."

Silence echoed in the tunnel, the only sound the *drip drip drip* echoing through the silence. Rhi could feel the tension in the team behind her.

Sona's gaze finally lifted, fixing on her. "I had no choice."

"You had a choice," Rhi snapped, thinking of how her voice rose that day, ringing out loudly, because it was the only child's among a sea of men's. "You think they didn't order *us* to cheer? You think we weren't punished when we refused to betray our sisters?"

"What do you want me to say?" Sona demanded. "That I was a child? That I was weak and terrified and brainwashed? That I didn't want my father to beat me again? All that is true, Rhi. What's also true is that day changed me forever. Watching the twins, watching all of you—" Her lips pressed together as her eyes grew bright. "You all showed me what it looked like to be brave."

"I'm so glad my friends' murder was educational for you," Rhi snapped.

"It was," Sona said, and Rhi went for her,

her nails slashing Sona's cheek before Scott pulled her back.

Sona touched a hand to her bleeding cheek. "I'm sorry the twins' murder was my wakeup call," she said. "But from that moment on, I understood the nightmare I'd been born into, the nightmare you were all suffering. Then I began to plan. And now I'm here."

"Yes, in this very impressive cave. I'm in awe," Rhi said, wiping the blood dotting her fingers on her pants.

"Come with me, and you will be impressed," Sona said.

"We're not going anywhere with you." It wasn't Rhi who said it—it was Jella. She stepped forward, away from Amadeus and past the rest of the team, coming to stand next to her.

"She's supposed to be dead," Jella said to Rhi. "The government reported she fell off a cliff on a walk with her father almost two years ago."

This was news to Rhi. She hadn't seen that bulletin, but Miss Egrit shared only select ones with them in the Maiden House. Rhi raised an eyebrow expectantly at Sona.

"Well, as you can see, I'm alive," Sona shrugged. "Are you surprised the government lied?"

"You could be working for them," Jella insisted.

"And if I was, I'd be reporting to *your* Keeper, the security secretary, so you'd know about it."

"He's not my Keeper anymore," Jella said. "He's not *anything* anymore."

"You got rid of Marson?" Sona asked, and then she

whistled, impressed. "Ansel's hair is gonna be smoking, he'll be so mad."

"I don't trust you," Rhi said.

"Well, you're going to have to," Sona replied. "Because I know where your brother is."

26

FOR A tense moment, they stood there, staring at each other. Their roles in life should have taken them on very different paths—Sona as the Damarian wife, Rhi as the Inhuman slave—but their mutual strength and stubbornness had brought them here, instead, to this place, with the same goal burning inside them: freedom.

"If you know where Zeke is, just tell me," Rhi demanded.

Sona shook her head. "We need to talk. You and me. No one else."

"Not happening," Carol said instantly.

"No way," Amadeus added.

Rhi appreciated their protectiveness, but her teammates were outsiders here. This was between her and Sona. "Fine," she said. Jella made a noise of protest next to her, but Rhi shook her head.

"Then all of you, come with me," Sona said,

pointing her torch toward the tunnel that led out of the cavern. It was narrow, with car tracks set deep into the stone, and they had to move single-file through it, half stooped in places.

"What is this place?" Amadeus asked.

"The Field of Fire was once a sprawling mountain range, before the ancient Damarians mined it to death," Sona answered. "The tunnels the miners built are what's left of their spoils. They lead all the way to the coast, but most people have forgotten about them, so we were able to take them over."

"We?" Rhi heard Carol mutter to Mantis, who whispered back, "There are at least a hundred of her people, probably more. I can feel them from here."

Rhi tensed, wondering whether they should be preparing for an attack. Part of her wanted to believe Sona, that she had truly been changed by witnessing the twins' execution. But all she could see was the image burned into her memory: Sona's arm raised, her fist thrust in the air obediently as her voice rang out in triumph alongside her father.

Rhi still had the scars along her spine where Miss Egrit had dropped beads of ember gel as punishment for each girl who refused to cheer.

Soon, she thought, picturing Miss Egrit's gaping smile in her mind, *you'll pay*.

But did *Sona* deserve to pay? That was the question. Was she evil? Was she good? Could she have truly broken free of the poison that was beaten into her?

Sona led them to the left into a huge cavern, this

one three times the size of the first—large enough for a small city. Tents and buildings cobbled together from whatever scrap could be scrounged dotted the expanse in crooked rows. Laughter filled the air, and Rhi watched as a little boy chased his sister down one of the rows, their mother following, telling them to slow down. The smell of grilled meat wafted in the air, clotheslines were strung between the houses and tents, and the heat towers set in the makeshift streets glowed softly.

"Welcome to the Hub," Sona said.

Jella's hand closed around Rhi's and squeezed it. Fern had fallen asleep in Jella's arms sometime during their walk, her cheek smashed against the older girl's shoulder.

Rhi looked at Fern and knew she couldn't resent her for Umbra's sacrifice. All she could do was be grateful to know the love of someone so giving, and hope she'd be worthy of it… and that somehow, someday, she'd be able to touch it—*her*—again.

Rhi didn't want to let Jella go as Sona led their group through the lopsided rows of homes. To shield pedestrians on some of the busier "streets," oiled canvas tarps were strung up under especially drippy spots.

"How many people live down here?" Carol asked.

"Over two hundred, last count," Sona replied. "We have women and men and people who don't feel those identities fit their true selves living here. Damarians from all over the planet come to us, seeking a life free from the Keepers and Council, from the strict binary they insist our lives and loves and selves must follow. This place is one of acceptance and learning. Of understanding." They passed a group of men who nodded their heads in respect as Sona passed. "The Hub is our home, but we have outposts on two other continents as well."

People peered curiously out of their homes as they passed, but no one spoke to them. Rhi and her group followed Sona down the path to the end of the row, where a crooked sign marked *RISE* in big block letters stood on a half-metal, half-wood building with a tarp roof.

"The rest of you can stay here. There's food and drink inside; Lola will give you anything you'd like. Rhi and I will return after we've had our discussion."

Rhi smiled reassuringly at her friends, but an uneasy tension was building. After a nod of approval from Carol, the team disappeared inside the makeshift restaurant. Jella followed with Fern after squeezing Rhi's hand a final time, but Carol remained on the street, looking up and down at Sona.

"In the museum gardens, you saw what I can do," she told Sona.

Sona inclined her head, a graceful movement that came only with hours of practice. "I did."

"Just so we know where we stand," Carol smiled, a dangerous edge to it that made Rhi feel warm and safe. "I will blast your little tent city to smithereens if you so much as touch her."

"We will just be talking, Captain," Sona assured her.

"So glad to hear that," Carol said, her smile

sharpening the threat in her voice. A shiver traveled down even Rhi's spine.

"We'll be fine," Rhi told her.

She followed Sona, leaving Carol standing guard at the end of the street like the soldier she was. The girls ascended the crude steps carved in the cavern wall that led up to a ledge overlooking the expanse of little houses, shacks, and tents. There, Sona led her into another tunnel cut into the stone, this one wider than the last, large enough to stand up in. Rhi drew her jacket tighter around her, Ansel's book digging into her ribs as she did.

The tunnel opened to a smaller cavern, where a rustic rug woven from leather and rags was spread across the damp stone floor, a desk made from crates and a rough-hewn slab of red stone laid across them. A bed was tucked in one corner, covered with furs that looked like Sona might have tanned them herself.

"Not what you expected?" she asked Rhi, sitting down behind her desk and gesturing to the rickety chair across from it.

Rhi ignored her. "Where is my brother?"

"Please, sit down."

She remained standing. "I don't think you understand, Sona." She began to circle her hands, the tug inside her splitting and growing, sparks gathering in the air. "I don't have an implant anymore. And that weapon that shuts down our powers? I'm pretty much immune to it at this point." She stretched her hands out, a rip tearing through the atmosphere. She fed into it, letting it grow, lengthen; it spun darker, closer to Sona.

Sona's hands gripped the edges of her desk, her eyes wide with fear. "You throw me in that," she gritted out, "you never find Zeke."

Rhi let go, and the rip unraveled, closing with a wobble just inches from Sona's face.

"I've had a bad day," she said, and it wasn't an apology—it was a warning. "So lay out your terms."

Sona slumped and sighed—in relief, but also in defeat—and Rhi hated the fact that somehow, she felt for her.

"I didn't fall off a cliff like the government says, Rhi," Sona said, leaning her elbows on her desk. "My father pushed me."

Rhi hadn't expected that. The perfect Damarian princess—and her father had tried to kill her? She had just one word. "Why?"

"Because he found out what I was doing," Sona explained. "After the twins' execution… I was being honest when I told you it changed me. I wanted… I *needed* answers. My father was preparing me for a political marriage. He wanted me to understand Damarian history to be the best wife I could be to whoever he chose as my husband, so he let me read a lot more than most girls."

"What does Damarian history have to do with any of this?" Rhi demanded, frustration hooking inside her. "All I want is to know where my brother is."

"My father tried to kill me because I uncovered the truth about the afflicted and why they died," Sona said.

"And I was close to finding the proof—proof that he once had before it was stolen from him."

"The truth?" Rhi echoed, still not understanding.

"They've always told us that the suns bless only men with the flame," Sona explained, intoning, "*As it is now, and how it always has been, and will always be.*"

"Yeah, yeah… *Women are too weak to bear it*—I know the script," Rhi waved her off.

"It's a lie," Sona said. "Hundreds of years ago, women held the flame, too. And in women, the flame wasn't limited to just pyrotechnics. I found scant references—sketches of powered women in ancient texts, letters mentioning women with abilities like healing or telekinesis—going back thousands of years."

"Then what happened?" Rhi asked, thinking about the afflicted and their myth about the woman who fell from the stars. "Why are only men powered now?"

"Because they slaughtered the women," Sona went on. "The group of men that would form the first Council after the war, they systematically ended every family line that contained the genes that give women the flame. Then they made up a story about a woman from outer space to blame their genocide on. And they told it so well and so many times for so many years that it became 'history.'"

Rhi stared at her. Sona was sitting there, looking at Rhi like she expected this news was going to shatter her world. But Rhi laughed—harsh, angry, and mocking. Sona jerked back, frowning.

"Seriously? Your dad tried to kill you because you

finally figured out that the obviously fear-mongering myth was just that—fake? Of *course* it's fake! Of *course* it's propaganda! Of *course* the woman who fell from the stars isn't real! I figured that out the second or third time they tried to shovel it down our throats. What's wrong with you that it took you all this time?"

Sona was up out of her chair, both palms flat on her desk, her eyes flashing. "How dare you…" she started to say, but Rhi slammed her own fists down on the desk, leaning into Sona's face and growling, "*Where is my brother?*"

"If you'll actually listen to me and give me what I want, then I can tell you!" Sona roared back.

"Sona." A male voice cut through their mutual fury, and they both turned as one, which made Rhi even angrier that she was somehow on the same wavelength as Sona. A tall bearded man was standing there, with two little girls—no older than three—holding each of his hands.

Twins. Rhi could see it in their faces. She looked at Sona, wondering whether this was some kind of sick game.

"Girls." Sona hurried around her desk, bending down to hug them. The man touched her shoulder briefly, and Rhi could see the bonding bracelets that matched Sona's own on his wrists. This was her husband. Were these her children? "Can you show Rhi your trick?"

The girls exchanged a look—a conspiratorial grin that sent Rhi's heart reeling. Then the girl on the right flicked her fingers, fire sprouting from them. Her sister giggled, reaching out and snatching the fire from her sister's fingertips as if it were a piece of candy, and the flame sprouted along her own palm.

Rhi sagged against the edge of the desk, the air punched out of her.

"Excellent work, girls!" Sona smiled. "Now go with Daddy. Get ready for dinner."

"You all right in here?" her husband asked, side-eyeing Rhi.

"We're fine," Sona said firmly.

She kept her back to Rhi until they were gone, and then she let out a long sigh, her shoulders slumping. "The genetics spontaneously appear mainly in twins, or at least we think they do. I don't have a lot of data on it other than my own, and a lot of my early journal entries are just, *Oh no, my babies are shooting fire out of their fingers!*"

"You…" Rhi didn't know what to say. "Are there more?" she blurted out, thinking of darker repercussions. If Ansel knew about this…

"We have four girls who hold the flame, including my two. And three little boys as well. My girls are pyrotechs, and so are the boys. The Laya twins, they're fifteen. Gretta can heal people, and Junie can cloak places. Which is why the Keepers haven't found us."

Rhi stared at the spot where Sona's daughters had been, thinking about how they had giggled together. How it had been fun, not frightening, to use their powers. "What are you going to do?" she couldn't stop herself from asking.

"What are *you* going to do?" Sona shot back. "You're in the same position I am. You can choose to look out for the few or to defend all. Neither path is easy. One seems impossible, and both are dangerous."

Rhi couldn't answer that—she couldn't bear to. Especially after the chance to free Umbra had failed because she'd put the *all* before herself.

Umbra would like Sona, she realized with an uncomfortable jolt. If she were here with Rhi, she wouldn't have been suspicious like Rhi was. Umbra would be sympathetic. She would help Sona, give her what she wanted, if she had it.

Rhi finally took a seat in the rickety chair, trying not to smile when Sona's ruddy eyebrows shot up in surprise. "What do you want from me?"

Sona leaned against the edge of her desk, folding her arms across her chest. "Years ago, before Ansel was president, he asked you to find something for him—a book. Do you remember?"

"I do," Rhi replied carefully.

"That book belonged to my father. It's the last official record of the *real* history of Damaria. The only one written not by the male victors, but by the few women and men brave enough to record their experiences for posterity, no matter the risk."

"And you think that if you get this book, you can, what—undo things? Break the system? Punish the Keepers?"

"Truth is power. And fear and hate are *taught*, Rhi. We aren't born with it, even if men like my father and

Ansel want us to think we are. And if hate is taught, it can be unlearned, and replaced with understanding."

Sona stared down at the ground, her hands cupping her elbows, almost cradling them, like she'd gotten used to hugging herself for warmth on the cold nights struggling for survival. "I know that to you, it seems ridiculous that a mythic woman cursing the world was so real to me. But think about that—think about all the women across Damaria who are certain that power and choices would destroy them... and about the men who push down their instincts 'for the betterment of all'— even though that's a cruel lie. But we're told, over and over again, that it must be true because there is no other option, even though the system hurts men and women and all who do not subscribe to those labels.

"So you ask what does it matter if I have proof that it *isn't* real? That it was a cover-up to explain mass murder? That might be the spark that will fan the true flame to wrest the Keepers' control away from the Damarians *and* the Inhumans. If you could help me find the book..." Sona almost pleaded. "It might... no, it *will* change things."

The passion in Sona's voice reminded Rhi of Umbra. She thought of Alestra and Zeke, of their growing baby, unaware of the oppression possibly awaiting her. She thought of her sisters back in the Maiden House. Of the Damarian girls, tucked away in their own Maiden Houses—not as horrific as theirs, but still prisons. Of all the women living on this monstrous planet—Inhuman and Damarian—all of them locked into lives of servitude, all of them forced to give up their daughters.

None of them had a choice. And Sona wanted to give them one.

Which meant Rhi had to make a choice, too.

She had started this journey determined to trust no one. But she had learned that was no way to end it.

Making her decision, she pulled the book out of her jacket, unwrapped it from the plastic that protected it, and held it out to Sona.

"I have to admit, you've got stellar timing."

"Is that—" Sona's face twisted in confusion melting into astonishment, and her fingers closed around the volume gently, as if she was afraid it would vanish beneath her touch. Her intensity reminded Rhi so much of Ansel's reaction she had to bite back bile to remember Sona would use it for good—not evil.

Sona stammered, "The title... the star on the cover... This... this is *it*! I can't believe it. I just can't— how did you get this?"

"I broke into Ansel's house tonight. And burned it down."

Sona's eyes widened in shock. "You... *what*?"

Rhi was at a loss to explain how it happened. She didn't know how to begin to describe Hepzibah— how her joy and freedom were so infectious, making a person feel like they could do anything. Finally she just said, "It's a long story. I found the book when I was searching Ansel's office for information on Zeke, and I remembered the time years ago Ansel had me find it, and I knew it must be important, so I took it with me."

"This is… you have no idea…" Sona stammered.

"I do," Rhi cut in. "I gave you what you wanted, Sona. Which is why you're going to tell me where Zeke is. Now."

"Of course," Sona replied, getting up to set the book carefully on the desk, like a precious jewel. "The Resistance has friends inside the government. I got word that the prison transport your brother's on will be stopping to pick up more fuel cells tomorrow morning. I have the route and the times. You should be able to intercept them." She pulled a map from a stack on her desk, laying it flat on the stone surface. "I can go over the route with you, if you'd like."

Rhi leaned forward, her eyes tracking the dark-blue line Sona had traced along the road.

"I'd like that," she said.

27

CAROL SEEMED surprised to see Rhi and Sona emerge an hour later, not exactly smiling, but definitely not primed to pummel each other. She hadn't seen that kind of animosity simmering in Rhi before, but once the story behind the twins' execution was told, she understood. And she felt a corkscrewing horror for both Rhi and Sona, for all they had endured—the two sides of the Damarian coin, where no woman won.

The tent-and-shack city inside the cavern was dank and smelly, but alive with activity: small street markets thrumming, children's laughter echoing from a makeshift playground of repurposed odds and ends scavenged from the world outside, and music floating above the haphazard tents and buildings as the night unfolded. The team unwound as much as they could inside the restaurant, which was just a lunch counter with a still in the back.

Amadeus, being Amadeus, had instantly engaged the bartender in questions about said still; by the time Rhi returned, he was on his back underneath it, Scott handing him a tool to replace one of the broken coils and chatting with the grateful owner.

Mantis had found a bench for Fern to lie down on and was hovering over the child, occasionally pressing her hand to her temple to chase away bad dreams. Jella was asleep in a chair next to her, the events of the day finally catching up to her, her hands shaky until Hepzibah poured her a cup of strong Damarian tea and commanded her to drink it.

"I'm going back to the shuttle to get some sleep," Rhi told Carol. "Will you walk with me? I want to talk to you."

Carol nodded, rising to her feet. "I'll be back," she told Scott and Hepzibah.

She had expected Rhi to be angry or despairing, peppering her with questions about Umbra, but their walk through the dark tunnel back to the cavern that housed the shuttle was silent. Rhi made no move to go inside the shuttle when they reached the cavern. Instead, she found a rock to sit on, folding her legs beneath her.

"I'm sorry, Rhi," Carol said, figuring she might as well start.

Rhi shook her head. "It's not your fault."

"I handed her the EMP patch, instead of just putting it on her arm," Carol admitted. "I didn't even think—"

"—that she'd sacrifice herself," Rhi finished. She

gave a shrug, her hair swinging down her shoulders at the movement. "That's my fault. I should've warned you. She... she's kind of amazing like that."

"So I learned." Carol leaned against a pillar, staring up at the dripping stone, glowing red even deep underneath the earth.

"I don't blame you at all," Rhi said. "I blame myself."

"What—"

"She always said that we couldn't leave without *everyone*," Rhi continued, staring at her hands, thinking of the last time Umbra had held them, the night before Ansel came to take hold of her. Umbra had kissed each finger and whispered, *I'm coming back, I promise* to her skin, because she couldn't say it to Rhi's face.

"And I always told myself that when the time came, she'd come. That she'd let herself be selfish. But that's not the girl I love. The girl I love gave her freedom away to a little girl who doesn't even understand her own power. Because it's the right thing to do."

Carol's eyes shimmered in the dim light. "She told me to tell you this: *We do what we must.*"

Her words wrenched a half-laugh, half-sob from Rhi. "Damn her," she muttered. "Damn her." She buried her face in her hands, the pain working its way through her, never again to surface. When the last tear finally fell, she wiped it away and squared her shoulders.

"Ansel's already adding maternity wings and nurseries to some of the empty Maiden Houses," she said. "I found his plans when I was searching his office. He's calling them 'Heritage Houses.' Even if we get Alestra away, off the planet, there are going to be countless others left behind to suffer the fate we save her and her baby from."

"That bastard," Carol muttered.

"I don't know what to do," Rhi said. "I thought that I could get my friends and my brother out, and that the rest… the Inhumans, the Damarians, they would have to find their own way."

How could she stay? But how could she go? Either way felt impossible.

"And now?" Carol asked, swinging her arms back and forth as she pushed off the column and began to move around the cavern, pacing in tight little circles that spoke of her restlessness. Rhi knew the lack of flight was bothering her terribly.

"I don't know," she answered, feeling suffocated by hopelessness. "Did you see them?" she asked, looking up at Carol. "The little girls who hold the flame?"

Carol nodded. "Cute kids. Very… fiery. I suppose we shouldn't be surprised. If the flame really is a genetic trait passed down, it was only a matter of time before it reappeared in a female line. Like gender, genetics is a varied spectrum."

"Sona wants to overthrow the Council. She wants me to help her lead the revolution to free Damaria."

"You definitely bring a lot to the table," Carol remarked.

"I don't know how to lead," Rhi blurted out.

"That's them talking, Rhi, not you." Carol said it so softly, with no pity, but it made Rhi flush all the same.

"You know, one of the most important things I've learned is the tricky relationship between being a hero and being a leader. You want to be both, of course, but sometimes leading means making a choice between sacrificing for the good of all or rising for the good of a few."

Rhi felt so small when she said, "I never asked for this."

"No… but the great leaders rarely do," Carol answered gently. "Those who are hungry for power rarely want it for good or right reasons. Those who respect power and use it with restraint to help others are the ones who do the most good for the greatest number of people over time."

Rhi stared upward. If she squinted, she could swear there was a crack at the very top of the cavern, a sliver where she could see the red sky.

She had dreamed of the stars. Of returning to them, and leaving Damaria and the hell it was behind. But she had also dreamed for years of green fields, and a girl who'd helped her make them so. A girl who'd want to stay, to help, to create change, to flourish.

The idea of staying was frightening, but Sona had said something she did believe: Fear was learned.

And fear could be conquered.

○────○

THE NEXT morning, the team gathered around the shuttle for a final check-in. Amadeus had washed off the salve that coated his burn, revealing new skin growth already covering most of the damaged area. He assured Carol he'd taken a sample of the stuff to bring back home.

"We're going to split up," Carol said. "We've got a lot to do in very little time. And now that Ansel knows what we're up to, we've got to make every second count. Amadeus and Scott will bring Jella to Fort Olvar to take out the suppression weapon. Rhi and I will intercept Zeke's prison transport as it stops to fuel up. Hepzibah and Mantis will get in position outside the Maiden House with Sona and the Resistance fighters."

"What about Fern?" Mantis asked.

"She's staying with Sona's daughters until we return," Jella said. "I do not like leaving her here, but she can't be anywhere near the fighting."

"Fern will be safe here," Carol said, and she believed that. "After the weapon's knocked out and Zeke's with us, we'll hit the Maiden House in a three-pronged attack: from below, from above, and on the ground."

"And we'll finally have Brawn on our side," Scott said, clapping Amadeus on the back. "Not that you haven't already saved our asses several times."

"I'm definitely feeling like I want to smash some things," Amadeus said. "And trust me, so is Brawn."

"I will not let you down," Jella put in solemnly.

"We've seen you in action," Amadeus smiled at the girl. "We know you won't. I would *love* to take some energy readings off you once this is all over. The atmosphere manipulation you can do is—"

"Not now, Amadeus," Mantis said, poking him

lightly. "We need to get going. It's a long trip to the Maiden House." She reached out, taking Rhi's hands in hers. "Be safe, Rhi."

"You too."

Hepzibah slipped something into Rhi's jacket pocket, and when she patted the spot, feeling the curve of an ember bomb, the Mephitisoid winked at her and hurried after Mantis. Rhi could hear the empath saying, "Where did you get that?" and Hepzibah sing-songing back, "Never you mind, Mantis, never you mind…"

"Sona's gonna show us the transport we'll be using, so we've got to go with her," Scott said, smiling at Rhi. "Kid, you've impressed the hell out of me this whole mission. You're gonna keep at it, right?"

She nodded, letting him hug her tight before turning to Amadeus.

"Umbra will be back with you soon," he said, making it sound like a promise. "We'll find a way."

She wanted so badly to believe him. But she also knew that as soon as the team had liberated the girls in the Maiden House, they had to get them off the planet immediately—especially Alestra. But Rhi would have to stay behind, because she couldn't leave without Umbra. And knowing what she knew about the horrors faced by all women on the planet, how could she leave at all?

But what could she *do* about it? Could she be the kind of leader who could help liberate Damaria? Did Sona and the Resistance have a chance? She couldn't decide.

Amadeus stepped away to give her and Jella some

space. The two Inhumans clung tightly to each other.

"I don't want to leave you again," Jella whispered. "The last time…"

Rhi's fingers clenched Jella's waist as she thought of that day. Secretary Marson and three guards had to drag Jella away. She'd screamed and kicked and scratched, even as they shocked her over and over again. Marson had laughed. But he wasn't laughing anymore.

"I'll be back," she said, wishing she could put the kind of reassurance in her voice that Amadeus did. "As soon as I have Zeke."

"You're a good sister," Jella whispered. "Zeke is lucky. And so are Alestra and the baby. Now go. Be strong. Be smart."

"Be strong. Be smart," Rhi repeated back to her as they broke apart.

Jella followed Scott and Amadeus out of the cavern, and Rhi turned to Carol, the shuttle below, ready to go, and their mission that lay ahead.

In her mind's eye, she could see her brother… his floppy hair that always seemed to need a trim. His boyish face encompassed their mother's eyes, blue and lively… and their father's crooked front teeth.

He was her family. A collection of traits and memories they alone in the universe shared. She loved him for his grace, for the core of sweetness in him that never seemed to turn bitter, no matter how much they lost. He was not made of stone and fire like the men of Damaria were supposed to be. But she would be the fierce steel instead, the fire needed to burn her brother free, to destroy any who dared to keep him from her.

She thought of the flames last night burning Ansel's island to ashes, remembered her laughter, so free, ringing in her ears, and she smiled.

"I'm ready," she said to Carol. And for the first time in her life, she believed it, too.

28

CAROL AND Rhi left to intercept Zeke's prison transport when it was still dark, the shuttle soaring so quickly over the Field of Fire that the spiky landscape melted into a blur as they passed. Carol was back in the cockpit, Rhi at her side, as the eroded mountain range finally gave way to the sprawl of sand dunes and desert.

"How much time do we have?" Rhi asked yet again as the twin suns peeked behind the sandy horizon. The desert reminded Carol a little of the Sahara—its vastness, how small it made you feel when you stood amid its glory. But here, the sand was red and black, glittering like a pool of blood speckled with ash.

Carol spotted the road weaving through the sand dunes, the snaking twist of white pavement standing out against the ruby red and jet black. She checked the coordinates Sona had given Rhi and activated the ship's radar. The screen beeped as it detected an energy signature ten miles ahead and moving fast toward them.

"They're coming," Carol said. "We've gotta go. Now."

She set the shuttle down behind a sand dune, shards of rock pinging against the shuttle windows so hard Carol had a feeling she was going to owe Hepzibah a special detailing job after this. She grabbed her bag as they hustled out of the shuttle, heading to the road. The wind carved through the desert sand and wound through the surrounding mountains; it whipped at their faces and clothes like a Fury, blowing sand *everywhere*—hair, mouth, fingernails. The one benefit to a second-skin uniform like Carol's? It was airtight.

Together, she and Rhi laid the sonic strip on the road. Carol adjusted the frequency to the highest level as she heard the first rumble of distant engines coming closer—fast.

Rhi dove for cover behind a sloping hill of sand, and Carol hit the power button on the sonic strip before rolling down the embankment, out of sight. She came to a stop next to Rhi with a grunt.

"How does this work again?" Rhi whispered as Carol handed her the special earplugs to block out the frequency. The transports were gaining ground; in her earplugs, Carol could detect at least three unique engine sounds. That meant three sets of guards at least, maybe more, depending on how dangerous the Damarians thought Zeke was—or how convinced they were that Rhi would come for him.

"It's a high-tech version of a nail strip," Carol explained. "Their vehicles will pass over the strip, which activates the frequency, which will scramble their brains. It hurts like hell, too, so they won't be able to fight back. That should give us enough time to get Zeke out and back to the shuttle."

"If you say so," Rhi said skeptically as Carol raised her head, peeking up the embankment. The first transport—a panel security van, blocky with armor—had rounded the curve and now was in sight. Two more transports appeared behind it; the one in the rear was identical to the first, but the middle transport sandwiched between them was larger—and shining with the glow of a force field.

Gotcha. Carol smiled. "Get ready."

The first transport passed over the sonic strip, the tech activating an instant assault on the driver's ears. Carol heard the surprised yell, the squeal of brakes, the screech of metal crashing into metal as the middle van plowed into the first. The force sent the head transport skidding down the road like a bowling ball spinning out of control; the backup transport swerved on two wheels to avoid it, flipped off the road, and was half buried in a sand dune as the engine squealed, choked, and died.

"Now!"

She and Rhi leapt to action, galloping up the sandy embankment. The two guards in the lead transport had crawled out of the vehicle—one dragging himself across the surface belly down like road kill before he lost consciousness, the other clutching his bleeding ears as he rolled back and forth, trying to shake the sound away. Rhi hurried up to the conscious guard and kicked him in the head with the kind of precision that would've made Hepzibah proud. Hell, it made Carol proud.

Carol ran up and blasted the remaining doors of each transport, the heat of her photonic energy sizzling the metal and trapping the rest of the guards inside. But they barely noticed: The sonic strip was, as Amadeus had put it, turning their brains into scrambled eggs. The driver in the middle transport slumped over the wheel, already passed out; the two guards in the backup transport, stuck back in the sand dunes, were pressed against the windows, the pain too severe even to scream.

With the guards secure, Carol stomped on the sonic strip, turning it off. She didn't care much for the guards' wellbeing, but she did care about Zeke, and he had to be in that middle transport.

"All good?" she called to Rhi.

"All good," Rhi replied, finishing binding the unconscious guards' hands. She jogged back to stand behind the first, overturned transport, using it as a shield as she examined the other vehicle ahead, her face alight at the thought that her brother might be inside.

It reminded Carol of a flatbed truck. The square container—the miniature prison—lay on a shimmering force field instead of a flatbed, the cab in front large enough for just one driver.

Carol could hear footsteps inside the container. More than one set.

"Stay behind me," she whispered. "I'm going to draw whoever's in there with Zeke away, then you can go inside to free him. Grab him and run to the shuttle. I'll follow as soon as I can."

Rhi nodded.

Carol held up a finger. One. Two. Three.

She launched herself over the transport they were using as a shield and darted down the road toward the force field. Fire sprang up along the ground, surrounding the transport, but Carol kept going, leaping through flames that scorched her boots as the Keeper inside the transport fed more of his power into the flame.

Smoke and heat swirling around her, Carol charged ahead, looping to the back of the container, where she grabbed the red-hot handle and yanked the whole door off its hinges with a pop. She tossed it backward through the flames like a regular human would toss a tissue. Through the heated, rippling air, she could see Rhi peeking around the corner, ready and waiting.

The flames began to recede around her, sputtering down from above her head to her waist, then her knees, and then just smoldering at her ankles. Whoever was inside was slowing his roll, preparing for his grand entrance. Well, she wasn't going to give him the pleasure.

"Come out, come out, wherever you are," she called, backing up a few steps. "Or are you really that scared of a girl?" It was a precise blow, designed to lure through mockery, and she knew he'd take the bait.

She'd known it'd be him inside.

Ansel was a man with all kinds of obsessions, and Rhi was a threat to every one of them. He thought he could take her down with a few guards and himself, but his hubris… it'd take him down in the end.

Carol was going to make sure of it.

Smoke wafted in charcoal waves around them as he stepped out of the transport. Carol stood tall, every part of her body screaming, *Attack!* But she waited, her hands on her hips. She knew that Zeke was inside. And Ansel could set the entire transport on fire in the blink of an eye if he wanted to.

Ansel stepped away from the transport, flames licking his feet, his eyes fixed on her.

"So you're the one giving orders," he said.

"The one and only," Carol replied as they slowly circled each other. If she drew him far enough from the transport, Rhi could dart in and free her brother without interference. "I heard about your house. Pity."

He jerked visibly, his nostrils flaring. She smirked, knowing condescension was the easiest way to get to him. A man like that had thin skin. He'd set up the world based on sacrificing the blood of others—so he'd never bleed, and so no one would dare to even prick him. By the time she was done with him, Carol thought with grim anticipation, she would slice his sense of self to ribbons. She stepped back again, her heel landing off the pavement and sinking into sand. Just a few more steps, and he'd be completely turned away from Rhi— and then she could grab Zeke.

"Who *are* you?" he demanded.

"We went through this the first time we spoke, don't you remember?" Carol said, *tsking* softly. "I'm your fake history made flesh, Ansel. Your worst nightmare, here to free the women of Damaria and give them back their power."

Fire exploded from his hands. Carol ducked, the heat blasting over her back and striking the sand behind her, turning it instantly to glass. "Tell me who you really are!" he hissed, anger flaring in his eyes.

One more step. If he took just one more step toward her, the way was clear. Out of the corner of her eye, Carol could see Rhi tensing, readying herself. Ansel kept his attention trained on her, fascinated, a covetous light gleaming in his dark eyes… the same way he looked at Umbra. This man loved power over all else. And he wanted all of it for himself, even if he had to enslave the more powerful to get it.

"I'm a lot of things," Carol said. "Captain. Commander. Hero. But all you really need to know is this: I'm the woman who's going to kick your ass."

She lunged for him, and his hands flew up—not to shield himself, but to shoot more fire at her. He didn't expect her to punch him.

Unfortunately for him, he was wrong.

That first crunch of her fist against his cheekbone felt joyous, like coming home. Powered by her rage, her skill, and her blended Kree and human blood— the impact singing through her like a battle cry—she watched in satisfaction as his head snapped back. The blow sent him spinning before she yanked him back by the shoulder.

Fire sprouted across his body, blooming wherever she touched him, and then leaped to her. She could feel the sleeve of her suit heat up, the material stretching, the fibers starting to shrivel under the high-temperature onslaught.

Her fist smashed into the side of his head this time, and she heard his teeth clack together before he yelled and reached out, grabbing her hand. Fire tunneled and rose between them like the cyclone from the botanical gardens, but now she was in the eye of the storm.

Ansel's flames surrounded them in a swirling cloud of acrid orange and red. She couldn't see through it—couldn't tell whether Rhi had rescued Zeke. Suddenly, her feet were swept off the ground and she went flying into the air, caught in the spin of the flames as Ansel's power fed into them. The fire grew stronger, higher, faster.

For a brief moment, all she could think of was the thrill of being in the air again—suspension, the hot wind below her, the sky above. Then she jolted back to reality, where she was inside a fire cyclone, in the grip of a sociopathic pyrotech hell-bent on dragging her to her death.

She yanked her arm free and kicked him away, thrusting both her hands out to fight the fire's trajectory as the heat tore through her suit. Meant to destroy her, the energy filled her, fed her, strengthened her. Power raced along her veins, illuminating them under her skin. She could feel it: the tang in the back of her throat signaling that point when she became even *more*. When she was just beaming out pure energy.

Ansel's fire pulsed, trying to resist the pull of the power inside her, its inexorable beckoning. But nothing can resist the stars for long. And she was made of battle-worn starlight—her own kind of fire, one that never went out.

His, on the other hand...

With each pulse of power Carol drew into her body, the cyclone of flame sagged and jerked until finally it broke apart, sending them flying in opposite directions. Carol fell to earth and rolled across the sand, her shoulders slamming into the overturned transport.

The swirling heat and energy she'd drawn from the fire tornado was a restless, living thing inside her chest—eager to burst free, to dance along the metal, to scorch and singe. Her skin buzzed as she got to her feet, her teeth chattering—not from the heat, but from the adrenaline shot of power. She staggered over to the transport, only to find it was empty. Rhi and Zeke had got out.

Relief washed over her like a warm waterfall. When she heard the rattling behind her, she turned in time to see Ansel—bloodied and battered from the spill to the ground—trying to rise to his feet and failing.

Time to finish him off. She knew Rhi wanted to do it, but Carol believed in taking advantage of openings.

"You know," she said, pulling the energy inside her, focusing on her hands as they lit up, glowing redder than the suns above. "On my planet, we have a saying.

Behind every great man is a woman. You're vile, far from great, but I did think you'd be harder to beat than this. I guess Umbra's the real power behind the presidency."

"You think I didn't have a contingency plan?" he slurred, spitting out a mouthful of blood and teeth. He pulled out a comm, chucking it at her. She caught it and looked down at the screen.

Arrival Time: 10 minutes.

"The strike team is very talented," Ansel said. "Well trained. By my estimation, it'll take precisely twenty-three seconds to kill each girl, but if they finish the job sooner, they get a reward."

He smiled, a slick bloody thing that turned Carol's stomach and made her stop in her tracks, a shiver going down her back.

"Your move, *Captain.*"

29

SCOTT PULLED the transport into a gully behind the tall security fence surrounding Fort Olvar and powered it down with the flick of a switch. The fort was composed of a series of domes grouped around an oasis in the desert. Spiky trees with lush green leaves and pockmarked bark were planted in a circle around the perimeter fence, which rippled and sparked every few seconds with the power of a force field.

His stomach thrummed with excitement and eagerness to jump into the action. Not being able to hold his Ant-Man form for long was getting to him. He loved his suit, loved the amazing—and sometimes hilarious— abilities it gave him, and it rankled him that he felt like he hadn't been enough help on this mission.

Not about you, buddy, is what Carol would tell him, but still… He glanced over at Amadeus, wondering whether he felt the same way.

This place had made him grateful for Earth, grateful for Cassie's childhood on it—and despite their differences, grateful to Peggy for being a strong example for their daughter.

"It's still early—hopefully we won't run into too many Damarians," Scott said.

"You ready, Jella?" Amadeus asked.

She nodded from her spot next to Scott, unbuckling the seatbelt. They piled out of the transport, and Jella cast an uncertain look at Scott. "I'm not sure how long I can conceal both of you, even when you're in your ant form, Scott. But I'll hold it as long as possible."

"And I'll try to stay small as long as I can," Scott promised. "Hopefully, that'll make it easier."

Amadeus hurried over to the fence and pulled out a small case he flipped open to reveal three magnets. He held one an inch from the fence and let it go, the chain link drawing the magnet to it with a snap, and the force field rippling at the addition. He set the other two magnets at the bottom; when the last one snapped into place, a beam of orange light seared through the force field. The metal smoked as Amadeus kicked open the hole he'd just carved out.

Scott hit the button on his wrist. He'd told Carol it was like walking through wet cement, and it was—everything felt *wrong*. Normally, he tunneled down with a whoosh, glorying in the rush of it—the sheer joy of looking up and seeing the world turned gigantic, the individual blades of grass towering over him like trees… there was nothing like it.

A finger—Amadeus's—dipped down, and Scott hopped onto it, running up Amadeus's arm and perching on his shoulder. As Jella began to manipulate the air around them, it wobbled like the horizon in a heat wave. They moved forward slowly, passing a platoon of guards heading to start their morning exercise, and not one head snapped toward them.

"Good so far," Amadeus muttered, looking down at his handheld scanner. "The biggest energy signature is coming from the small gray dome over there." He raised his hand to point, but Jella shook her head and he dropped it quickly, not wanting to breach the protective barrier she was manipulating around them.

Scott tugged on the collar of Amadeus's shirt. "We need to hurry." He could feel his hold slipping, his muscles tightening with the need to change back, to grow.

Jella sped up; just as they turned the corner, with the gray dome blocking them from view from the recruits lining up in the exercise yard, Scott lost hold. As he popped back to regular size, he dove forward off Amadeus's shoulders and out of Jella's range. When he turned back, he couldn't see them at all, Jella's power blending her and Amadeus perfectly into the gray of the dome. Now if they just stayed there, this might work.

Scott's jaw ached from the sudden snap back to large, his bones creaking from the strain—not from old age, as Cassie liked to needle him. God, he missed his kid. He was going to hug her extra tight when he got back. The image of Fern with her father would haunt him for the rest of his life.

"Scott!" he heard Amadeus's voice hiss, and he didn't even look up, just hit the button on his suit and popped back to ant size at the warning. His eyes scrunched up in pain, and his head felt like someone was driving an ice pick in his ear. That damn weapon; he wanted to take a baseball bat to it—*soon.*

He looked up just in time to dive out of the way as the sole of a boot came crashing down, laces swinging. To his right, Jella and Amadeus were flattened against the dome, still obscured by her power, staying stock still. To his left were two Damarian soldiers, one of them writing something in a notebook while the other scrolled through his comm.

"These early morning shifts are killing me," one said.

Scott hopped onto the man's boot, leaping up and grabbing the end of the shoelace. With visceral memories of those rope-climbing tests in gym class in his mind, he scrambled up it—take *that,* Coach Stafford!—before untying the knot. The laces flapped free, and Scott swung down onto his right boot to untie those, too.

"Thought your promotion would be coming through soon," said the notebook holder. "Damn pen." He shook it, a drop of ink splashing on Scott's head, the world going blue for a second before he wiped his visor free.

"That's what they keep telling me," the other soldier grimaced as Scott took the opposite laces from both the soldier's boots and tied them together with a knot that'd make an Eagle Scout weep.

The pain in his head was making Scott grind his teeth so hard he could taste blood. He wouldn't be able to hold on much longer. He dashed across the ground.

Here we go.

His body shifted, his muscles lengthened, and in an eye-bulging stretch, he popped back to normal size right behind the soldier.

"Hi," he said, as the guy whirled around, his notebook dropping to the ground. He punched him—a jab to the solar plexus that had him reeling, gasping for breath, his eyes rolling back when Scott delivered a quick kick to the temple.

The second soldier lunged toward him. But he went flying, his laced-together boots hampering his steps. He face-planted in the dirt, his forehead bouncing off the ground with a loud smacking sound. Blood trickled down the man's cheeks, and Scott winced out of pure reflex. He'd feel worse if these guys weren't such monsters.

He bent down, stripping the specialized heat glove off one of the soldiers' hands. Putting it on his own, he pressed his palm to the sensor on the dome they were crouching behind. Its door slid open, and Scott looked toward where he thought Amadeus and Jella were, pointing at the opening as he grabbed the unconscious soldiers and dragged them inside the dark dome.

When he turned around, Jella and Amadeus were standing there, visible again.

"That was so clever, Scott," Jella said. "Your power would be very useful in the spy trade."

"Well, once upon a time, I was a thief," Scott said, trying not to brag. "You and I could trade tips later."

"It's gotta be around here somewhere," Amadeus said, pulling a glow stick out of his pocket—he had clearly been a better Boy Scout than Scott—and snapping it, activating the light. The neon beam lit the room with an alien glow as they moved deeper into the dome, eyes peeled for any sign of the weapon. Lights suddenly turned on as the floor changed from cement to tile. In the brighter light, Scott could see they were on a railed observation platform that circled the entire dome. Looking down…

"There it is," Amadeus said, peering over the railing. "You owe me ten bucks, Scott. I told you it'd be a sphere."

Scott stared at a giant glowing orb perched on a sturdy steel stand in the lab below. "I think the technical word for something so fancy is *orb*," he hedged.

Amadeus shook his head, laughing. "I'm still collecting."

"Fine, fine," Scott said as they headed down the stairs that led to the lab. "Jella, you ever dealt with this thing when they were forcing you to spy on people?"

She nodded. "It's not anyone's top priority because they've had it so long. But they do regular maintenance."

Scott couldn't exactly tuck the orb under his arm and hightail it out of there like it was a basketball—the thing was car-sized, so you'd need a few people to move it, but he'd imagined something bigger… and maybe with spikes.

"Do you know its origin?" Amadeus asked, waving his tablet a few inches around the orb to scan it.

"It's said that the ancient Damarians mined the contents from inside the suns themselves. But I don't think that's actually possible, is it?"

"Well, whatever's inside it certainly came from space—the radiation's off the charts," Amadeus mused. "No force field or anything protecting it. Maybe a field would block its effects? You know," his head tilted as he regarded the orb, "it reminds me of their ember bombs." He reached out, tapping it with the edge of his tablet; when it rang out like glass, his mouth twisted. He looked up, eyes scanning the dome's ceiling.

"What are you looking for?" Scott asked.

"Sprinkler system—all labs have them, even a pyrotech lab. And… there it is." He pointed to the pipes painted the same gray as the inside of the dome.

"You want to set off the sprinklers?" Scott asked, not getting it.

"Yep!" Amadeus said. "Come on. We need to get back up to the platform."

But as they turned to do just that, something whizzed past Scott's cheek.

"Get down!" he yelled, pushing Amadeus and Jella forward toward the stairs before diving behind an overturned lab table. He chanced a look around it as he heard the soldiers' shouts and thumping boots approaching. Amadeus and Jella had made it halfway across the room in the first round of bullets. From where they were crouched behind the stairs, out of sight of the soldiers, Amadeus stared at Scott through the gaps between steps.

"*STAY WHERE YOU ARE!*" An authoritative voice rang out as soldiers filed along the platform, aiming their guns at Scott. With Amadeus and Jella tucked behind the stairs, Jella could make them disappear at any moment—this was all on Scott. So he slowly stood up from behind the lab table, lacing his fingers behind his head.

"Okay, okay," he said, registering six guns pointed in his direction. No Keepers—if any of these goons had powers, they would've blasted him with fire by now. Behind his head, he stretched out a finger to his opposing wrist. "No need to shoot me. See? I'm surrendering."

Click. He shrank, bouncing down onto the tile, then jumped up and raced across the floor as confused shouts filled the air. *Hold your fire! Where did he go?*

Popping back to normal size behind the stairwell, he leaned forward for a moment, panting, his hands on his knees. "We gotta do something, fast. Any ideas?"

"I need a gun," Amadeus whispered.

Jella pulled one out from her long jacket. Amadeus's eyebrows rose. She shrugged. "Hepzibah gave it to me."

"Of course she did," he smirked. "And we're lucky to have it. Both of you, back up as far away from the orb as possible."

Jella grabbed Scott's hand, and the air wavered as their bodies and shadows melded into the wall. Amadeus aimed the gun and squeezed the trigger, emptying a slew of bullets into the orb; it shattered, a powerful pulse of energy sending him and everyone else in the room flying backward off their feet as the glowing orange stuff that had been contained in the orb—what the hell was it, magma or something?—oozed across the floor. Alarms blared, lights flashing, and the sprinklers above activated, drenching their heads and the floor. The orange goop sizzled and turned gray as soon as the water touched it, foaming sluggishly.

Instantly, Scott's headache disappeared. "Seriously?" he shouted, getting to his feet, his hair dripping in his eyes as he looked for Amadeus. "You just *shoot* the damn thing and add water, and that's it? *I* could've done that!"

But Amadeus didn't answer. A rumble filled the air… a growl that raised every hair on Scott's arms as the soldiers' authoritative yells gave way to panicked screams.

Scott turned slowly, his gaze rising up. Brawn's fists were clenched, and his thick, flat brows drawn together. The change never failed to punch the air out of Scott's lungs even now, when he'd spent so much time getting to know Amadeus.

"Hi," Scott said, as the soldiers scattered on the platform, regrouping in defensive positions now that a massive green guy who could tear them limb from limb had appeared. "You feeling better?"

Brawn sniffed, turning his head to focus on Scott. "I was stuck." He smiled, a toothy, mischievous grin.

"But not anymore."

He whirled toward the soldiers with the speed of a much smaller creature, his fists raised. Scott thumbed his suit and shrank down, excited to notice no pain, no fuzziness, and they got to work.

30

AS THEY huddled together inside the shuttle's kitchen, waiting for Carol to return, Rhi couldn't stop staring at Zeke. She reached out and touched his face again and again—gently, because it was bruised, as if the Damarian guards had taken turns on him. When she'd pulled herself up into the transport and he first caught sight of her, she had wanted to cry—and she knew she did, too—but they didn't have time. And as Ansel's fire cyclone exploded, Rhi did one of the hardest things she'd ever done—she'd trusted Carol's words and obeyed her orders. She'd done the thing she knew Carol never would: She stayed at her post, watching her leader go fight Rhi's greatest enemy.

She felt torn in two—part of her desperately wanted to be outside helping her friend, but the other part knew she should stay here with Zeke, who was still reeling from the effects of the sonic strip.

"I'm sorry," Rhi said again, dabbing at his ears where blood was still trickling. "I'm so sorry."

He grabbed her hand, squeezing it, shaking his head. "You saved me."

"We still haven't freed Alestra," she said. "The baby... She's going to start showing soon."

"We'll go free her together." He laced his fingers with hers, gripping tight in promise.

"We're going to get her right now!" Carol's voice burst out as she pounded onto the ship.

She was back! Her suit was streaked with black, one sleeve sheared off completely from Ansel's fire. "Zeke, nice to meet you, glad you're okay," Carol yelled over her shoulder as she dashed past them straight to the cockpit, and Rhi shot a worried look at her brother.

"Stay there," she told him.

She hurried after Carol, who'd thrown herself into the pilot's seat and was going through the launch procedure in double-time.

"What's wrong?" she asked.

"Ansel had a backup plan," Carol said, flipping on the ship's comm. "Hepzibah, Hepzibah, do you read me?"

There was a crackle, then, "Loud and clear, Carol."

The thrusters lit, and Rhi strapped herself in hurriedly as they lifted off, Carol not even waiting for all the systems to go completely online. "Are you in position at the Maiden House?"

"Sona, Mantis, and I are, but the Resistance fighters are still an hour away. The caravan got stuck in a sandstorm and had to wait it out."

"You three need to go in. *Now*. Get those EMP patches on the girls' arms, because Ansel's sent in a strike team to kill them all. They're only ten minutes out."

"What?" Rhi asked, her heart jolting. "*No!*"

"I'm counting on you, Hepzibah," Carol went on. "The girls need to be able to fight back, even if Scott and Amadeus don't get the weapon turned off by then. We're headed to you now, but I'm not sure we'll get there in time."

"They will not touch one hair on their heads," Hepzibah said fiercely. "Do not worry. I must go."

"Fly fierce," Carol said.

"And you."

Carol's fingers clenched around the shuttle's controls, pushing the engine to full throttle as the red and black sand below swirled in the smoke.

"They *can't* kill them," Rhi said.

"They won't," Carol said, and Rhi wanted to believe her, but she feared she couldn't.

"Where are we going?"

Rhi turned around, saw Zeke standing in the doorway of the cockpit, and her stomach fell. She reached out a hand; he took it, meeting her eyes, blue on brown—like their mother, like their father. "We're going to fight," she said. "And we have to win."

———◦———————◦———

IT TOOK twenty minutes to get to the Maiden House. Twenty agonizing, mind-numbing minutes while her heart pounded out of control and Carol's knuckles blanched whiter and whiter around the shuttle's controls. The silence pressed in on them, but Rhi couldn't bear to break it as the shuttle rocked to and fro, bucking its way through a small sandstorm.

She used to watch the storms from her sliver of a window in the Maiden House, set high in the wall. If she stacked her table on the bed and stood on tiptoe, some nights she could just catch a glimpse of the lightning and whirls of sand.

When the way cleared, the storm fading as they flew through it, the Maiden House came into sight. Rhi gasped at the sight of smoke spiraling off the roof in thick black clouds. The electrified fence surrounding the brick building was crumpled and gaping open, as if someone—Hepzibah, most likely—had rammed a truck through it. A Damarian ship was parked in the bay next to the exercise yard—the strike team had already arrived. Rhi's stomach dropped—she wanted to scream, but she couldn't.

She wouldn't. This wasn't over. He hadn't won yet. Not before she tried to… not before she'd done all she could.

Swearing at the sight of the Damarian vessel, Carol flew the shuttle in a tight loop around the Maiden House, scanning the perimeter. The smoke made it hard to determine where the fire was coming from— the ground floor or an upper one.

"We've got life signs!" Carol called out as the scanner beeped, little dots moving around onscreen, relief thick in her voice. "Lots of them! This isn't over yet."

"What do we do?" Zeke asked, looking from Rhi to Carol.

"Zeke, you taught Rhi to fly, right?" Carol asked, as the shuttle dove and came to a stop in front of the Maiden House. Gravel crunched under the thrusters as they powered down and folded into the ship.

"I did."

"Okay, you're gonna be our pilot. I've coded the launch sequence into the panel," Carol said, pointing to the screen. "All you've got to do is press this"—she pointed to the cloaking button—"as soon as you see one of the girls come running out. That'll deactivate the cloaking tech so they can see the ship. And then, once they're all on board, you pull this." She flipped open the tab near the bottom of the panel to reveal the emergency-takeoff lever. "When you've got all the girls, you take off, no matter what, okay?"

"You want me to sit here while you fight?" he asked. "No, I need to—"

"You need to be their getaway driver, Zeke. Like you and Rhi planned originally. Remember?" Carol asked.

He swallowed. "But Alestra—"

"She will be with you soon," Rhi promised.

"What about you?" Zeke demanded, fixing her with an urgent stare.

"I'm not leaving without Umbra," Rhi said. "I can't."

"Rhi… I just got you back…" His face crumpled, and he turned away, trying to gather himself.

She blinked back tears, unable to apologize for

what she had to do. Before she could say anything, there was an echoing boom; the shuttle rocked and shuddered, sending them scrambling to starboard, one of the comms spilling off its hook. Someone was firing at them.

"Time to draw them away," Carol said, climbing past Zeke out of the cockpit. "Rhi, you still have the gun Hepzibah gave you?"

Rhi nodded, pulling it out from beneath her jacket. She squeezed Zeke's shoulders as she passed him, unable to look him in the eye. She had to focus. For him. For her. For all of them.

"I love you," she said.

"I love you, too."

She nodded, telling herself that it wouldn't be the last time she saw him. Then she turned and followed Captain Marvel out into the smoke.

31

THEY TORE across the exercise yard as fireballs were falling around them, dodging flames spreading greedily across the gravel and heating the rocks to burning shards. Carol slammed through the double doors of the Maiden House, shattering the glass insets into pieces that crunched under their feet as they descended into the halls of the prison that had been Rhi's home for a decade.

Three bodies lay in the hallway, men with heavy tactical gear, totally unconscious, smears of green across their faces. Carol looked down at them, kicking one lightly to make sure he was out, before shooting Rhi a look. But all Rhi could feel was relief—because these men, the way they were rendered unconscious, meant that Mazz was alive. That her implant wasn't working.

"What happened here?" Carol asked.

"Mazz is kind of poisonous. Or her saliva is. She didn't give them enough to kill them."

"That's handy."

The power was out, and only the backup lights flickered down the dim hall. Rhi smelled smoke and heard yelling and loud footsteps above her head.

"Tell me where to go," Carol directed Rhi, her hands glowing with power. "Third floor, right?"

"Yes, upstairs."

Rhi took them two at a time, right behind Carol, climbing two flights to the third floor, but they skidded to a stop when they rounded on the corridor.

A riot of half-burnt vines blocked the hall. Slumped on the ground, tangled in the smoking brambles, was another unconscious guard, this one with a thorn as thick as Rhi's arm speared through both his arms, trapping him to the foliage. Rhi tentatively reached out, brushing her hand over the vines; they stirred, the thorns sharpened, stretching toward her for just a moment, before pausing as if they recognized her.

"Tarin?" Rhi whispered.

The vines rustled, pulling apart to reveal a hole big enough to pass through. She and Carol ducked inside, and what she saw made her heart flip in her chest.

Tarin was sitting in the center of the hallway, alone, her eyes closed. Her ragged hair, long and matted to her head, was spilling down the back of her thin shift, her spindly arms and legs caked with dirt. And on the inside of her wrist was a patch of blue.

Hepzibah had gotten to her. She'd freed her. But

where was Hepzibah—and the rest of her sisters?

"You came back." Tarin stated it flatly, still not opening her eyes. Rhi rushed forward, kneeling down in the spread of flowers that surrounded Tarin like long-lost friends. She cupped the girl's face, praying that when she opened her eyes…

But when Tarin finally did, her gaze slid away from Rhi's, unfocused, fixed on a distant spot beyond her. As always, she was lost in the haze that had settled over her long ago, when the Keepers had deprived her of the plants that fed her heart and her power. Perhaps it had been silly to hope that just by freeing her power, Tarin would be freed from the pain that had stolen her sanity. But it didn't matter, Rhi told herself. She was here. She was still Tarin.

"They came back to me, Rhi," she said, trailing her fingers on the ground in a swirl. Flowers—daisies and violets—sprouted in their wake. "The Keepers said the flowers wouldn't come, but look—they did."

There was movement at her back through the vines blocking the hall from the rest of the Maiden House, and then a slicing sound—the wall of thorns tearing through flesh—followed by a guttural groan and a wet splash of blood. Rhi glanced over her shoulder, knowing it was only a matter of time before they broke—or burned—their way through Tarin's barrier.

"I know they did," Rhi said. "I told you they would, remember?"

Tarin nodded, her eyes sliding back to the riot of color blanketing the ground around her. She began to hum, the smell of violets and charred flesh blending in the air.

"Tarin, where's Tynise?" Rhi asked, peering over her shoulder down the empty hall. "Where's your sister?"

"Tynise," Tarin echoed, a rose sprouting next to her foot. She plucked it, heedless of the razor-sharp thorns. "She's with the skunk lady. But I wanted to come back here, so I snuck away. The thorns aren't going to grow themselves."

"Hepzibah," Carol said, as Rhi gently took Tarin's elbow and pulled her up. Tarin stood, holding the rose, still fingering the petals.

"Where's the skunk lady, Tarin?"

A smile crept across Tarin's face, her head tilted. She giggled, plucking a thorn off the rose. "Tables turned," she sang out. "Now Miss Birdie's going to learn a lesson."

<hr />

RHI DIDN'T wait for Carol. She didn't wait for Tarin.

She bolted down the familiar hall turned strange and spooky with Tarin's garden, a mix of plants she remembered from Attilan—ivy and blackberry brambles and flowers of all kinds—and Damarian monstrosities that snapped and twitched as she passed, their spiky tendrils reaching for her.

Several guards were slumped across the floor— just unconscious, but... at least two had come up against Alestra. They had blood trickling out of their ears.

Rhi didn't hesitate. She ran, focused: the end of the hall. The red door.

Miss Egrit's room. The only door without a heat sensor.

Rhi turned the knob and pushed open the door, slipped into the room, and closed it quickly behind her, afraid of what she might find.

"Rhi!"

She sagged against the door, relief knocking her knees together, stealing her breath, and filling her with the kind of joy that made her dizzy. They were all there: Alestra, her hands and dress spattered with blood. Tynise, towering over them all, her broad shoulders blocking Rhi's view of Mazz, who rushed toward her, crying her name, and threw herself into her arms.

Rhi held her tightly, her hands cradling Mazz's brown curls and trying not to break down. She hadn't realized just how surprised she was to see them again, when something inside her had never expected she'd ever succeed. The rest of the girls rushed to her, embracing her tightly, as Hepzibah, Mantis, and Sona hung back, letting them enjoy their hard-earned reunion.

It was the best feeling in the world, being there with them. And the most frightening. Because this wasn't over… and within minutes, they could be scattered in the wind again. Or dead.

After they'd come this far, she couldn't—*wouldn't*—

let that happen. She *had* to get them onto that shuttle.

"Zeke's waiting for us," Rhi said, and Alestra gave out a little sob of relief, leaning against Tynise, who hugged her tight. "You all need to go out front where the shuttle's waiting before they send more strike teams."

"We can handle the strike team now," Tynise snarled, holding out her arm, the blue EMP patch blazing against her skin.

"Alestra needs to get away from here," Rhi stressed. "The baby… all of you have to go."

"We can't," Alestra said. "Not yet."

Rhi frowned. "But—"

Then the group parted, revealing what the girls had been blocking… *who* they'd been blocking.

And Rhi stared at Miss Egrit, bound to her chair, with tears staining her face and a gag stuffed in her mouth. She went cold and then hot, like her body didn't know what it wanted: to be still and frozen, or angry and heated.

"We waited for you," Alestra said.

"We want you to decide," Mazz added.

"What to do with her," Tynise finished.

Rhi stared at Miss Egrit, at her crushed curls— messier than Rhi had ever seen them—and her crooked skirt, and the tear in the elbow of her sweater. She remembered viscerally for a moment that day she'd met them. The first day she'd tried to break them with the myth, the way Sona had been broken all those years ago. The way all Damarian girls, human and Inhuman, had been broken.

Then she looked at her friends—at the two women who had helped bring her here, and the woman who had been raised here.

Hepzibah moved to stand behind their captive, her arms crossed, her stance wide. "I have told your friends that I will not interfere," she said. "Your captive, your choice. It is the only just way."

"And I made myself perfectly clear how I feel about this sort of thing to Jella and Marson," Mantis declared with a permissive nod.

Sona said nothing, and Rhi arched a brow. Was she going to be the judge?

Sona licked her lips, her breath hitching as she said, "Your move, Rhi."

Miss Egrit whimpered, and the sound was so much like the sound Rhi made when she'd dropped the ember gel on her skin. That bit-back, oh-so-scared but oh-so-determined-to-hide-it sound you couldn't stop from bubbling to your lips. In Rhi, the sound had meant strength. But here, in Miss Egrit, it was all weakness.

She heard footsteps—Carol bringing Tarin back to them. Her heart creaked in her chest like a door shutting on something good. To have Tarin watch this… to have Mazz participate… to show Carol who she *really* was…

Could she do it? *Should* she?

She hooked her finger on the rough cotton gag shoved in Miss Egrit's mouth, pulling it free. The woman spat, her pink lipstick—almost the same color as her mouth—smeared across her skin.

"You could have been kind," Rhi said. "You could've been drawn to this, to us, out of the goodness of your heart. But you weren't, were you? You wanted power. And you didn't care who you hurt to get your shred of it."

"Why would I be kind to *things* like you?" Miss Egrit shrilled, but her voice cracked on the words, and Rhi noticed her lips were trembling.

"You're scared now," Rhi said. "You're thinking it through—all the things you did to us. Do you even remember them all?"

Around her, her sisters stirred as they remembered. But she could see it, underneath the terror in Miss Egrit's eyes: she didn't. The horrors of the last ten years had blurred together, because they weren't horrors to her. They were just a means to power, to the only kind of freedom a Damarian woman could get.

"You should be very scared," Rhi said. "*We* were."

Tables turned, indeed. Tarin was right.

"The Council will burn you for this, just like the twins," Miss Egrit snarled. "You're no better than them, Number Five. You're *nothing*." The words, as always, were spoken to hurt her, to bring her low, to remind her.

They didn't hurt her, but they did remind her. Of how she was smart. Of how she was strong.

There was an ember bomb in her jacket pocket. The one Hepzibah had slipped her. She pulled it out, tilting it back and forth, letting it catch the light. Miss Egrit went rigid, her terrified gaze fixed on the bomb, her chair rattling on the ground with the convulsions of fear wracking her body.

"I could drop this, and that would be it," Rhi said. "A few minutes of agony as it eats through your flesh and bone, and then you would be... gone. You would feel nothing." She tucked the bomb back into her pocket. "I don't want that," she said, her words directed toward her sisters, not to Miss Egrit. "I want her to suffer for much longer," she told them. "Every day. Every hour. Every breath that she takes, I want her to remember not only what she did, but also what she's *lost*: her freedom, the only thing she actually values." She leaned forward, her voice lowered, feeling Carol's gaze blazing down her back. "Killing is too good for you. Punishment is much crueler. And unfortunately for you, I learned from the best. Because you may not remember all that you've done to us, but we do."

Miss Egrit shuddered as Tynise's hand clamped down on her head, forcing her to stare straight ahead as Alestra leaned forward and hummed a simple lullaby into her ear.

The woman's head dropped, Alestra's powerful voice sending her into slumber before the last note was sung. Relief bubbled inside Rhi like water boiling over, hissing and splashing through her body.

"An appropriate punishment," Hepzibah told her, nodding in approval.

"A leader's choice," Carol added under her breath, for only Rhi to hear.

Mantis stiffened next to Hepzibah. "A ship is

coming," she said. "I can feel the people inside. We need to leave this place before another strike team arrives."

"The shuttle," Rhi said. "It's parked out front. Zeke's waiting." She shared a special smile with Alestra and then turned to her friends, her heart thumping wildly in her ears. She looked in their faces and finally said the words she'd dreamed of saying for so long: "Are you ready to go?"

Tears glittered in Mazz's eyes. "I'm scared," she confessed as Alestra drew her tighter against her.

"I was, too," Rhi told her, holding out her hand. "But I'm not scared anymore."

But before Mazz could reach out and take it, an electronic shriek sounded throughout all floors of the Maiden House, and then a crackling voice echoed out of the speakers tucked in the corners of each room.

"Rhi, I know you're in there."

Ansel's voice. All the triumph that had rushed through her just seconds before, all the relief and joy, snuffed out like a candle. Rhi's eyes widened in horror, and her jaw dropped when she saw a *smile* on Carol's face.

"You didn't kill him?" she hissed. She hadn't even thought to ask. She'd just assumed.

Carol shook her head.

Betrayal flashed through her, so deep and so wounding she could barely breathe around the hurt. *I trusted you...*

Then, Ansel's voice boomed out again, "I have her right here, Rhi!"

Umbra. Rhi's stomach churned as she staggered out

of Miss Egrit's room to the right, where the lone dingy window was cut into the brick. She was barely aware of Carol following her out and everyone else hanging back as she stared through the glass.

Ansel was standing in the center of the exercise yard, Umbra's arm clutched in his. The sight of her in his grasp, head bowed… it broke Rhi's heart.

"I knew he couldn't resist," Carol explained, looking apologetic as Rhi shuddered. "I knew if I let him go, he'd bring her here."

It was smart. It was reckless.

It was what a leader would do.

"I'm offering you a deal, Rhi," Ansel continued, his voice echoing through the halls of the Maiden House. "Quite a generous one, considering how much trouble you've caused today. I'll give you Umbra… if you hand over the captain."

32

"SEEMS LIKE a solid trade to me," Carol drawled. "Let's do it."

Rhi stared at her. "I can't just… go down there and *trade* you," she protested. She hated that there was a small part of her that leaped with a horrible eagerness at Ansel's proposal. The idea that he'd ever even *suggest* letting Umbra go…

"Well, of course not—it's a trap," Carol said. "He's got Flame Keepers on each sand dune surrounding the place. Look." She pointed, but Rhi couldn't see what Carol saw even when she squinted. She guessed having super-vision did have its perks.

"I can't see them."

"They're there," Carol assured her. She ducked away from the window as Ansel's head tilted toward it. "He's gonna start a countdown soon," she said. "Give you thirty seconds to come down or something.

We need to make a plan fast."

"We can help," said a voice behind them.

Rhi hated that it was Mazz who said it. Hated that she was so willing to fight. Hated that she *had* to. She thought of Fern, tucked away in the caverns below the Field of Fire, oblivious to the kind of pain her sister Inhumans were going through. She was glad for Fern. She was jealous of Fern. She was terrified for her… for all of them.

"You have to get to the shuttle," Rhi repeated. "Zeke can take you away. Get you out. Just like we planned."

"Rhi, this is nothing like we planned," Alestra said gently, her hand resting on her belly, just barely showing a slight curve. "It's time for a new plan. One where we work together—all for all."

"I agree," Sona said.

"We have talked before about needing a strong team at your back," Hepzibah added solemnly. "We *are* that team, Rhi."

"I don't want anyone to get hurt," Rhi said, hating how weak her words sounded, how pitiful the excuse. They were already hurt.

"Too bad," Tynise said bluntly. "We're willing to get hurt to help each other. That is what family is."

"We need to take out the Keepers on the dunes," Sona said. "That'll reduce the threat to only Ansel. I can load us in my transport and head over there, pick them off one by one."

"Do you think you can take them?" Carol asked— not just Sona, but the women behind her.

"Absolutely," Alestra said, and Rhi felt an involuntary frisson at the conviction in her voice. Could a united front really work?

"Then go," Carol said. "Hepzibah?"

"I will accompany them."

"Mantis?"

"I'm staying here," Mantis said. "You need backup. And firepower that isn't flashy."

"Fair enough," Carol said.

Rhi knew there was no time for goodbyes, but she slipped the chain carrying the ID tags off of her neck and placed it in Alestra's palm. Alestra looked down at the tags as Rhi curled her fingers closed around them, making her grasp them tight. "To remember, in case I don't come back."

Alestra didn't protest. She didn't tell Rhi she'd come back. She kissed Rhi's cheek. "You are strong," she whispered. She kissed her other cheek. "And you are smart." She pulled back, her eyes blazing. "Now go show him that."

○────────○

RHI WALKED onto the exercise yard flanked by Carol and Mantis like a leader with her army. She felt no fear—she couldn't afford it. This was a battle she had to win.

Ansel's fingers dug into the nape of Umbra's neck as the three women emerged from the Maiden House, wisps of smoke curling all around them as they strode across the gravel walk.

"Just like old times," he called. "Do you remember, Rhi? We met in a place much like this."

"I could blast him right now," Carol muttered, but Rhi shook her head. She might hit Umbra. Or Ansel might light her on fire and burn her to a crisp before Rhi could even cross the yard to stop him.

They had to get her out of his grip—and put an EMP patch on her arm. They each had one. It was just a matter of getting close enough.

"One wrong move," Ansel warned, "and they'll fire." He jerked his head backward at the Keepers positioned above them on the dunes.

"You might want to look again," Mantis said.

He cast a glance over his shoulder. Thick red smoke was rising off two of the dunes. Then a third.

Four to go.

"Isn't that their distress signal?" Mantis asked, head cocked in mock puzzlement. "Oh dear. Should've brought more backup."

"My contingency plans are way better than his," Carol commented. "Mine involved a notorious space pirate."

"Agreed," Mantis sighed.

Their needling was purposeful, if ridiculous to Rhi's ears in that tense moment. And it was getting to Ansel. He didn't like being ridiculed to his face—who did? She knew she didn't—she'd endured ten years of it. He could survive a few minutes.

Not that he'd be surviving much longer than that.

She looked at Umbra, whose eyes were glassy

with panic, staring at Rhi as if to say, *Run! Why aren't you running?*

Because you taught me there was more to life than just helping me and my own… that it must be more, Rhi responded, if only in her mind.

"Any closer, and I'll kill her."

"You'd never." It wasn't Rhi or Carol who said it— it was Mantis.

The empath's shoulders squared as Ansel's gaze fell to her. "You know, deep down, that she's more powerful than you. I can feel it. In those dark places even you don't go."

"Silence!"

A ball of fire shot toward Mantis, and Carol darted forward, shielding her by taking the brunt of the blow, letting the ball smash against her shoulder, the flames dancing along her exposed skin.

Annoyed at Carol's act of heroism, Ansel pressed his lips together tightly and grabbed Umbra's arm, thrusting it out, activating her powers. Carol could shield Mantis from a ball of fire, but the wall of ice that sent Rhi flying forward to avoid it was another matter. Her cheek pressed into the sharp gravel, she scrambled up. The wall was stories high—and blocking her from Carol and Mantis, who were on the other side.

She backed up, her shoulders hitting the wall as she heard muffled voices on the other side and the thump of someone's fists on it. The chill of the ice blasting around her was strange in the dry heat of the desert, but Rhi made no move toward Ansel. Behind her, the ice lit with a red glow—Carol was melting it, trying to break through to help her. But even as water trickled down the wall, it began to freeze again. Umbra whimpered as Ansel pushed more and more power into the wall of ice, thickening it so even Carol's powers would take time to break through. A hush fell over the yard that reminded her of before, of the day she and Ansel met, when they had stood on a similar field.

It was just them now.

But it wasn't just her anymore.

She had her sisters, fighting on the dunes beyond them, fighting for their freedom. She had her team— their skills, their stories, their failures, and their strengths. The heroes of the universe and beyond had helped her return here to free her sisters. Now she must use what they'd given her to free Umbra and take them all to safety.

He hasn't seen anything like me, Carol had said once. And that was true: She was unique—one of a kind.

And so was Rhi.

It was time to show him that.

Something danced at the edges of her fingers like a haunting melody she couldn't write down correctly… the space in-between, both the darkness and the light that it encompassed. She spun the edges of the atmosphere apart, ripping through it as if her fingers were a knife; as she spun, the sparks twirling like a miniature galaxy between her hands, she walked away from the wall of ice and toward Ansel.

His eyes, fixed on the tear, glowed with the

reflection of the sparks shooting around them. When his gaze focused on her face, he looked awed, shocked... *furious*.

She smiled. "I told you once that you couldn't hide forever," she said. "But I hid well from you, didn't I, Ansel?"

"What—" he started to say, shaking his head, his grip on Umbra tightening. She cried out, and Rhi's focus split, just for a second. The rip narrowed, and a triumphant smile spread across Ansel's face as he raised Umbra's arm and pointed it right at her.

"No!" Umbra screamed, sweat pouring off her face as she fought the implant's control. Her eyes began to roll back in her head, electricity sparking where their hands were joined. Her knees buckled, ice spears shooting from her hands and plunging into the ground at Rhi's feet—instead of *into* Rhi— as she slumped down onto the gravel.

"Useless creature," Ansel sneered, stepping over her twitching body as if it were a piece of trash. "I have to do everything myself."

Rhi's hands began to move again, gripping the atmosphere, slashing the rip in the air right between them like a shield. He came to an abrupt halt, staring into the void, his hand reaching out involuntarily for it as if he couldn't help himself, and then jerking back.

"How did you hide this?" he marveled. "I admit it was foolish of me to kill your parents so quickly. I should have taken my time and tortured them to get all the information about their daughter I needed."

This time, the rip didn't wobble or narrow. This time, his cruelty hit its target—but instead of wounding or weakening her, it did the opposite. Behind her, she could hear water trickling in a rush—Carol was close to breaking through, and more columns of red smoke curled in the air beyond the Maiden House fence.

Carol and her team were winning. And he knew it.

Umbra was still on the ground behind him. Her eyes had fluttered shut, ice frosting over her eyelids, but she was breathing—wasn't she?

Sweat trickled down Rhi's face as she struggled to tear the rip larger. She could do it—she'd squeezed a damn ship inside one once. Her finger muscles cramped, the power racing through them enough to shatter most people's bones.

"I'm going to kill you," she gritted out. "Just like you killed them."

He laughed. "An admirable sentiment," he said. "But we both know you aren't capable of such things."

"You really want to bet on that?" Rhi asked. "Did you think I was capable of stealing your ship? Burning down your house? Taking that precious history book you had hidden away? Because I did all that and more."

His eyes widened, his brows drawing together at her last question. "You—"

"I gave it to Sona Lee," Rhi continued, enraged delight dancing through her at the way his face drained of all color. "You're going to die knowing that I caused your worst nightmare. I made your silly little myth reality. I brought not just one star woman here, but *many*. And every single one will put power back in the Damarian women's hands. We will work together—Inhuman, Damarian, Earthling—until every woman… every person on this planet has the power of choice and the power of *freedom*."

He screamed, swiping at her, his fingers almost brushing against the rip. Just a little closer…

Her hands trembled, her fingers curling to claws as she stretched and pulled the rip wider and wider. The darkness yawned between them, sparks lighting his face, creating deep shadows and crevices, so he resembled the predator he was.

Was he right about her? Could she kill him? Jella had killed Marson, and she didn't regret it. Rhi had hesitated when given the same opportunity inside with Miss Egrit. But she hadn't spared her because of mercy—she wanted the evil woman to pay for what she'd done.

Ansel's payment couldn't be merely death, but total annihilation: of the beliefs and the system and edifices he had established and imposed, and of the future he'd planned to make even more monstrous.

Ice shattered around them, an explosion of shards she couldn't run from. She gasped in surprised pain, her head whipping to the side to shield her eyes—and in that split second of self-protection, Ansel leaped.

His hand closed around her wrist, pulling her forward, trying to break her connection with the rip. But she couldn't let him. If she did…

So she did the only thing she could think of, as

blue and red and gold blurred in the edge of her vision. She flung her free hand wide, the rip widening, and she *yanked* with the hand he was gripping.

They tumbled into the rip, into the in-between, and the last thing she saw was the dawning of a new era—*their* era, not his—rising in his horrified and beaten eyes.

33

"RHI!"

Carol yelled as Ansel yanked the girl forward. The rip quivered and then widened around them as Rhi twisted in his grip, tipping backwards, *into* the rip, pulling him with her.

Carol ran, ice crunching underneath her boots as she pelted across the yard, diving toward the rip as it began to narrow and close. Behind her, she heard Mantis yell, but she didn't turn, she just leapt, not hoping but *knowing* it would return to her. That she could break free.

She had been born for this. And no weapon and no man could contain her.

Her feet left the ground—and they didn't return. Her heart soaring, her chest tight, she flew into the shimmering black rip just as it narrowed.

It was darkness unlike anything she'd ever

experienced, even in the farthest reaches of space. Her hands lit her way as she spun—floating on her back, staring up at the deep black lit with the glow of red coming from her—when something drifted past. A doll, one of those hand-sewn patchwork ones. She blinked, confused, flipping over, her gaze lifting as she searched for Rhi. She didn't find her. Instead, a wedding band slid past her, followed by an orange hat that had seen better days, a constellation of gold coins and jewels that looked ancient—and oh, her heart twinged, a set of dog tags like the ones back around her neck. She almost reached out to them to read the name.

Just some of the lost things of the universe.

Carol twisted up, soaring through the dark, the cold frosting her lips. It felt *heavy* here. Like time had stopped around her, but not *in* her.

She dodged around an ancient ship—the old-timey wooden pirate kind—the gaping hole in its hull telling her exactly how it got lost. An odd spinning hexagon of light that spit blue sparks when it neared Carol made her back up a little—she didn't need trouble right now. She just wanted to find Rhi. She dodged around a grandfather clock, flying forward, her heart beginning to thump in her ears.

"Rhi!" she called—and to her surprise, her voice echoed like she was in a hall, bouncing off the lost objects around her. The ice particles on her lips thickened with each breath she took as she surged forward.

A hand closed around her ankle, jerking her down and back. She kicked out *and* propelled forward at the same time, spiraling through the darkness, dragging her attacker with her. She glanced down, catching sight of white hair and bulging, infuriated eyes.

"You really don't know when to stop, do you?" she snarled at Ansel.

She whipped him into the grandfather clock with a crash, the clock's chimes clanging and echoing in the darkness. He grunted in pain, but kept his hold on her, clawing at her, but his hands didn't heat or light on fire.

It was too cold.

"Where is she?" Carol demanded, planting the foot he wasn't gripping against his throat, adding enough pressure to make him gurgle.

She could feel his laugh vibrating through her foot. It made her skin crawl. But it also confirmed something: He'd put her somewhere. And he couldn't have got far, floating, caught in the gravitational pull of this place.

"I need to know," he gasped out.

She glanced down below them to where he'd grabbed her. The old ship was the obvious choice—which is why she discarded it. Her eyes fell on the trunk floating in the distance, bringing to mind the gold coins and jewels that had glided past her earlier. Like someone had emptied a treasure chest.

"I need..." His hand tightened around her ankle. "Who are you?"

Her lip curled. "You tried to take their names from them," she said, remembering Rhi's story. How she had been Number Five. "You don't deserve the privilege of knowing mine."

She kicked him, a perfect snapping blow to the jaw, and he shrieked as he lost his grip on her, the sound like nails on a chalkboard—the last gasps of a man who knew he'd be lost forever, drifting among things long forgotten. He flip-flopped through the darkness, spinning away, trying to catch hold of something to slow his trajectory and failing, his voice fading, fading… lost.

Carol shot forward, away from him, toward the trunk floating in the distance. The wrought-iron bands keeping it shut were old and rusted; they creaked as she flipped it up, and she couldn't stop the relieved gasp that tore from her throat when she saw Rhi was curled inside, a lump on her forehead.

"Rhi." She shook her gently, and then a little harder. Rhi's eyes fluttered, and then slowly opened. She jerked up, too fast, panicking until she met Carol's eyes.

"Carol?" her voice broke. "You—you're flying!"

"And I found you," Carol laughed, lifting her from the trunk. "But you've got to rip us a way out of here. It's getting a little chilly, even for me."

The smile Rhi gave Carol was brilliant—shining so bright it lit up the in-between, the lost things vibrating like they knew she'd finally been found. Her hands lifted, her fingers poised, almost delicate as they plucked the atmosphere apart like parting silk curtains. And together, they soared into a new world.

○———————○

Three weeks later

"I'M GOING to miss you," Rhi said, watching Carol zip up her bag and set it on the bunk.

"I can stay longer if you want me to," Carol said.

Rhi smiled. "It would be selfish of me to keep you here."

"And a leader can't be selfish," Carol added.

"You taught me that," Rhi pointed out. "And you're a *commander*."

"Just a fancy word for a lot of paperwork," Carol laughed.

The last three weeks had been like a dream mixed with just a hint of nightmare. Recordings of the battle at the Maiden House had been spread across the planet, thanks to Amadeus and Sona, who was proving to be skilled at not only hacking the major networks, but also at the good kind of propaganda, if there was such a thing. The message of the Resistance was spreading like wildfire—and with the Damarian weapon destroyed, Ansel and Marson gone, and proof of the true Damarian history reaching people's ears, demands for change were being made, and women were already appearing alone in the streets—even speaking publicly.

The Council was no longer—with Marson and Ansel's murders, the more cowardly members had fled, going into hiding, replaced by an interim government appointed by a team headed by Rhi and Sona, and made up of representatives from each continent and string of islands. The old guard would soon be found and tried for their crimes, alongside Miss Egrit and all the workers in the Maiden Houses. The few who remained were trying desperately to hold on to some kind of power—but that would prove impossible after the second week, when the Inhumans on the Forgotten Islands breached the force fields and returned to the continent in full force.

Rhi and Sona had been waiting for the Inhumans, determined to prevent more bloodshed. The two women and their separate followers, Rhi suspected, would soon just become *the people* as they moved forward to create a better future, together. For the most part, they'd succeeded—so far.

She knew it wasn't going to be easy. She knew there would be violence on both sides. Revolutions weren't fairytales, and they didn't happen overnight. They were hard-won. They took time. They caused trouble. And they were worth it. She had to believe that, now that she'd chosen to stay. She had to believe in creating the kind of change that would give everyone on the planet a better life—turning the oppressors' cruel lie into the honest truth: *for the betterment of all.*

"I don't know how I could've done it without you," Rhi said to Carol.

"You would've figured out a way," Carol replied, with so much confidence that it warmed her.

"I'll never forget you."

"Hey now, that makes it sound like I'm leaving and

never coming back," Carol said, wagging her finger at her as they got up and headed out of Rhi's new rooms toward the hangar bay where Hepzibah's shuttle was being readied for takeoff. "I said I'd come back next time I was on leave, and I will."

"And Amadeus said he'll come, too," Rhi added. "There's a lot of excited talk going round the Hub about Brawn coming back to smash any remaining Council members."

"I'm sure he will. And we've burned all the Maiden Houses," Carol said, smiling at the memory. "Hepzibah does have a flair for the dramatic."

"Always," Rhi agreed. They paused at the top of the stairs leading down to the hangar bay. The entire team was waiting for them there, the ship packed and ready.

But she wasn't ready to say goodbye to any of them. Her throat burned as Mantis met her eyes, smiling as they embraced.

"You're going to do great things here," Mantis told her. "And you will always have a friend in me, and any help I can give you and your people."

"Thank you for caring enough to come find me," Rhi said, and Mantis cupped her cheek for a moment before letting her go.

"Don't forget, intergalactic book club is on the third Thursday of each month, Earth-time," Amadeus said. "I set your office computer up so you and Umbra can video in."

"We'll be there," Rhi promised. "And you'll be back soon?"

"You're not done with me yet," Amadeus promised, and she had to blink back tears.

"I don't know how to thank you and Amadeus," Rhi said to Scott, who clasped her hands in his. "We all owe you two and Jella such a huge debt for destroying the weapon."

"Well, it was kind of easy once we got inside before everyone started shooting," Scott demurred.

"There's nothing easy about a chemical reaction!" Amadeus argued. "I made some very precise calculations and hypotheses to come to the conclusion that—"

"Shooting the glass orb and making it rain was the way to go?" Scott asked innocently.

Rhi was trying not to laugh as Hepzibah swept her into a tight hug, and then let her go just as abruptly. "We will meet again," she told Rhi. "Perhaps I will come to teach the little one," she nodded over Rhi's shoulder, where Umbra and Fern were waiting for her. "Some proper skills."

"We'd love to have you."

"I *am* a delight," Hepzibah said blithely, but then she sobered. "You did very well, my friend. I am proud to be able to call you that."

Rhi hugged her again, unable to say anything else without crying. The team filed down the stairs, toward the ship, and she turned to Carol, the only one left.

Rhi swallowed, the lump in her throat making it a challenge. What could she say that could encompass what this woman had done for her and her people? There was just too much, and mere words could never express it.

"You changed my life," she began, because she had. Carol had taught her not only what freedom was, but what freedom could be. Her team had shown her joy and unbridled compassion, the kind of strength and unity that the bravest person in the world would envy. And Rhi would carry the lessons and love they'd taught her all the days of her life. "You changed *everyone's* lives."

"No, Rhi, *you* did that," Carol replied. "You reminded me of what I fought for when I was your age—the things I hoped for and believed in. Teamwork. Sisterhood. Freedom. I can't tell you how grateful I am that *you* crashed into *my* life."

Tears pricked at the corner of her eyes as she and Carol embraced.

"Send me messages whenever you want," Carol urged. "I want to hear how things are going. And if there's trouble…"

"I'll call Hepzibah first, because she's got the secret stash of ember bombs," Rhi finished for her.

Carol threw back her head and laughed. "I never could tame her sticky fingers." She looked down at her team, who had just finished loading their equipment into the shuttle.

"You should go," Rhi said, never in a million years thinking she would be saying that. But she knew Carol had a life to get back to—just like she had a life to build here. With Umbra and Fern. With Zeke and Alestra and their baby. With Jella and Mazz and Tarin and Tynise. With the Inhumans who were still learning how to be around others after years in exile. And with Sona, her family, and the other members of the Resistance. Rhi and her friends had a *society* to rebuild here, where Inhuman and Damarian would live side by side in harmony.

"I should." Carol squeezed Rhi's hand. "Keep in touch."

Fern's delighted applause when Carol floated down the stairs instead of walking filled Rhi with happiness as she approached the two of them, taking Umbra's hand, watching Carol near the group awaiting her on the tarmac.

"She'll be missed," Umbra murmured, leaning her head against Rhi's shoulder.

"She'll be back," Rhi said, surer of that than almost anything else in her life.

She waved as the rest of the team piled into the shuttle. Carol was the last to board; she paused on the stairs, looking back at where Rhi and Umbra stood.

"Hey, Rhi!" she yelled.

Rhi stepped forward, Umbra's hand still in hers.

"You're strong and you're smart!" Carol called out, her words ringing out like a blessing. "Don't you forget it!"

Rhi smiled, a brilliant bright crook of her mouth that said it all.

"I won't."

ACKNOWLEDGMENTS

TEAMWORK IN writing is almost as important as teamwork in super hero pursuits. A book, like most successful operations against invading aliens, is a collaborative effort. My most grateful thanks to the team that helped bring this book into the universe:

Steve Saffel, editor extraordinaire and guiding light, and the rest of the amazing team at Titan Books, Cat Camacho in particular for all her guidance and help. Caitlin O'Connell, Jeff Youngquist and the lovely team at Marvel for all their expertise and ideas. My wonderful agent, Jim McCarthy, who rolls with the punches of publishing in a way Carol would admire. Natasha MacKenzie for creating such a phenomenal cover, and Hayley Shepherd for her eagle eye for detail. My dear writing friends, who are patiently used to me being evasive and slightly secretive about what I'm working on: Elizabeth May, Charlee Hoffman, Paul

Krueger, Dahlia Adler, Jess Capelle, Kelly Edgeington Stultz, and EK Johnston. And my husband, who drove an extra thousand miles over the weeks to fetch me endless rounds of takeout while I wrote this book—the true hero I needed in my pursuit for out-of-this-world barbecue. I love you.

ABOUT THE AUTHOR

BORN IN a mountain cabin to a punk-rocker mother, Tess Sharpe grew up in rural northern California. Living deep in the backwoods with a pack of dogs and a growing colony of formerly feral cats, she's the author of the thriller *Barbed Wire Heart*, the critically acclaimed YA novel *Far From You*, the *Jurassic World* prequel, *The Evolution of Claire*, and co-editor of *Toil & Trouble*, a feminist anthology about witches.